To

my wife, Deborah

Who puts up with a lot

Symington Smythe, ostler and would-be thespian, and ling playwright Will Shakespeare are now firmly ensconced in a theater company . . . but unfortunately all of London's theaters have been closed because of the plague. The players are now broke, forcing our intrepid duo to seek employment in other lines of work—Smythe smithing and Will poetizing.

A murder rocks London.

A handsome young craftsman kills a wealthy and somewhat mysterious merchant trader in what was apparently an argument over the reputation of the trader's daughter, a beautiful, dark lady to whom he was engaged. It has all the elements of classic Greek tragedy and in no time at all our out-of-work thespians are making much ado about murder.

Also by Simon Hawke

Much ado About Murder

Simon Hawke

A Tom Doherty Associates Book

NEW YORK

MUCH ADO ABOUT MURDER

A Forge Book
Published by Tom Doherty Associates, LLC
175 Fifth Avenue
New York, NY 10010

www.tor.com

Forge® is a registered trademark of Tom Doherty Associates, LLC.

ISBN 0-765-30241-1 (hc)
ISBN 0-765-30836-3 (pbk)

First Hardcover Edition: December 2002
First Paperback Edition: January 2004

Printed in the United States of America

0 9 8 7 6 5 4 3 2 1

Much Ado About Murder

1

IT WAS A QUIET NIGHT in the taproom of the Toad and Badger as Tuck Smythe sat down to a simple supper of dark oat bread, ale, and pottage. A quiet night at the Toad and Badger tavern, however, did not necessarily mean the night was quiet in any generally accepted meaning of the phrase. It simply meant that no crockery was being hurled, no furniture was being overturned, and no skulls were being broken. (Admittedly, broken skulls did not occur as frequently as broken furniture and crockery, largely because players, as a rule, had less of a tendency toward violence than histrionics.) Smythe knew that the occasional broken bone or two was not altogether out of the question, but then such incidents did not often involve actors, who usually knew well enough to make a timely exit to the wings whenever the action center stage became a bit unruly.

Despite the general tumult over which the ursine Courtney Stackpole presided as the innkeeper, Smythe took comfort in the fact that the Toad and Badger was not really the sort of tavern where blood could flow as freely as small beer. Those sorts of places could more readily be found in Southwark or Whitechapel, where seamen from the trading ships and mercenaries from the foreign wars often brawled with the weatherbeaten rivermen and tough drovers from the Midlands. In such places, on any given night, blades could be drawn as readily as ale. The Toad and Badger, fortunately, was not that sort of tavern. It was rowdy and boisetrous, to be sure, but for all that, it was more loud than lethal and its charm lay primarily in the eccentricities of its patrons, most of whom were simple tradesmen and entertainers.

On this particular occasion, the atmosphere within the tavern was unusually subdued, in large part because the fortunes of the Queen's Men were lately in decline. The previous summer, they had gone out on tour throughout the English countryside, but their performances had not brought in nearly as much as they had hoped. The harvests had been poor for two years running, and while people in the countryside were generally starved for entertainment, many of them were also quite literally starving and could scarcely afford even the very reasonable price of admission to a play.

In many villages where they had stopped, rather than set up in the courtyard of a local inn, as was their custom, the Queen's Men had erected their stage out in a village square, then played for free to gain an audience. Afterwards, they would simply pass the hat. All too often, unfortunately, they had found that the number of people in their audience had well outnumbered the few coins that they had left behind.

To add insult to their injury, there were numerous bands of cozeners, vagabonds, and sharpers traveling the countryside of late, posing as legitimate companies of players. They would herald their arrival in a town with a fanfare of cornets and sackbuts, then with dramatic gestures, posturings, and declamations, the imposters would announce themselves as "the famed and legendary Queen's Men," or "the illustrious and acclaimed Lord Admiral's Men," or "the Earl of Leicester's Own Grand Company of Players," when, in fact, they had no legitimate noble patron whatsoever and thus possessed no right under the law to perform anywhere as players. Nevertheless, that did not stop scores of enterprising scoundrels from banding together in companies, stealing some wagons and some horses, then dressing up in motley and passing themselves off as legitimate players out on tour from London.

These rogues would come into a country town and stage some sorry travesty of a production they had cobbled together from bits and pieces filched from various plays that they had seen in London or, worse still, put on a play that they had stolen in its entirety by attending several performances en masse and committing different parts to memory. Much of the time, a play that was stolen in this manner resulted in a production that was a hopeless mish-mosh of misremembered lines and markedly inferior performances, which would have been bad enough, thought Smythe, if fraud were the only crime being perpetrated. Unfortunately, no sooner would these imposters leave a town that they had visited than numerous thefts and other crimes would be discovered, leaving little doubt as to the culprits.

Needless to say, the victims of these roving, thieving bands were not very well disposed toward legitimate companies of players who came to visit afterward. The Queen's Men had been driven from three villages they came to on their tour and Smythe still had some bruises left from being pelted with sticks and stones hurled by the angry townspeople at their last stop.

At least London's critics did not hurl anything more hazardous than a few well-turned epithets.

When the company had finally come home to London, they quickly discovered that things there were not much better. The playhouses were all closed down, in part because of plague, and in part because of rioting apprentices who had taken to roaming the streets of the city in large gangs and getting into violent, bloody battles with their rivals on the slightest provocation. There had been numerous complaints of damage done to property by these roving bands of hooligans, not to mention damage done to life and limb, as well. Smythe could not see what the players had to do with it. As he saw it, the blame lay with the guildsmen to whom these roaring boys had been apprenticed. They clearly failed to exercise the proper amount of supervision with their charges and allowed the boys too much free time. But rather than place the blame where it belonged, the authorities had apparently decided that any place where large numbers of citizens could gather was a potential breeding ground for violence, and so the playhouses had all been closed down til further notice.

Smythe thought that it was terribly unfair to penalize the players by denying them the ability to make their living, even though they were entirely innocent of any wrongdoing . . . however, there was nothing they could do about it. Between their unsuccessful tour and the playhouses being closed, most of the Queen's Men were now dead broke. They had lost several members who had left the company to pursue other work, and those with any money left would soon be penniless themselves from sharing the little they had with their less fortunate comrades. Even the meanest of them was not above standing a fellow to a meal or a drink. Adversity seemed to bring out the best in them, Smythe thought. The players took care of their own.

He recalled the way his father had railed against them when he first found out about his son's dream of joining a company of players. "*Players!*" Symington Smythe the elder had exclaimed, his voice dripping with scorn as he lifted his chin and gave an elaborate sniff of disdain. "Naught but a frivolous, immoral lot of dirty scoundrels, every last man jack of them! Degenerate and drunken wastrels, all of them, a foul and pestilential pox upon society! No son of *mine* shall ever be a player! Mark me well, boy, I shall strip the hide right off your back afore I allow you to disgrace the family name in such a manner!"

Well, Smythe thought wryly, as things turned out, his hide was still intact, which was certainly more than he could say for his father's fortune or good name. The old fool had squandered all his money in his vainglorious attempts to gain a knighthood. Now he had little left to show for all his efforts save for his precious escutcheon, which he had bribed and cozened the College of Heralds into granting him, thinking that once he was a proper gentleman, a knighthood would soon be within his grasp. Alas, Symington Smythe II's lofty ambition had overreached him and his dreams had fallen into dust. He had only narrowly avoided debtor's prison and was now living mainly on his younger brother's charity.

Meanwhile, Symington Smythe III took satisfaction in the knowledge that he was realizing his own dreams. He had left home for London, where he had found and joined a company of players, and though his current state of fortune was not much better than his father's, at least he was living the life that he had chosen for himself. "Life," as his Uncle Thomas used to say, "is much too short to be lived for someone else. Go and live it as you like it."

Smythe often missed his Uncle Thomas, who had always been more of a father to him than his own father had been. Thomas Smythe had never begrudged his older brother his inheritance. He was a simple, unassuming man who lived his own life and was content to make his own way as a farrier and blacksmith in their small village. He had liked nothing better than standing at his forge, his powerful arms corded with muscle, his bare chest, covered only with his well-worn leather apron, glistening with a sheen of sweat as he labored at his favorite task, the careful crafting of a blade. Though he had shod more horses and forged more iron tools than weapons, Thomas Smythe could also forge a blade that could rival the finest fighting steel from

Toledo. No less a connoisseur of weapons than Sir William Worley, master of the Sea Hawks and courtier to the queen, had admired his work.

And if it wasn't for his uncle's tutelage, Smythe knew all too well that he would have gone hungry on this night. He had been completely broke, but had luckily managed to make some money earlier in the day by shoeing horses and helping out a local smith named Liam Bailey, who had found himself suddenly short-handed when his young apprentice became caught up in a street brawl and had his head busted for his trouble.

"Damned bloody foolishness, if ye ask me," the big old smith had sworn, running his rough and liver-spotted hand over his spare and close-cropped, grizzled hair. "Dunno what in blazes is the matter wi' young people these days. Why, in my day, a young man counted 'imself lucky to 'ave someone take 'im on an' teach 'im a good trade. But, blind me, these young scalawags today 'aven't got the sense God gave a goose! Not like you, now. I can see straight off that someone's taught ye well. Ye know yer way around a forge an' ye 'ave a way wi' horses, lad. Ye 'ave a fine, thick, brawny arm an' a big, strong chest, all the makin's of a proper smith. Ye know, ye could do worse than to throw in yer lot wi' me."

Smythe had thanked him warmly and explained that he already had a job with the Queen's Men, quickly adding that he was very grateful for the work because the playhouses had been closed and times were lean, but that he hoped to be on the boards once again before too long.

"A player, is it?" Liam Bailey shook his head, sadly. "Ah, well, 'tis a waste of good brawn, if ye ask me. Still an' all, 'tis yer own life, an' I'll not be tellin' ye how ye should live it. Come around any time ye need some extra work, lad. I can always use a good strong arm."

It was a kind offer, to be sure, and the way that things were going, it looked as if he would be spending a lot more time at Liam Bailey's smithy if the playhouses were not reopened soon, for after settling accounts with Stackpole for a couple of his fellow players who were most in need and then standing them to inexpensive ordinary meals, he barely had enough remaining to pay for his own supper.

He did not even want to think about the rent.

He mopped up the last of the juices from the pottage with his final crust of bread and gazed ruefully at the empty bowl. He was still hungry. He knew that Stackpole was an understanding soul and would allow him to have some more upon account, but he was reluctant to ask. He had already seen too many of his fellow players run up bills to the point where Stackpole had stopped extending further credit to them until they had paid up what they owed. He did not wish to find himself in a similar position. Understanding could extend only so far, and then a man had to take care of his own business.

Smythe recalled how his father had overextended himself into poverty and had no intentions of repeating his mistakes. Unfortunately, his growling stomach had no such scruples. As he stared longingly at the big iron kettle over the hearth where the pottage was simmering, he couldn't help but think that, surely, just a small bill on account could not truly be so bad.

As his stomach wrestled with his conscience, Smythe felt his resolve weakening as his appetite increased. He was sorely tempted to give it up and go ask Stackpole if he would let him have another tankard of ale and bowl of pottage on account, but was distracted when the tavern door swung open with a bang and Will Shakespeare entered with a flourish of his dark red cloak, swept off his hat dramatically, and called out, "*Hola*! Drinks and food for everyone, my good Stackpole! Gentlemen! Good news! Tonight we feast and stuff ourselves!"

For a moment, everybody simply stared at him with disbelief, and then they fell over one another in a race to take advantage of the very generous offer, shouting out their orders and hammering their fists upon the tables for attention from the serving wenches. As Shakespeare spotted Smythe, waved jauntily, and made his way over toward his table, he was surrounded and deluged with questions concerning his sudden good fortune.

"You came into some money, then?" asked Augustine Phillips, one of the senior members of their company. "Who died?"

"Whose pocket did you pick, you rascal?" Thomas Pope asked, clapping him upon the shoulder. His tone was jocular, but the look he gave the poet indicated that he might not have been surprised if that was exactly how Shakespeare came by his good fortune. Times were certainly desperate enough to warrant it. It might have been safer not to ask.

"You had a run of luck at cards?" asked John Fleming, one of the senior shareholders of the Queen's Men.

Dick Burbage, whose father owned their playhouse, was a bit more practical in his concerns. "You did not sell a new play to some rival company, I trust?" he said, eyeing Shakespeare with an anxious frown. "You promised that we would be the first to see any of your efforts."

Ever since Shakespeare had started doctoring some of the old plays in their repertoire, the Queen's Men had been anxious to see any original work he might attempt. He had produced such strong improvements in some of their old standbys that they had made him the bookholder for the company and he was now taking a key role in the staging of their productions. Smythe was pleased for him, for Shakespeare was his closest friend, but at the same time, he felt a little envious. Unlike his friend, he had no skill with words and knew that his own acting abilities left much to be desired.

"Ease yourself, Dick," Shakespeare replied, patting Burbage on the shoulder reassuringly. "I have, as yet, written no play of my own that can withstand close scrutiny, much less production. When I do, then you shall be the very first to see it, that I promise you."

"Then to what do you owe this sudden turn of good fortune?" Burbage asked, perplexed.

"I have sold some of my sonnets," Shakespeare replied, as they both sat down across from Smythe. "You may recall my having mentioned to you that I had several times before written a few verses on commission. Well, I had thought little enough of the endeavor at the time. 'Twas nothing more than simply a means of making a few extra shillings now and then."

"Aye," said Burbage, with a wry expression. "The fashionable young noblemen do dearly love to speak of the poets whose muses they inspire. They commission a few laudatory verses from some poor and starving poet, then pass them around or recite them to one another in the same spirit that a country squire may show off his sporting hounds to all his friends."

"Well," said Shakespeare, raising his eyebrows, "I do believe 'tis the very first time that I have ever been likened to a hound, but then, my dear Burbage, every dog must have his day . . . and lo, here is mine. Behold!" He dropped a weighty purse onto the wooden planking of the table and it fell with a rather satisfying thud and a metallic clinking.

"Good Lord!" said Burbage, picking the purse up and hefting it experimentally. "All *this* from a few sonnets?"

"Odd as it may seem, my verses are apparently becoming popular among some of the young aristocrats," said Shakespeare in a bemused tone. "You see, like a good harlot, my poetic sighs inflame their passions with themselves and thus create increased desire for more. Hence, each commissioned sonnet begets another dozen. All I need do is wax poetically about the graceful charms and charming graces of some overdressed young milksop with more money than good sense and afore you know it, all his friends start lining up and wanting similar effusive verses written about themselves, as well. Being of sound mind and empty purse, I was only too happy to oblige. And so now, like a good harlot," he added, wryly, "I require some ale to wash the taste out of my mouth."

"*Ale!*" Burbage cried out, happily. "We must have more ale! 'Allo, Molly, my sweet! Our tankards want refilling!"

Shakespeare's gaze fell on the empty bowl, from which Smythe had mopped up every last bit of juice, so that it was now dry as the proverbial bone. "I should say that wants refilling, too," he added, pointing at the bowl. "Yon Tuck has a lean and hungry look, methinks."

"Aye, he frequently looks hungry," Will Kemp agreed, archly, "but I have yet to see him looking anything near lean."

"Well, we are all looking a bit lean these days," said Shakespeare as he paid Molly, the serving wench, adding a gratuity that won him a beaming smile and a kiss upon the cheek. "With any luck, however, that may be changing soon. There is word that they may soon be reopening the playhouses."

"*What! When?*" asked Burbage, eagerly.

"Where did you hear of this?" echoed Robert Speed, whose financial situation, like most of the Queen's Men, had long since passed the point of being precarious. They all gathered round to listen.

" 'Twould seem that the well-to-do are growing bored," Shakespeare told his captive audience. "Her Royal Majesty, as you all know, is still out on her progression through the countryside with her entire court, thus there is little of social consequence happening in London. No one is holding any balls or masques; they are all saving up their money for when the court returns and they must once more start spending lavishly upon their entertainments, trying to outdo one another in attempting to impress their betters. Aside from which, need one even remark upon the folly of holding a social event of any consequence while the queen is out of town?"

"Oh, so true," said John Fleming, nodding in agreement. "Even if Her Majesty did not deign to attend, 'twould be social suicide to hold any event to which she could not be invited, and most especially if dancing were involved."

"Indeed," said Burbage, nodding at the reference to the queen's well known passion for dancing. "A fall from grace such as Lucifer himself could not imagine would almost surely follow."

"So then, what does that leave for the jaded pleasures of the wealthy?" Shakespeare continued. "They cannot take in some sport down at the Bear Garden, for that arena has been shut down along with all the playhouses, and one can only take the air at St. Paul's so many times before the amusement starts to pall, so to speak."

"Ouch," said Smythe, wincing at the pun. Several of the others groaned.

Shakespeare went on, blithely. "The brothels are not without their risks, of course, and tend to become tedious, especially to noblemen who prefer some breeding in their women. Though not all do, one may suppose. The ladies in waiting to the queen are all traveling with Her Majesty and are therefore unavailable, aside from which, pursuing them might well land one in the Tower, as Her Majesty prefers to have her young glories unsullied by masculine attention. So, what to do? Playing primero every afternoon grows tiresome. What other diversions does that leave? There are, at present, no fairs being held anywhere within a reasonable distance of the city, so what, I ask you, is a proper and fashionable young gentleman to do in order to amuse himself?"

"Take in a play!" Thomas Pope exclaimed with a grin.

"Ah, but the playhouses are all still closed by order of the city council," Shakespeare said, with an elaborate shrug. "Whatever is a rich young gentleman to do?"

"He could always try to bribe a councilman or two," said young George Bryan, with a grin.

"Why, George, I am deeply shocked at your suggestion!" Shakespeare said, gazing at him with mock outrage. "I will have you know that the members of our august and honored London city council are all fine, upstanding citizens of absolutely impeccable character and reputation!"

"How many have been bribed thus far?" asked Burbage, dryly.

"About half of them, I'm told," said Shakespeare.

Smythe joined in the laughter, gladdened to see that everybody's spirits were so much improved. "And from whence comes this most welcome news, Will?" he asked.

"From a certain young nobleman who would prefer not to be known to share such confidences with a mere poet," Shakespeare replied. "And as my present livelihood—to say nothing of our suppers, my dear friends—depends to a large degree upon his generosity, I am bound and beholden to be respectful of his wishes."

"So then it would appear that you have found yourself a patron," said Burbage.

"Well, in truth, I would not say so," Shakespeare replied. "At the least, not yet. This gentleman is merely one of several who has commissioned sonnets from me. He has introduced to me to some friends of his, and has taken an interest in my work, though he prefers to remain anonymous, at present. A true patron would not hesitate to have his name attached to those who would benefit from his support. He enjoys having it be known that he is a benefactor of the arts. Such is the nature of that sort of relationship."

"Perhaps Will has found another sort of relationship entirely," said Molly, with a sly smile and a wink, as she set fresh tankards full of ale before them.

"Why, you cheeky wench!" Shakespeare exclaimed, as the others burst out laughing. "I have a mind to turn you over my knee for that!"

Molly gave him a saucy grin and tossed her fiery red hair back out of her face. "I may have a mind to let you," she replied.

"Well, if I tried, then you would probably just run away," said Shakespeare.

Molly looked him up and down. "Nay, good sir, methinks I'd stand and fight."

The other players laughed again. "Looks like she's got your measure, Will," said Speed.

"Aye, and a very small measure it is, too," Molly added, holding her thumb and forefinger about two inches apart.

"Mayhap a measure large enough to fill your cup may one day come along," said Shakespeare, with a bow, "but until then, 'twould seem that none may measure up to you, milady."

The players laughed at the riposte, but before Molly could reply, Shakespeare continued, adding in a casual tone, "None, that is, save perhaps for a certain former armorer's apprentice recently returned to England from the wars."

Smythe noticed that Molly looked completely taken aback for a moment, then as quickly as the reaction had come over her, she recovered her habitual pose of saucy insolence and went on wiping off the table.

"And what would I have to do with foolish young apprentices who knew no better than to leave their trades and go running off to war?" she asked.

"Well, far be it from me to know, Mistress Molly Beatrice O'Flannery," said Shakespeare, "save that 'twould seem I had heard in passing somewhere that you once had a deal to do with this particular apprentice . . . or former apprentice, I should say, as he has by all reports proven himself a brave and stalwart soldier, having much distinguished himself in feats of arms on foreign soil."

"Good Lord! You are not speaking of Ben Dickens?" asked Will Kemp.

"Indeed, I do believe that was his name," Shakespeare replied.

"What, our own Ben Dickens?" asked John Fleming.

"The very same, by his own report," Shakespeare responded.

"You saw him, then?" said Speed. "You spoke with him?"

"I did, indeed, both see and speak with him," said Shakespeare, "and you may know he did inquire after all of you, as well, and did bid me give you all his warm regard and, furthermore, this message: that he would come here and call upon you all this very evening."

"Oh, now that *is* good news, indeed!" said Burbage.

"By God, that calls for another round of drinks!" said Speed. And then he glanced uncertainly at Shakespeare, all too mindful of his own empty purse. "That is, of course, assuming your good graces . . ."

"Oh, by all means, Bobby, have another round on me," said Shakespeare airily, with a wave of his hand.

"Your newfound wealth shall not last out the night, at this rate," Smythe cautioned him.

"Oh, 'tis a weighty purse, and there is always more where that came from," said Shakespeare, lightly.

"Just the same," said Burbage, "we would be poor companions if we drank up all your earnings. 'Tis good news, indeed, that the playhouses may soon be open once again, but have a care, Will. We do not yet know how soon that 'soon' shall be. Unless, that is, you happen to be privy to more knowledge than you have thus far shared with us."

"In good time, Dick, in good time," said Shakespeare. "For now, let the lads enjoy themselves. 'Tis money well spent if it gladdens them, for then it gladdens me. I shall not begrudge them so much as a farthing."

"Who is this Ben Dickens of whom everyone is speaking?" Smythe asked, puzzled. "I do not recall the name."

"That is because you have never met him, Tuck," Burbage replied. "He was with the company some years ago, when he was just a lad. Fleming took him on as an apprentice, to play the women's parts, but he left us before you and Will came to join the company."

"Do you mean to tell me that he left the players to become an *armorer's apprentice*?" Smythe asked, with surprise.

Burbage chuckled. "You know something of the armorer's trade, so you are thinking, no doubt, that Ben Dickens left an easy trade for one much more laborious. However, in truth, his heart was never in the player's life. He was a real roaring boy, and playing at adventure on the stage never truly suited him when there was genuine adventure to be had. Besides, his voice changed early on and grew much too deep to play the female roles, though he was still too small to play the adult male parts. We would still have kept him on, of course, for we all loved him well and he would have grown into his voice soon, but then he found an armorer to take him on as an apprentice and so he chose to leave us, thinking to learn the trade of arms from the crafting to the plying of them."

"We parted on the very best of terms," added John Fleming, "and he still came to see us now and then, whenever he could spare the time, but then one day his master fell to a palsy and the shop was closed, so Ben went off to war with some of the soldiers he had met."

"How did you happen upon him?" asked Burbage, turning to Shakespeare.

"He was part of the company at dinner with the gentleman who was kind enough to give me this," Shakespeare replied, picking up his purse and tossing it lightly in his palm to hear it jingle before putting it away. "When he discovered that I was a player with the Queen's Men, he introduced himself and greeted me with such warmth and affection as to win me over on the instant."

"Aye, that's Ben," said Fleming, smiling. "He faces all the world with open heart and countenance. I have never met a man who from the start could not perceive his merits."

"Nor has Ben Dickens ever met a man to whom he would not recite them," Molly added wryly, as she swept by with several tankards.

"Nay, Molly, you do him an injustice," said Will Kemp. "Ben was ever modest to a fault."

"If he were modest to a fault, then he would find it needful to abandon modesty, the better to be faultless," she tossed back over her shoulder.

"He never held himself to be so," Kemp replied.

"Why blow your own horn when you can have heralds trumpet all your fanfares for you?" Molly said, as she served some patrons at another table. "Ben gathers friends who extol his virtues the way a vain woman surrounds herself with mirrors, the better to bask in her reflections. Much as you all seem to love him, I vouchsafe he loves himself the better."

" 'Twould seem as if you have some grievances against him, Molly," Smythe said. "Has the man done you some injury?"

"Oh, no injury was done to me, though one might think his own vaunted opinion of himself effects an injury to good prudence," she replied, as she retrieved some empty tankards and wiped off a table. "As for grievances against Ben Dickens, I have none. Why should I? What is Ben Dickens to me? I pay no more heed to him that I would to the wind which constitutes the greater part of him."

"The lady doth protest too much, methinks," said Shakespeare, in an aside to the others. "If she truly cared so little for Ben Dickens, 'twould seem she would not speak so much of him. Or, perhaps, so ill."

"She does seem to dislike the fellow," Smythe said.

"You must not mistake her, though," Burbage replied. "There always was a kind of merry war betwixt them, and they never met without some skirmish of wit between them. In truth, I do believe that Ben and Molly share a more than passing fancy, though neither would admit to so much as a brass farthing's worth of fondness for the other."

"Well, disdain is oft the obverse of the coin of fondness," Shakespeare said. "And skirmishes of wit can oft preclude the larger and more earnest battle of the sexes, known as marriage."

"I like that," Burbage said. "Skirmishes of wit precluding the battle of the sexes. Perhaps we can use that line somewhere."

" 'Tis yours, my dear Burbage," said Shakespeare, with a magnanimous gesture. "Make what use of it you will, so long as you put to good usage."

"So then, who else was present, Will, 'mongst this distinguished company where you met our Ben?" asked Fleming.

"Well, now let me put memory to the test," said Shakespeare, frowning. "There were several in the company, along with the gentleman I mentioned, among them a stout, older, balding fellow called Master Peters by the others, by which title and by whose fine apparel and accoutrements I would infer that he must be a guildsman of some standing in his company, though which company that was I cannot say."

"Oh, well, I can tell you that," interjected Burbage. "He is a master in the company of goldsmiths. He likely has more journeymen and apprentices in service at his shop than any other hammerman in Cheapside. He comes often to our theatre, where he takes a box up in the galleries and entertains his friends. Word has it he may soon be made a peer, for he surely has the means and the connections to move up. You *were* civil to him, I trust?"

"I am civil to the world, Dick," Shakespeare replied. "And as Master Peters was civil in regard to me, so was I to him. Never fear, I did not embarrass your fine patron, nor did he give me cause to. He had with him a handsome young man by the name of Corwin, whom I might have taken for his son, but for the lack of any resemblance between them, for his manner toward the lad was very much that of a father or perhaps an uncle."

"There, too, I may supply elaboration," Burbage said, "for I have met the young man of whom you speak. Master Peters might indeed show favor to him, for Corwin is a journeyman in his shop, lately raised up from an apprentice. His work as an artisan in gold and silver has garnered much praise and is thus a favorable reflection on his master."

"He seemed to be on close terms with your friend, Ben Dickens," Shakespeare said.

"They doubtless knew each other when both were still apprentices, albeit to different masters," Fleming said.

"Aye, that would account for it. They seemed to be old friends," said Shakespeare. "There was one other present in the company, a dark and foreign-looking fellow by the name of Leonardo. He wore a seaman's boots, and spoke English passing well, but with an accent that sounded Genoan to me."

"Him I know not," said Burbage, "but if you say he is a seaman, and a Genoan at that, then I would venture that he must be a merchant trader, doubtless the master of his own ship, for I cannot quite see Master Peters breaking bread with common seamen. Methinks that he would find their company a bit too coarse for his tastes."

"Why, no more coarse than the company of players, I should think, eh, Burbage?" a deep and resonant voice came from behind them. "A man who would suffer the company of players might well be said to suffer the insufferable."

"*Ben!*" cried Fleming, jumping to his feet and rushing to embrace him. The older players eagerly surrounded him as well, while the younger ones who had joined the company after he had left looked on with interest, having heard so much about him.

"Odd's blood!" Will Kemp exclaimed, embracing him in turn. "Look how you've grown, my boy! How time hath flown! Step back now and let me look at you! How you have changed!"

Ben Dickens grinned at him. "And you have not changed at all, Will Kemp. Tell me, are you still as cantankerous as ever? Or has time's passage mellowed you, like wine?"

"Soured him like vinegar, more like, if ye ask me," said Speed.

"Bob Speed, as I live and breathe!" said Dickens, clapping him upon the shoulders. " 'Tis good to see you, my old friend. How well I remember all you taught me!"

"Do ye remember how to drink, then?" asked Speed.

"Often and prodigiously," Dickens replied, with a grin.

"Marry, then you remembered the most important part," said Speed, slapping him upon the back. "Come join us!"

"That I will," said Dickens, "if you wouldst allow my good friend Corwin to join your merry company, as well." He indicated a young man who had politely stood back a bit while he had greeted all the others.

As Ben Dickens made the introductions, Smythe took the measure of both men. They each looked to be roughly the same age as himself, which would have put them in their early twenties, and they both looked very fit, though of the two, Ben Dickens seemed somewhat more robust and carried himself with a greater air of confidence. Perhaps that was not surprising for someone who had fought on foreign soil and distinguished himself in battle. Many men never had such a chance to prove themselves, thought Smythe, and Dickens had the air and bearing of a man who had faced up to the test and passed with colors flying. He bore himself with self assurance but not arrogance, and his manner was open, natural, and direct, rather than forced, studied, or pretentious. His chestnut colored hair was worn loosely to his shoulders and he took no trouble to arrange it beyond simply combing it to keep it neat. His brown leather doubtlet was likewise simple, functional, and unpretentious, as was most of his apparel. Like his woolen cloak, it matched his boots and breeches, and the only touch of bright color in his clothing was his crimson shirt, visible through his fashionably slashed sleeves. He wore a blade, as did most men in London, but it was a utilitarian rapier rather than a showpiece, well made, probably of Spanish origin, with a basket hilt and no fancy embellishments for decoration. It was the sort of blade a soldier would wear, useful, but not ostentatious.

Corwin, on the other hand, took rather more trouble with his appearance. His dark blond hair was worn longer, down below the shoulders as was fashionable among many of the young aristocrats at court these days, and his short, elegant beard and moustache were carefully trimmed in the French style. He obviously spent more money on his clothes, as evidenced by his three-piled, burgundy velvet doublet with twin rows of pewter buttons and slashed sleeves displaying a black silk shirt, his new black leather kidskin breeches, his fine hose in the dark eggplant color known among the fashionable tailors as "dead Spaniard," his stack-heeled shoes with silver buckles, and his silk-lined burgundy wool cloak. He looked very pretty, Smythe thought wryly, like a journeyman who spent all his money on his clothes and skipped meals in order to look prosperous. Save that in Corwin's case, he corrected himself, it was very likely that he might not have to skip meals, if what they said about his work was true. Either way, thought Smythe, it still looked as if he were trying a bit too hard, and next to Dickens, he still came up a little short, despite the plainness of the latter's apparel. All in all, a decidedly odd couple, it seemed. Somehow, they were not two men he would have put together.

Corwin greeted everyone politely, yet without the same warm enthusiasm as did Dickens. True, these were not old friends of his, thought Smythe, but at the same time, he marked how Corwin's gaze held a touch of condescension in it that he either disguised poorly or else made a poor effort to disguise. And there was a smug superiority in his manner for which Smythe did not much care. His recent elevation from an apprentice to a journeyman must have made him dizzy, so much so that the height seemed rather greater to him than it was.

At that moment, Molly came out from the back. She saw Dickens and her step faltered for a moment, though Smythe did not think that anyone but he had noticed, and then she swept into the taproom, carrying her tray, her manner blithe, carefree, and a touch sardonic, as usual.

"Hark, I thought I heard the door fly open and a great wind come blowing through," she said, without even glancing at Dickens.

Dickens turned and saw her, cocked his head, and smiled. "What, my dear Lady Disdain," he said, insouciantly. "Are you still living?"

"Now how could disdain die with such abundant food as you to feed it, Ben?" she countered, as she went about her work.

"Oh, marry, that was well struck!" said Shakespeare. "Would that I had thought of that!"

"Never fear, doubtless you shall," replied Smythe, with a smile.

"Burbage, strike him for me," Shakespeare said. "He sits too far away, I cannot reach him."

"Not I," said Burbage, shaking his head. "He would make two of me."

"Two of you? He looks more like three of you," said Speed.

"I am not too far away to reach *you*, Bobby," Smythe cautioned him good naturedly.

"Then I shall bestir myself and get me hence," said Speed, changing his seat to a nearby table. "Here, Ben, take my old seat, next to this stout infant."

"I shall, indeed, afore yon lady's lashing tongue doth trip me up," said Dickens.

"It takes no tongue lashing from the likes of me to do that, Ben," Molly said. "I must have seen your own tongue trip you up a thousand times."

"A thousand! Zounds, a thousand, you say?"

"Well, at least a hundred, surely."

"Look how she retreats from her first estimate," he said to the others.

"But never from my first impression," Molly added, to the amusement of the others.

"Tart," said Dickens, with a wry grimace.

"What speech is this?" asked Molly, rounding on him, her eyes flashing.

"I said that I do believe your wit has grown more tart."

She grimaced. "As yours has grown more stale."

"Have a care," said Smythe. "Another moment and they shall come to blows."

"Oh, not I," said Dickens, shaking his head emphatically. "I fear I may be overmatched."

"You need fear no match for bluster, nor yet for arrogance," said Molly.

"The lady would seem to bear you little love," said Corwin to his friend.

"Bear you a mountain, sir," she said to him, "then I assure you, 'twould be as a kernel next to the love he bears for his own self."

"I would my horse had the speed of your tongue, Molly," said Dickens, throwing his hands up in surrender. "I know you of old, and I see now you have not changed."

"Aye, nor have you, and more's the pity," she said, as she picked up the empty tankards and departed.

Dickens looked after her and sighed. "Go as you will, Molly," he said. "Keep your way, for I have done."

"And well done, I should think," said Corwin. "The lady's temper is as fiery as her hair."

"Ah, you noted that, did you?"

"I did, indeed. As I did also note that Master Leonardo has a daughter of surpassing beauty. I meant to ask you about her. Did you mark her when they left together in his carriage?"

Dickens shrugged. "I recall a dusky-looking wench with long, dark tresses, but beyond that, I did not mark her in any one particular. In truth, she did not strike me as any great beauty."

"Then you must not have marked her well," protested Corwin, "for to me she was the sweetest lady that ever I had looked on, a girl with a temperament as modest as your Molly's is tempestuous."

"Think you so?" He turned to the players with a smirk. "How do you like my friend here? So astute a judge of character and nature is he that he may deduce a lady's temperament merely by observing how she sits inside a carriage! Faith, and I would swear that she did never utter but one word, modestly or otherwise, in the brief time that we saw her!"

"You may jest, Ben," said Corwin, "but her demeanor was

demure and sweet, 'twas clear and evident to me. I tell you that I have never seen such a rare jewel."

"You speak as if this were a jewel you would possess," said Dickens.

"Indeed, I would, if there were a way to make her mine," said Corwin, "for after seeing her, I do not believe that I could suffer to have any other man but me possess her."

"This lady must be a jewel of great rarity, indeed, to make a man so covet the possession of her," Smythe said.

"Had you but seen her, sir, then you would have had no doubt upon that score, despite what my friend Ben says. He sees no special virtue in any one woman, as he loves all the fair sex equally. Or so he claims."

"Well, some better than others," Dickens said, with a grin. "Or at least more often."

"Again, you jest, but I remain in earnest," Corwin said. "I was hoping that you would speak on my behalf to Master Leonardo."

"Odd's blood, but you must truly be in earnest! Do you mean to turn husband, then?"

"Though I had often sworn the contrary, I daresay I would forswear myself if sweet Hera would agree to be my wife."

"Good Lord! Has not the world but one man who will wear his cap with suspicion? Shall I never see a bachelor of threescore again? Why do you come to me with this? Why not ask Master Peters to speak on your behalf, instead?" asked Dickens.

"I shall, indeed, ask him to speak for me. But Master Leonardo knows you better, and I could see that he held you in high respect."

"You flatter me from selfish motives. I see you are a knave, sir."

"Nay, Ben, truly—"

"Oh, very well then, thrust your neck into a yoke and wear

the print of it if that is what you wish. I shall speak to Master Leonardo for you."

"Who is this Master Leonardo, Ben?" asked Burbage.

"He is a merchant trader with his own ship, lately come from Genoa," Dickens replied. "I sailed from the Netherlands with him. He has made his fortune in voyages to the New World and has now come to make his home in London."

Burbage looked as if he might have had another question, but at that moment, their attention was distracted by all the noise coming from outside. The sounds of people shouting, screaming, and running rose rapidly outside on the street, followed by the sounds of hoofbeats clattering on the cobblestones.

"Another bloody riot," Courtney Stackpole said gruffly, coming out from behind the bar with a thick adze handle in his hand. "If they break my windows once again, so help me, I'll have somebody's guts for garters!"

"It sounds as if the sheriff's men are riding them down to break it up," said Fleming.

No sooner had he spoken than the front door was flung open with a bang and two tough-looking young men came stumbling in, out of breath from running. They slammed the door behind them and leaned against it, as if to hold off pursuit. One of them, Smythe noticed, was brandishing a club, while the other held a good-sized dagger.

2

"I'LL BE THANKING YE TO turn right around and haul your carcasses back out into the street, afore I break both of your heads open," Stackpole said, in a voice that clearly brooked no argument.

The two apprentices glared at him belligerently, but his imposing presence made them think twice about making any rude retorts. "We want no trouble, see?" one of them said. He smiled and made a show of sheathing his knife. He put his hands out to his sides, then nudged his pockmarked friend to drop his club. "Nice and peaceful, eh? We have no quarrel with you, Innkeeper, nor would we be wanting one. We'd just like to buy ourselves a pint or two now, with your kind permission, and then be on our way, right?"

Stackpole pointed at them with the adze handle. "A pint apiece," he said gruffly, "and then be off with ye. And mind, I'll be remembering your faces. If I get me windows broken once again, 'tis you that I'll be looking for."

"Well now, what if 'twasn't us who broke 'em then, eh?" the pockmarked apprentice said. Smythe noted that he had one of those unpleasant, sneering sorts of faces that wore a perpetual expression of insolent aggression.

"I suppose 'twould add incentive then for you to persuade

the other Steady Boys you run with to leave Master Stackpole's windows well enough alone," said Dickens.

They glanced toward him sharply, then Smythe saw recognition dawn on both their faces. "Well, smite me, if it ain't Ben Dickens!" the first one said. Unlike his pockmarked friend, he was rather handsome in a pugnacious sort of way, with a thick shock of black hair and deeply set, dark eyes that glinted with insolent amusement.

" 'Allo, Jack," said Dickens. " 'Allo, Bruce."

"When did you get back, then?" asked Jack, approaching him.

"Only just this morning," Dickens replied.

"Come back to visit some of your old friends, I see," said Bruce, who seemed to have a whiney, spiteful tone no matter what he said. "But there were some old friends I suppose ye couldn't be bothered with, eh?"

"Nothing of the sort," Dickens replied. "I first went to pay my respects to Master Peters, as 'twas only right and proper. 'Twas there I encountered my new friend, Will Shakespeare here. Upon discovering that he had joined the Queen's Men, my old company, why I at once informed him that I would next be coming here to pay them my respects. Now, had I encountered you and Jack first, then I might well have stopped by at your shop before ever coming here, although 'twould seem from what I heard outside just now that I would not have found you there. Either way, lads, never let it be said that Ben Dickens would slight any of his old friends. Not even you, Bruce."

"Oh, and what's that supposed to mean then, eh?" asked Bruce, taking a step towards him belligerently. However, his fellow apprentice quickly intervened.

"It means that he remembers his old friends, Bruce. Just as he remembers still how easily you can be baited. Don't get your back up. It's just our old friend Ben, see?"

"Well, 'tis growing late and I really should be going," Corwin said, getting to his feet. "You *will* speak on my behalf to Master Leonardo, won't you, Ben? You did promise."

"I promised that I would and so I shall, my friend," said Dickens, holding out his hand. As Corwin took it, he added, "And if my word bears any weight, why then, you may soon receive permission to go courting your young goddess, Hera. After that, why 'tis up to you, entirely."

"I could never ask for more," said Corwin with a smile. "Gentlemen, I bid you all good night."

"Good night, Corwin," Shakespeare said.

"And good luck in your suit," added Burbage, with a grin. "Come and bring your pretty Hera to see us at the theatre when we open once again."

"If her father proves agreeable, why then I may even spring for a box up in the galleries," Corwin replied with a smile.

"So speaks the prosperous new journeyman," said Jack, with a heavy touch of sarcasm in his tone. "One might think that you could easily afford box seats at each performance with all of your success these days. Or perhaps 'tis an apprentice's frugality that still lingers out of force of habit?"

"Frugality is not a habit that I would discard as easily as some might discard a perfectly good cloak merely because it has gone slightly out of fashion," Corwin replied, with an obvious reference to Jack's brand new velvet cloak. "The habit lingers because it makes good sense, for either an apprentice *or* a journeyman, and 'tis a habit, I might add, that you might do well to emulate. Good night, sir."

"Do you presume, then, to instruct me?" Jack called after Corwin as he left. "You are not a master guildsman *yet*, sir! It ill behooves a man to put on airs above his station!"

"Oh, enough of that, now. Come sit down and have a drink, lads," Dickens said, good naturedly. "Gentlemen," he said, turning to the others, "allow me to present Jack Darnley and Bruce McEnery, old friends of mine from my apprentice days."

"Well met, lads," Burbage said jovially, moving over to make room for them, though Smythe did not think that he was truly eager for their company. Nevertheless, Burbage politely introduced himself and all the other players in their group. Stackpole brought the drinks himself, giving the two apprentices a wary eye in the process. Smythe had the distinct impression that they were no more eager for the company of players than the players were to sit with them. However, Ben Dickens seemed to provide a sort of buffer between them, acting as a conversational go between in a way that seemed to lessen the tension.

As they talked, Smythe could not decide if it was all a skillful display of diplomacy or merely a natural way that Dickens had of controlling the flow of conversation around him. The discussion centered, for the most part, on his experiences as a soldier and the things that he had seen while he was away in foreign lands. When he did not actually dominate the conversation, Dickens seemed to steer it in directions that were basically innocuous and safe, allowing the others to take part without ever losing his command of the discussion. Smythe could easily see why Ben Dickens had been so well liked by the members of the company. He possessed an easygoing charm and had a way of creating a sense of cameraderie around him. It was clear that he would have been a natural as a player. He had the way about him.

Not so Bruce and Jack, Smythe noted. They nursed their drinks, mindful that they would only be allowed the one pint each, and as they listened to Ben talk, the envy was clearly written on their faces. In the case of Bruce, it was more than merely envy; it was spiteful resentment, and ill-concealed at that.

Smythe thought it rather strange. Here they were, senior apprentices still enjoying their rowdy youth while on the threshold of becoming journeymen—which would bring them a good living and in time, with diligence and perseverence, would likely bring them wealth—while on the other hand, there was Ben Dickens, a mercenary soldier whose prospects, unless Fortune were to smile upon him, were very poor, indeed. He could only sell his sword arm to whoever needed fighting men at any given time, and while the world had not yet banished war, the employment of a soldier was often interspersed with protracted periods of peace. At present, there was no shortage of soldiers in the city searching for employment, not all of it gainful, nor even honest work. And few soldiers of fortune, a misnomer if Smythe had ever heard one, were fortunate enough to live to a ripe and whole old age. Of those who did not die in battle, many became maimed or crippled and were reduced to begging in the streets. He saw them every day, dressed in their worn-out soldier's motley, many of them missing arms or legs. It was not a life for anyone to envy. And yet, as he watched Bruce and Jack listening to Dickens, he could see they envied him. True, he was still young and whole and healthy, but his future was as uncertain as their futures seemed assured. But perhaps they could not see that.

What they *could* see, though, was Molly. Perhaps because of the words she had with Dickens, or perhaps because Stackpole had chosen to serve them himself, so as to keep an eye on the troublesome twosome, Molly had not come near their tables since the pair came in. But they both noticed her, all right, and their gazes followed her everywhere she went. Smythe saw Shakespeare notice it, as well, but it did not seem as though anybody else did.

"So then," Dickens said to them, as he finished off an anecdote, "if memory serves me, you lads should both be nearing the completion of your apprenticeships with Master St. John, is that not right?"

"Indeed, I have but a few months to go," said Jack, "whilst

Bruce, here, has a bit less than a year remaining. Then we shall both be journeymen, as you could have been by now, Ben, had you not run off to war."

"Run off?" said Fleming, rising to the defense of his former protege. "By Heaven, I daresay I would scarce call putting life and limb at hazard 'running off!' Life in London poses fewer risks, by far, than what life as a soldier would entail. Now who could gainsay that?"

"Not I," Jack hastily replied. "Do not mistake my meaning, good sirs. Odd's blood, Ben always was the man you wanted at your back when things got nasty. Why, I remember that time we had a set-to with the Paris Garden Boys and that rotter, Mercutio, God curse his swarthy Roman forebears, slashed me with his stiletto. I still have the scar, see?" He pulled back the long hair from his forehead, revealing a livid scar that ran across his forehead to his temple. "Damn near took me ear off. He would've done for me for sure if Ben here hadn't pulled him off and slammed his face into a wall. Blind me, you should have seen him! Mashed his nose right flat, he did, and knocked out his two front teeth. We dusted 'em off right proper that night, didn't we, Ben? Those were the days, eh? The Steady Boys owned the streets then, didn't we?"

"Well, you seem to have somewhat fonder recollections of those days than I," said Dickens, wryly. "All told, we were fortunate not to have wound up in prison or, worse yet, cut up and with our skulls busted in some alleyway."

"And how is it any different for a soldier?" asked Bruce, with a sneer. "Tell me that, then."

"Perhaps 'tis not so different after all," Dickens replied, "but at least a soldier gets paid for risking life and limb, though not nearly enough, if you ask me. And truth be told, if I knew then what I know now, why, 'tis doubtful that I would have made the same decision. Either way, when I was with the Steady Boys, as I recall, we risked life and limb for no more reward than the thrill of breaking someone else's skull. Even back then, I thought 'twas rash and foolhardy to behave so, although I went along with all the others. And 'twould seem that with your apprenticeships nearly completed, 'tis even more rash and foolhardy to take such chances now. Odd's blood, why risk your future, lads? You've worked hard for all these years, and the payoff is now nearly at hand. Why risk throwing it all away for a few thrills?"

"Well, smite me!" said Jack, with surprise. "I must say, you certainly seem changed, Ben. That does not at all sound like the Ben Dickens I once knew."

"Perhaps he *has* changed, then. Perhaps he came back from the wars because he lost his nerve," said Bruce, contemptuously.

"Here now . . ." Fleming began, but Dickens put his hand out, forestalling his comment. He fixed Bruce with a steady gaze, transfixing him with an unblinking stare the surly apprentice gamely tried to meet, but after a moment, Bruce found himself forced to blink and look away.

"I do not need some lickspittle street brawler to tell me I have lost my nerve," said Dickens, softly. "When you have seen men dying on the field of battle by the thousands, when the stench of bodies swelling and bursting in the sun assails your senses til your head reels and your eyes burn, when the buzzing of the flies over the carrion fills your ears, so that you go on hearing it for days and days after the battle has been fought until you think you will go mad with it, when you have seen women and old men searching for their fallen sons' amongst the corpses and when you have heard their wails of grief on finding the mutilated objects of their quest, why, *then* you can come and speak to me about my nerve. Until then, apprentice, best stick with your clubs and daggers and your cocksure roaring boys, posturing and puffing out their chests, and speak not to me of things that you cannot even begin to understand."

Bruce rose to his feet with a snarl, reaching for his dagger, but before he could unsheath it, Jack grabbed his hand in both of his, preventing him from drawing it.

As Smythe and several of the others leapt to their feet, Bruce sputtered with rage as he struggled angrily against his friend. "Let me go, damn you!"

"Don't be a fool," Jack replied in a steady voice, maintaining his grip and strengthening it by pressing his body up close against his friend, immobilizing his arms between them. "You only have your dirk, whilst he wears a rapier. Aside from that, in the event you have not noticed, we are quite outnumbered here."

"That *does* it!" Stackpole said, hefting the adze handle once again as he came out from behind the bar. "Out with you! And don't be coming back!"

"You've not seen the last of us, old man," said Bruce, sneering at him.

"Old man, is it? I'll bloody well show ye who's old, ye miserable guttersnipe!" He swung the adze handle and it made a sound like the Grim Reaper's scythe cutting through the air. It narrowly missed Bruce as he ducked at the last instant, barely avoiding having his skull split. Before Stackpole could swing again, Jack shoved Bruce toward the door and quickly followed.

"You shouldn't turn your back on your old friends, Ben!" he called back over his shoulder. "You were one of us, one of the Steady Boys, and we ain't never let you down!"

"You just did, Jack," Dickens replied, with a wry grimace. "You just did."

"*Out, I said!*" roared Stackpole, brandishing his adze handle.

Bruce held up two fingers and went out the door, with Jack on his heels.

"And good bloody riddance!" Fleming said, emphatically.

"And those were truly *friends* of yours?" asked Burbage, with distaste.

"Aye, at one time," said Dickens. "And great good friends they were. Or at least, so I believed back then."

"And now at last you see them for what they truly were," said Fleming, with a righteous air.

Dickens smiled. "Perhaps," he said. "But if so, John, then I see myself for what I truly was, as well."

"Well, now, methinks you judge yourself a bit too harshly, lad," Fleming said, patting him on the shoulder. "I never knew you to be a coarse, ill-mannered ruffian, like that lot. And even if you once did have some common ground with the likes of those two scalawags, why, you have been out to see the world and you know much better now."

"Do I?" Dicken said. "I wonder. 'Tis indeed a thing devoutly to be wished, however things may stand. A man can only hope to grow wiser as the years accumulate, though I fear not all men do."

"And in that observation, there is wisdom, Ben," said Burbage, with a smile, "so 'twould seem that you are on the right path after all."

"I wish I felt as certain of that as you, old friend," Dickens replied.

Burbage frowned. "What do mean by that? You mean to say that you have doubts about the course you chose?"

"I have been giving it much thought of late," said Dickens, nodding. "And especially so on the voyage home with Master Leonardo. He has made his fortune on his voyages and now seeks to settle down to a gentleman's life. He desires to use some of his profits to invest in business. 'Tis possible that his interests and mine may coincide in some degree."

"So then you plan to give up soldiering and remain in London?" Fleming said.

"Well, I have, as yet, made no firm decisions," Dickens answered, "but I have found that the adventuring life has lost much of its allure for me. It feels good to be back home in England once again, amongst old friends. And new ones, of course." He smiled at Smythe and Shakespeare and the other players who had joined the company since he left.

"'Tis good to have you back, as well, Ben," Burbage said. "And if, by chance, your plans with Master Leonardo do not come to fruition, although we wish you all success, I am sure that we could find a place for you with the Queen's Men once again, at the very least until you should decide upon which path your future lies."

"I'll drink to that!" said Speed.

"So shall we all!" said Fleming. "Stackpole, my good man, more ale, if you please!"

Later that night, as he lay in bed upstairs, Smythe thought about the events of the evening, feeling an unsettling disquiet that he could not account for. It was not simply that Bruce McEnery had tried to draw steel in the Toad and Badger. At least, Smythe did not think that was the reason for his apprehension. Although that sort of thing did not usually happen downstairs in the tavern, it was not entirely unheard of, and it was not the sort of thing that made him feel particularly squeamish. He had seen tavern brawls before and on occasion been involved in them. On at least one of those occasions, that memorable day when he and Will had first arrived in London and met Chris Marlowe and Sir William Worley at the Swan and Maiden, both blades *and* blood were drawn. On that day too, as he recalled, a street riot had preceeded the festivities, setting the tone for the violence to follow. Mob violence always seemed to get people's blood up, even if they were not themselves involved. But there was something else that gnawed at him, maybe something unrelated that he could not quite put his finger on. Something about those two apprentices, perhaps . . .

"Well, all right, what *is* it?" Shakespeare said, putting down his quill pen and turning round from his work desk to face him.

"What? I said nothing," Smythe replied, glancing at him with surprise.

The gentle glow of candlelight illuminated Shakespeare's face as he sighed and rolled his eyes. "I know," he said. "You *said* nothing, but your restlessness spoke volumes. You grunted and you sighed, time and time again, and as if that were not enough, you keep squirming on that mattress like a nervous virgin on her wedding night. By Heaven, for all the noise you're making, 'tis like trying to work with a bull grazing in one's bedroom!"

"I am sorry, Will. I did not mean to disturb you at your work."

"Aye, you never mean to, and yet you always do." He removed his ink-stained writing glove and tossed it on his desk. The kidskin glove had no mate, for he had made only the one, expressly for the task of keeping ink stains off his fingers while he wrote, so that people would not constantly mistake him for a scribe. It also served as a reminder that if he did not become successful as a poet or a player, there was always his father's trade of glovemaking to go back to, something he earnestly wanted to avoid.

He sighed wearily and ran his hands through his thinning, chestnut hair. "I do not know how I shall ever manage to write anything at all with the likes of you about. At this rate, I do not think that I shall ever manage to get past 'Act I, Scene I, Enter funeral.' "

" 'Enter funeral?' Well, there's a cheery opening. What happens in Act II? A war?"

"What, are you a critic now? 'Strewth, you may as well be.

You cannot write, you cannot act; clearly, you have all of the right qualifications. You even add a new one; you review my play before I have even written it. A brilliant innovation, I must say. Just think of all the time it saves."

Smythe grimaced. "Never mind, go back to work if you are going to be so surly."

"Well, now that you have muddled up my muse beyond all recognition, you may as well tell me what is on your mind, for clearly, something troubles you. I know that mien of yours when something preys upon your brain. The very air around you is turbid and oppressive. So, come on, give voice to it, or else neither of us shall have any peace upon this night."

"To be truthful, I am not quite certain what the matter is," Smythe said, with a grimace.

"Hmm. 'Twill be like pulling teeth, I see. Very well, then, what does it concern?"

"Not what so much as whom. Methinks 'tis your new friend, Ben Dickens."

"Ben? Why? He seems like an absolutely splendid fellow."

"Oh, I grant you that," Smythe replied. "He does seem like a decent sort, yet there is still something about him . . . something . . . I do not know what; I cannot quite put my finger on it."

"You are not envious of him, surely?"

"I should not like to think so. I but bemoan my own shortcomings, as you know, and I admit them freely. Now that you mention it, however, I can see how others might well envy Ben his winning ways. To wit, those two apprentices, Jack and Bruce, his friends of old."

"He would be better off without such friends, if you ask me," said Shakespeare, disapprovingly.

"Oh, I quite agree," said Smythe. "A thoroughly unpleasant pair, they were. You saw the way they looked at Molly?"

"Aye," Shakespeare replied, with a grimace of distaste. "The way a hungry wolf looks upon a lamb. Especially that Bruce. And did you mark how she never once came near our table after those two came in?"

"So you noted that, as well. I thought you did."

"I did, indeed. And from it I deduce that Molly is an excellent judge of character. But what has any of this to do with Ben?"

Smythe shook his head. "I cannot say." He frowned. "And yet I feel a disquiet in my soul about him."

"A disquiet in your soul?" Shakespeare grinned. "Odd's blood, have you developed poetic sensibilities?"

Smythe snorted. "If so, then 'tis entirely your fault, for you are a bad influence. The way you walk about, mumbling verses to yourself, 'tis bound to rub off on one sooner or later."

Shakespeare raised his eyebrows. "I mumble verses?"

"Constantly. Under your breath, sometimes even in your sleep."

"Indeed? I had no earthly idea. In my *sleep*, you say?"

"Aye. Not all the time, but often enough that you wake me upon occasion."

"Truly? How extraordinary. When I do so, would it trouble you to write it down?"

"Now there speaks a writer," Smythe replied. "Not 'I am sorry, Tuck, for troubling your sleep with my dreamful babble,' but 'Would it trouble you to write it down?' Selfishness, thy name is poetry!"

"Oh, say, that is not bad at all! Wait, let me set it down . . ."

Smythe threw a pillow at him.

"Zounds! Watch out, for God's sake! You will upset my ink-well!"

"If I do, then 'twill be the first time that any ink was set down upon that page this night," Smythe replied, dryly.

"Sod off!"

"Sod off yourself. You are getting nowhere and you seek to blame it all on me, when in truth the fault lies entirely with you. I *can* see, you know. You sit there and stare off into the distance, as if your very gaze could penetrate the ceiling and look out upon the starry firmament, and your lips move as you mumble softly to yourself, and then you make a motion as if to set your pen to paper, but soft! You pause . . . your quill hovers as if in expectation, and then you set it down once more and stare off into the distance, and so it goes, with little variation, as it has gone so many nights of late, whether I have been plagued with restlessness or not."

"You are a foul villain!"

"And you are a prating capon."

"Dissentious rogue!"

"Soused goose!"

"Carrion kite!"

"Perfidious wretch!"

"Churlish minion!"

"Mincing queen!"

"Oh, you venemous monster! I do *not* mince! 'Tis but a slight limp in my leg."

"Limpness resides in more than just thy leg, methinks."

"You abominable apparition! Ungrateful bounder! Thus you impugn me when I have spoken up for you and fed you and defended you—"

"Defended me? 'Gainst whom?"

"Well . . . 'gainst certain individuals who wouldst' have others think base things of you."

"*What* individuals? *What* base things? *What* others?"

"Nay, now, let us speak no more of this. 'Twould serve no useful purpose."

"Who speaks ill of me?" persisted Smythe. "Someone in the company?"

"Well, now, I did not say that . . ."

"Not in the company? Then who . . . surely not Elizabeth!"

"Nay, not Elizabeth. What have I to do with her or she with me? It matters not. Forget I even mentioned it."

"But I do not even know what was mentioned!"

"So much the better, then. Let sleeping dogs lie. 'Tis for the best."

"*Will!*"

"Nay, I have said all that I shall say. Thus let there be an end to it."

Smythe folded his arms and gazed at him truculently. "Ah. So I see. No one has said anything, is that not so? You are but baiting me again, as is your wont."

"Just so, Tuck. You have found me out. See, you are much too clever for me. I cannot outwit you."

"Nay, you throw in your cards too quickly. Someone truly said something about me, did they not?"

"Not at all. 'Twas all in jest, I tell you. You had it right the first time. I did but bait you, as I so often do."

"Truly?"

"Truly."

Smythe lay back on the bed and put his hands behind his head, frowning as he stared up at the ceiling. He gave an irritated, sidelong glance toward Shakespeare, who had turned back to the sheets of parchment spread out on his writing desk. Smythe took a deep breath and let it out slowly. He cleared his throat. He wiggled his foot back and forth. He tried hard to lie still. He clicked his teeth together. Finally, he could stand it no longer.

"Will, honestly, tell me the truth. Who was speaking ill of me?"

Shakespeare ignored him.

"Will? Did you hear me?"

There was no response.

"*Will!*"

Shakespeare reached for his quill and held it poised over the parchment.

"Oh, very well, then," Smythe said, irritably, as he got to his feet and reached for his boots and short woolen cloak. "Be a stubborn jade! See if I care! I can find better things to do than waste my time with your nonsense!"

He slammed the door on his way out.

Without looking up, Shakespeare chuckled softly to himself. "Ah, would that 'twere all so simple and predictable," he said. And then he sighed. "Now then, where was I? Act I, Scene I. Enter funeral . . ."

3

THERE WERE STILL PEOPLE DRINKING in the tavern as Smythe came back downstairs, carrying his boots and cloak. Bobby Speed was among them, as well as George Bryan and several other members of the company, although they would not have much coin left among them to divide for drinking. Will's largesse notwithstanding, Smythe knew they would all have to make some money very soon, or else many of them would stand in danger of being thrown out into the street. Most of the players saved money by sharing quarters, as he and Will did, but things were getting tight, and with the shortage of rooms in London these days, if it came down to a choice, then it was better to starve and have a place to sleep than placate a growling stomach and risk losing a roof over one's head. With the recent setbacks they had suffered, even before the playhouses had been closed, they all needed to have the Theatre reopen very soon or else it might well spell the end of the Queen's Men.

Sitting on the bottom steps, Smythe pulled on his boots. He did not particularly feel like going back into the tavern. Drinking held little fascination for him. Until he came to London, he had never used to drink spirits at all. For a cool drink, he prefered spring water, and for a hot beverage, he had often enjoyed a healthful herbal infusion that a local cunning woman in his village had taught him to brew. He was still able to get the ingredients from Granny Meg's apothecary shop, but now he mostly drank it cold, after brewing it in an earthen jar on his window. More and more, however, he found himself drinking small beer or ale, primarily because it was what everybody else drank. Londoners had ale for breakfast, ale for dinner, ale for supper, and ale in between. Those who could afford it drank imported wine, but absolutely no one in the city drank water and the idea of brewing an infusion from "weeds" seemed very peculiar to most people.

Smythe had learned to drink ale in order to be sociable, but he was careful not to drink too much, because he knew he had no head for it. Shakespeare, on the other hand, indulged heavily, sometimes to the point of near insensibility, though that point for him was reached long after most people had become utterly paralyzed with drink. There were few players in the Queen's Men who could keep up with him and Smythe knew better than to try. He had learned that it was best to nurse his ale and drink sparingly, otherwise his head would pay the price.

It was a lesson a lot of people never seemed to learn. At this hour, Smythe knew those players still remaining in the tavern would be three sheets to the wind, and there was nothing quite as uninteresting as being sober in the midst of drunken revelry. Besides, he was not much in the mood for company. He felt like going for a walk. And in all fairness, Will needed his time alone, as well. Smythe knew that Shakespeare could work best when left completely on his own, without any distractions, which was perhaps the main reason why he seemed to work best during the night.

Will was still trying to work on several ideas for original plays, but much to his frustration, playwriting was not what was bringing in the money for him right now. Shakespeare's sonnets were becoming rather popular among some of the fashionable young gentlemen at court and if he kept on his present course,

there was a good chance that he would soon find a wealthy nobleman to be his patron. In fact, judging by what had happened
earlier that day, he may already have found one, though he was
being rather circumspect about it. Smythe could understand the
reasons for that, but if Will had found himself a patron, then it
could easily turn out to be a two-edged sword.

The other players were all happy for his good fortune, and
grateful that he chose to share the wealth, but at the same time,
Smythe could see that they were somewhat apprehensive. Will
had quickly become a valuable commodity to the Queen's Men.
He was industrious and capable of working quickly. He had already rewritten several of the plays in their repertoire, improving
them significantly in the process, and the proof was in the pud-
ding. Audiences had responded far more favorably to the rewritten versions than they had to the earlier ones, and Will had a
knack of revising as they went along, making alterations from
performance to performance by taking into account the reactions
of the audiences and the contributions of the players.

Unlike many of the university men, who often seemed to act
as if their words had emananted from a burning bush and thus
were sacrosanct, Shakespeare understood that plays were a col-
laborative effort, depending upon the contributions of everybody
in the company for their success. As a result, within a fairly short
time, he had risen in stature from ostler and hired man to book
holder and stage manager for the company. Both Burbages, father and son, were anxious to see what he could do when it came
to writing an original play.

However, revising the current plays in their repertoire had
taken precedence, for that was where the immediate improvements to their fortunes could be made. Now, with the playhouses
closed, even that work was being put off while Shakespeare had
to strike where the iron was hot. His writing of sonnets on commission was helping to support them all right now, so the other

players could hardly begrudge him his efforts in that regard. Yet, if his "strumpet sonneteering," as he called it, happened to secure a wealthy patron for him, which was the true heart's desire of every poet in London, then perforce that patron would be the one who called the tune, and he might well choose to have his house poet spend all of his time creating sonnets for publication, rather than writing plays or acting with a company of players.

On the other hand, it was also possible that a wealthy patron might enjoy having a poet in his service who wrote plays. Some of the university men, such as Kit Marlowe, had such patrons and were allowed considerable freedom in writing what they chose. Robert Greene, for instance, wrote not only plays and poetry, but also cautionary pamphlets on the art of "cony-catching." To Smythe, coming from the country, cony-catching had always meant hunting rabbits, but in the underworld of London's criminals, it had another meaning altogether.

To the cutpurses, foists, and alleymen of London, a "cony" was a victim, an innocent rabbit to be caught and skinned, whether by outright theft or trickery. And though Greene's plays had not impressed Smythe particularly, his pamphlets had proved very educational. John Fleming had told him that they should be required reading for anyone coming to London from the country and on his recommendation, Smythe had purchased several and found them well worth the few pennies he had spent.

They described how the criminals of London plied their trade, from the "lifters" who stole goods from shops by concealing them upon their persons, to "curbers" who used hooks on poles to steal things out of windows that had been left open, to the "jackmen" who forged licenses, to "divers" who used small boys to squeeze through windows or other narrow openings and steal for them, to "nips" and "foists" or cutpurses and their accomplices, Green's pamphlets described all manner of thievery and "cozenage," which was the art of gaining someone's confi-

dence so that the "cozener" or "con man" could then cheat or
steal from the "gull" or the person being deceived. There was an
entire language, called a "cant," that was spoken by the members
of the London underworld and doubtless, Smythe thought,
Greene was not endearing himself to London's criminals by ex-
posing so many of their tricks and secrets.

As he went outside, the bellman came walking by, carrying
his pike and bell and lantern. The city gates were closed at night-
fall and now he made his rounds, calling out the hour in his
singsong chant:

> "Remember the clocks, look well to your locks,
> fire and your light, an' God give ye good night,
> for now the bell ringeth, eight of the clock!"

As part of the watch, the bellman ostensibly patrolled the
streets in order to protect the citizenry at night, but in truth, he
provided little more protection than did the other constables of
the watch, which was to say practically none at all. His primary
value was in his ability to sound the call in case of fire, which
aside from the plague was probably the single greatest danger to
the city, especially with so much shoddy construction and the
buildings piled up so closely against one another. And in the
event of fire, there was usually not much that could be saved, for
the only recourse was to fight it with hooks and buckets brigaded
from the wells, and the buildings, for the most part, were so
cheaply made that they went up like kindling.

As he came out into the street, Smythe nodded to the bellman as he went by, then stood there for a few moments, enjoying
the cool night air. The stench of the streets was somewhat tem-
pered on this night by a good, strong breeze coming in off the
river, for which Smythe was thankful. He did not know if he
would ever become fully accustomed to the city's smells. The

little country village where he grew up was clean and fresh compared to London. Here, everyone simply threw their refuse out
into the streets, so that the cobbles were almost perpetually covered with a coating of slime, which was rinsed away only by a
hard rain, though not even a good downpour would wash away
all of the refuse piled up and stinking in the streets. And the
streets that were not cobbled were almost continually churned
into a quagmire, so that navigating them became a challenge to
man and horse alike. Here, where Smythe stood, the filth drained
down into a depression that ran down the center of the street,
and that in turn drained into Fleet Ditch, which stank so badly
that it made the eyes water and sting.

He hopped over the ditch as he crossed the street, thinking
perhaps to wander down by the river for a while, but then he
looked back and saw Molly coming out of the tavern, wrapped
in her threadbare, brown woolen cloak, her cap upon her head.
She did not see him where he stood. It looked as if she were
going home for the night, and Smythe thought that perhaps he
should offer to escort her, for being abroad alone in London's
streets at night was not safe for a woman. Especially a woman
as young and pretty as Molly. However, before he could go
across the street and make the offer, Smythe saw her meet a man
who had apparently been waiting for her outside.

In the darkness, as the man came up to her, Smythe did not
get a very good look at him, but he seemed to be a tall, long-
legged fellow, dressed in high boots and dark breeches, a long
dark cloak, and a wide-brimmed, rakish hat. From the way the
cloak poked out at the bottom, Smythe could tell that the man
also wore a sword.

The dark stranger and Molly acted as if they knew each other
as they walked off together down the muddy, refuse-strewn
street. Out of curiosity, Smythe followed. He liked Molly, as did
all the players, with whom she was quite popular for her vivacity,

ready smile, and quick, sharp wit. They all felt rather protective of her. On more than one occasion, he had seen patrons of the Toad and Badger try their luck with her, but all to no avail. Molly's heart was spoken for. He had heard it said that Molly had loved a soldier who had gone away some time ago to fight in foreign lands. Now, after the events of earlier that day, it was evident to him who that soldier must have been. Anyone could clearly see that Molly and Ben Dickens had a strong mutual attraction. Anyone, apparently, except for Molly and Ben themselves. For some reason, they seemed either unable or unwilling to admit it to themselves or to one another. And to a point, Smythe could sympathize.

There were certain things that he and Elizabeth could not say or admit to one another, too. Of course, their situation was not really the same. Master Henry Darcie's daughter could hardly be courted by a lowly player. Sometimes it seemed as if she might as well be one of the queen's glories, for all the chance he had with her. Indeed, she often seemed as far above him as one of the queen's ladies in waiting, though as a successful merchant guildsman's daughter, Elizabeth was not quite as inaccessible. Pursuing one of the queen's glories could get a gentleman at court accomodations in the Tower of London, for the queen preferred to keep her young ladies as virginal as herself. Paying court to Elizabeth Darcie was not going to land him in the Tower, but it could certainly bring him a great deal of trouble if her father's permission were not secured. And the only thing that stood between Smythe and receiving that permission was his standing.

Smythe had no doubt that if he were a gentleman, then he would be welcomed as a suitor in Henry Darcie's home. And if he had a title, why then, the match would have been assured . . . provided that Elizabeth agreed. For though it was certainly not common practice for a father to seek his daughter's approval before arranging a match for her, Henry Darcie had learned the hard way that disregarding his daughter's wishes in that regard could only bring disaster. Nothing would have made him happier than to have his daughter married to a nobleman, and he had done his best to put her on display before them, but Elizabeth was a very forthright and willful young woman, for which reason she was still unmarried. However, there was a limit to how much willfulness Henry Darcie would put up with. He owed Smythe a debt of gratitude, and so did not object to him too strenuously, but then neither did he grant him his approval.

What Henry Darcie did not know, he could not object to, and so he was kept ignorant of their occasional meetings at the bookstalls in Paul's Walk or at the Theatre while the players were rehearsing. Had he troubled to, Henry Darcie could have easily found out about their meetings. For a man of his means, having his daughter followed would have been a simple thing for Henry Darcie to arrange and after he had satisfied himself that she was having assignations with someone who was thoroughly unsuitable, it would have been equally as simple for him to have Smythe beaten senseless, whipped, or even killed. Smythe knew such things were known to happen to those who aspired to rise, so to speak, above their station. However, there was a curious sort of unspoken understanding between him and Henry Darcie.

Darcie understood that he was a well-intentioned and honorable young man who would never do anything to bring dishonor to Elizabeth, just as he had faith that, for all her stubborn willfulness, his daughter would never do anything to bring dishonor to herself or to her family. Thus, he tolerated their relationship, if not openly, then at least by pretending not to know about it. Henry Darcie still had hopes of making a good marriage for Elizabeth, one that would help advance him socially, and he firmly believed that in time, the right aristocratic suitor would come along and Elizabeth would come to her senses and forget

all about her girlish infatuation with a lowly player. In the meantime, he chose to look the other way, because he knew that neither of them would go so far as to take their relationship past
the point of impropriety. And in that, Smythe found both solace
and frustration.

With Ben and Molly, on the other hand, there were no such
impediments. There was nothing to prevent them from finding
happiness with one another . . . if that was truly what they
wanted. To Smythe, they seemed kindred spirits, an ideal couple,
and he found it puzzling that they fenced the way they did. But
if this dark stranger had replaced Dickens in Molly's affections,
then perhaps that would explain it.

Without really thinking about why, he followed them for
several blocks, at a discreet distance. If Molly had a paramour,
then it was certainly none of his concern, but now that he found
his curiosity aroused, he felt reluctant to stand off and let them
go, as he knew he probably should. Especially since Molly's companion was carrying a sword and he had not troubled to bring
his.

Smythe knew that sort of forgetfulness was bound to get him
into trouble one of these days, but he still found it difficult to
think about buckling on his sword each time he went out somewhere. It was second nature to him to carry his uncle's dagger
with him everywhere, for he had carried it since he was a boy.
However, until he came London, there had never been any real
need to go about armed with a sword. Most of the men in London wore swords, though often more as fashion accessories than
as practical weapons. An elegant rapier was considered an essen-
tial item of apparel for a proper gentleman, even if he did not
have much idea how to use one. But although Smythe was a
competent fencer, he had yet to fall into the habit of wearing a
sword on a daily basis and unlike the typical London fop, who
had mastered the art of posturing rakishly with one hand on his

hip and the other resting lightly on the pommel of his sword, when Smythe did wear one, he found that it was always getting in his way.

A few more blocks and Molly had arrived safely at her door, escorted by the dark-cloaked stranger. Smythe watched from a distance as they lingered, speaking for a few moments in the street, then they embraced and exchanged chaste kisses on the cheek before Molly went inside and the stranger went off down the street alone. Well, whoever the fellow was, Smythe thought, he at least appeared to be behaving properly. But it did seem as if Ben Dickens may have lost his charm for Molly Beatrice O'Flannery.

He debated for a moment whether or not to follow the stranger and perhaps find out who he was, but then decided against it. It was truly none of his concern whom Molly chose to see. So long as she was not in any sort of trouble and the man was not a villain or a bounder who was trying to take advantage of her. For all he knew, perhaps the stranger was her brother or an uncle or some other relative. She had reached home safely and that was really all that mattered. He decided that he might as well head back toward the inn. Whatever vague apprehension had been troubling him before seemed to have gone now, which suggested that it must not have been of any true concern.

He had gone about a block or so when two men stepped out in front of him from a dark side street, blocking his way. There was no mistaking their confrontational demeanor. Both men carried clubs. Remembering what he had read in Greene's pamphlets about how alleymen waylaid their victims, Smythe stopped and backed up slightly, then quickly spun around, drawing his knife as he turned . . . only to find the tip of a sword point pressed lightly up against his Adam's apple.

"Quick, laddie, very quick. But not quite quick enough, eh?"

The voice was husky, raspy, and low, and not in the least bit apprehensive. The tone was soft, relaxed, and confident. And the sword point held at his throat bespoke an excellent control. It could easily have pierced him through, but as it was, it exerted just the right amount of pressure to make him lift his chin. In the darkness, he could not quite make out his assailant's features, but by the clothes, he recognized the stranger who had escorted Molly home. He was also uncomfortably aware of the two men standing very close behind him.

"You've been following my friend and me ever since we left the Toad and Badger," said the stranger. "Now be a good lad, drop the dirk, and tell us why, eh?"

Moving quickly, Smythe used his knife to bat away the sword point from his throat, then in almost the same motion, struck out behind him with his leg, kicking back as hard as he could. He heard one of the men behind him cry out. Without pausing, he lowered his shoulder and slammed into the stranger in front of him, seized him, and then swung him around to use him as a shield, holding the knife to his throat.

"Bloody hell!" the second alleyman swore, standing there and holding his club, uncertain what to do. In an instant, the tables had been turned, and the cony had turned out to be not quite such a helpless rabbit after all.

"Now you drop *your* blade, my friend," said Smythe. And as he spoke, he suddenly became aware that the dark-garbed stranger was not a man at all, but unmistakably female. Her hat had fallen off and long, raven tresses tumbled to her shoulders. However, it was soft fullness in his grasp that gave the game away.

"Gently, laddie," she said, in her husky, raspy voice. " 'Tis not a cow's udder that you're milking, you know." Her sword dropped to the cobbles.

"My apologies," said Smythe, relaxing his grip a bit, but still maintaining it. "I did not expect a woman." He saw the other man make a move toward the sword lying on the ground. "And you stay right where you are, ruffler," he said to him. "Unless you want your friend to have her throat cut."

"You would cut a lady's throat?" the woman asked him.

"Not a lady's throat," said Smythe. "But I would have no compunctions about cutting yours."

"*Aargh, God's bollocks!*" the first alleyman swore, still doubled over and clutching at his shin with both hands. "The bastard damn near broke me leg!"

"I wish he *had* broken it, you simple-minded oaf," the woman said. "As for you, laddie, I take it back. You were more than quick enough."

"What do we do now, Moll?" asked the second alleyman, in a confused and frightened tone.

"Whatever he tells you to, you fool," she replied. "And keep your bloody mouth shut."

"Moll?" said Smythe. He recalled the name from one of the pamphlets he had purchased. A woman who went about dressed as a man, who fought with a sword as well as one, ran a school for pickpockets and lifts, dealt in stolen goods, and carried a great deal of influence in the thieves' guilds of London. "Moll Cutpurse?"

"You know me?"

"I have read about you, it seems."

"Ah. Greene and his damn fool pamphlets. Sure an' I should have drowned him in the river like a sack of cats long since. He'll get me hanged yet. So . . . now that you have me, what will you do with me? If you kill me, my boys will break your head, you know."

"Well, I suppose they can try," said Smythe, trying to mask his uncertainty. "But I could always call out for the watch."

She laughed. "Call all you like, laddie. They'll be gathered in some tavern, having cakes and ale. And if you try to take me in to them, you'll not get far, I promise you. My boys will see to that."

"What, these two sorry rufflers?" Smythe said. "They were not much help to you just now, were they?"

Moll whistled sharply through her teeth and a moment later, Smythe became aware of dark figures stepping out from the shadows all around him. There were at least a dozen of them or more.

"Oh," he said. "Damn."

"So, laddie, what do you intend?" asked Moll.

"Well now, 'tis an excellent question, Moll," he replied, uneasily. "To be honest with you, I do not quite know. But if I let you go, 'tis clear that things would not go very well for me, whereas so long as I have you, I have something to bargain with, it seems."

"Indeed," she said. "So then, what do you propose?"

"Right now, methinks I would settle for getting out of this with my skull intact," said Smythe.

"That sounds entirely reasonable to me," Moll Cutpurse replied. "You spare me throat, and I shall spare your skull."

"Ah, but there's the rub, you see," said Smythe. "What assurance have I that you shall have your men stand off if I should let you go?"

"You have my word."

"The word of a thief?"

"I may steal," she replied, "but I always keep me word. Ask anyone."

" 'Tis true," one of the alleymen replied.

"Well, with such an impeccable gentleman vouching for your honor, how could I ever doubt your word?" asked Smythe, wryly.

She chuckled. "Laddie, if I wanted you dead, I could have you followed, and then once I knew where you hung your hat, I could have you done in at any time. Anytime at all. Once all is said and done, what matters it to me if I am hanged for theivery or murder?"

"Your point is well taken," Smythe replied. "Well then, 'twould seem that someone is going to have to trust someone first, else we shall be standing here like this all night. And that would profit no one." He took his knife away from Moll Cutpurse's throat and stood back, cautiously, keeping his blade ready.

Moll stepped away and turned around to face him, her hand instinctively going to her throat to feel for blood. There wasn't any. Smythe had been careful not to cut her. The other men started to close in, but she held her hand up, holding them off. They stopped at once.

"Would you have done it, then?" she asked, softly. "Would you have cut me throat?"

"To be honest, I truly do not know," Smythe replied.

" 'Tis an honest man who can admit his own uncertainties," she said. She came up close to him, so she could see him better. She gazed at him thoughtfully. "I have seen you before, methinks," she said.

"I stay at the Toad and Badger," Smythe said. "And I am a player with the Queen's Men. So now you know where you can find me, if you truly wish me dead."

"If that were so, then you would be dead already," she said with a smile. "A player, eh? You are a strapping big lad for a player. You have the look of a man who does honest labor for his living."

"I apprenticed as a smith and farrier," he said. "Though I am no journeyman, I still do some work for Liam Bailey now and then, what with the playhouses being closed."

"Liam Bailey's last apprentice had his head broke in a fight, I heard," she said. " 'Twould be a shame to deprive him of another. He's not getting any younger."

"I would not say that to his face," Smythe said. "His arm is still twice the size of mine, and I do not yet see him entering his dotage. Not without a fight."

"He's a cantankerous old kite, sure enough. But though 'tis pleasant to stand here and pass the time, we still have unfinished business, you and I. What were you doing following me tonight?"

"Well, 'twas not you I was following so much as Molly," Smythe replied.

"Molly, is it? Are you her lover, then?"

"What, I? Nay, nothing like," said Smythe, a bit taken aback. "In truth, I love another. But Molly . . . well, we all . . . that is, all the players . . . we are all quite fond of her, you know. And when I saw a strange man . . . well, what I *thought* was a man, anyway . . . approach her in the street tonight and then go off with her, well . . . I was curious and merely wanted to be sure that naught would go amiss."

"I see." Moll stared at him thoughtfully for a moment. "Well, that has the ring of truth to it, I suppose. And you did seem surprised when you learned I was woman. What is your name, laddie?"

"I am called Tuck Smythe."

She held out her hand. "Moll Cutpurse is me canting name," she said, as he took it. "Someday, if I should get to know you better, I may give you me Christian one. And then again, I may not. But I shall keep an eye on you, Tuck Smythe. For me own sake and for Molly's . . . just to make sure that naught will go amiss," she added, giving him his own words back with a smile.

She reached out her hand and one of her men returned her sword to her. As she put it back into its scabbard, another man picked up her hat and gave it back to her. She put it back on, touched her brim to Smythe, and then one by one, they all melted away into the darkness without a sound.

"Hmpf. Now I know why they call them 'footpads,' " Smythe said to himself. He looked around.

The streets were dark and foggy, and it was difficult to see much more than a few paces ahead. However, despite that, and despite the lateness of the hour, he was nevertheless struck by the fact that on a street crowded with buildings, in a part of the city where rooms were often shared by as many as a dozen people crowded in together and sleeping on the floor, apparently no one had even opened a window and looked out during his encounter with Moll Cutpurse and her men.

He was also struck by how quickly she had been able to summon those men. Surely, she could not have had the time to do so in the brief interval between leaving Molly at her doorstep and accosting him only a few blocks later.

She had known that he had followed her and Molly from the Toad and Badger. She had said as much, though he did not know how she could have noticed him. He had never once seen her look around. But she must have known somehow that he was there, just the same, for she had to have sent word to those men, through some sort of signal . . . but to whom? And how? Once again, he felt out of his depth, a country bumpkin from the Midlands wandering through London like a perfect gull, ignorant and clueless.

He had never considered himself gullible or foolish, but then, he reminded himself, gullible and foolish people never do, do they? That is one of the things that makes them so. London truly is a different world, he thought. More than one, in fact. The worlds of London society were like layers. Begin to unearth and discover one, and soon another became revealed underneath it . . . an "underworld," so to speak.

He needed to obtain more of those pamphlets of Robert Greene's. He felt as if what he had learned from them had merely scratched the surface of London's underworld of thieves. How was it, he wondered, that Greene came by all his knowledge of the world of London's criminals? He was a poet, a university man who, one would think, would be much more accustomed to the ways and customs of the Inns of Court rather than the "stews" or brothels and "boozing kens" or alehouses of Cheapside and Southwark. He wondered if it would be possible to meet Greene somehow and ask him questions.

"Were I in your place, I should not bother," Shakespeare said, when Smythe returned home and put the question to him.

"Why not?"

Still at his writing desk when Smythe returned, Shakespeare had managed to get a number of pages written and felt pleased enough with his progress to retire for the night. They both prepared for bed, stripping down to their white linen shirts.

As Smythe sat down on the mattress and brushed off stray bits of rushes that had adhered to his bare feet, Shakespeare hiked up his shirt and urinated in the chamber pot they kept on the floor in the corner of their room. To help keep down foul odors, they avoided using the chamber pot for anything else, and instead shat in the jakes, a tiny room where Stackpole kept a close stool, which was nothing more than a small, crude, wooden box seat with a hole in the top and a lid, inside of which was kept a large chamber pot partially filled with water. In the interests of keeping his establishment as clean as possible, Stackpole dutifully saw to it that the jakes was emptied out into the street several times a day, and fresh rushes were strewn on the floors in all the rooms each morning, mixed with chips of wormwood to help keep down the fleas. It was, truly, among the cleanest inns that Smythe had seen in the working-class neighborhoods of London, despite its somewhat tumbledown appearance, and any tenant who violated Stackpole's scrupulous edicts on decorum by voiding, spitting, or vomiting upon the floor without cleaning it up was soundly boxed about the ears and then thrown out into the street. Consequently, most of Stackpole's tenants tended to follow his rules out of both self-interest and self-preservation.

"From what I hear, Greene has descended into dissipation," Shakespeare said, as he opened the window and flung the contents of the chamber pot out into the street.

"*Oy!*" someone yelled out from below.

Shakespeare glanced out briefly. "Sorry, Constable," he called down.

"Seems to me as if you have made that particular descent a time or two yourself," Smythe replied.

"S'trewth, I have enjoyed, upon more than one occasion, the happy state of drunkenness," Shakespeare replied, as he got into bed, "but I have never sought to wallow in the desolate depravity of dissipation. Greene, poor soul, has fallen to that saddest of all states wherein his talent, such as 'twas, has sailed away upon a sea of spirits. 'Tis not a pretty story, I fear. He is but six years my senior, and yet Dick Burbage tells me that he looks almost twice my age. He has fallen upon hard times, it seems, and taken up with still harder company. When I asked Dick the same question that you just asked me, Burbage cautioned me to give him a wide berth and from what he said, 'twould seem like very sound advice. I might recommend the same to you."

"Pity," Smythe said. "I have much enjoyed his writings. They have the mark of a well-educated man."

"Aye, they do at that," Shakespeare agreed. "The writings of well-educated men are oft' filled with their contempt for the common man, who does not share their education. Which, of course, is why they always fail to understand him. But then enough of Greene and all his ilk. Tell me more about Moll Cutpurse. I find her much more to my interest!"

"I can understand that well enough," said Smythe. "I could

easily see her as a character portrayed upon the stage. She is positively filled with the stuff of drama, from her head down to her toes."

"Go on! Describe her to me!" Shakespeare said, his eyes alight with curiosity.

"Well, to begin, she is quite tall for a woman," Smythe replied. "We are nearly the same height. I took her for a man, at first, because of the way that she was dressed. She wore high leather boots, dark breeches, and a long dark cloak together with a rakish, wide-brimmed hat, rather in the French style, with an ostrich plume stuck into the band. She also wore a sword. I did not have much opportunity to take the weapon's measure and make some determination of its quality, for at the time, I was rather more attentive to making certain that its point did not transfix my throat."

"What of her features?" Shakespeare asked. "How did she look?"

" 'Twas difficult to see well in the darkness, though we stood close enough that I do believe that I would know her if I saw her once again," said Smythe. "Her hair was dark, or it seemed dark, at any rate. I suppose 'twas possible that it could have been red or auburn, though I had the impression that 'twas raven-hued. Her skin seemed fair, and I could not discern a blemish nor any marks of pox or the like."

"Was she pretty? Or was she rather plain? Or ugly?"

"I would not call her plain," said Smythe. "Neither would I call her pretty. Nor ugly, for that matter."

"Well, what then?"

"Striking, I should say. S'trewth, she did not seem hard at all upon the eyes, but her face had rather too much . . . too much . . ." He searched for the right words as his hand floated up in front of him, as if grasping at something. "Too much *forthrightness*, I should say, to call it pretty."

"Ah," said Shakespeare. "A face with strength of character."

"Just so, precisely."

"Tell me about her gaze."

"Her gaze?"

"The eyes, when she looked upon you. . . . Did they sparkle with a pleasant humor? Or did they seem cold and distant? Cruel? Mocking? Lustful, perhaps?"

"Lustful!" Smythe snorted. "Surely, you jest! The woman had a *swordpoint* at my throat!"

"Well, with some women, that sort of thing might induce an . . . excitation."

"Odd's blood! I shudder to think what sort of women you must have known!"

"I shudder to think what sort I married," Shakespeare replied, dryly. "But that is quite another matter. What I meant was, did you have any feeling that having you so at a disadvantage gave her a sense of satisfaction or, perhaps, of pleasure?"

"She did seem to enjoy my discomfort, come to think on it," Smythe said.

"What about after you turned the tables on her?" Shakespeare asked. "When you had your knife to her throat . . . what then? Was she afraid?"

"Not in the least," Smythe said. "She was aware of the danger, I should say, and from what she asked me later, I do not think she was truly sure if I would have used my knife or not, but she seemed to take it all in stride. I found that quite extraordinary."

"Indeed," said Shakespeare. "The portrait you have painted has a most unusual aspect. And not at all unpleasing, at that. It brings to mind our mutual friend, Black Billy, doees it not?"

"Sir William's other self?" said Smythe. "Aye, there does seem to be a sort of family resemblance."

Shakespeare's eyebrows raised. "You don't suppose . . . ?"

"Certainly not!" Smythe said. "What an astonishing idea!"

"Any more astonishing than a knight of the realm galloping about the countryside as a common highwayman?" countered Shakespeare.

"Aye, perhaps not, when you put it that way," Smythe replied. "Still, they are much more different than the same. Moll's speech has a Highland ring to it, which tells me for a certainty that she did not grow up in England, as did Sir William. And their faces are both shaped rather differently. Sir William's has a sharp and hawkish cast, whilst Moll's is rounder, with somewhat gentler features."

"But you said that you could not see her all that clearly."

"I saw her clear enough to know her face again. I could not tell you for certain what the precise hue of her hair was, whether 'twas black or chestnut rather than auburn, or if she was more pale than ruddy, but I believe that I would know her features."

"Then you must be sure to point her out to me if we should chance to pass her in the street," said Shakespeare. "I wonder what she was doing with our Molly."

"I was wondering the same," said Smythe. "Moll and Molly. Two women with the same name, or near enough, and yet they could not be more different. Of course, 'twas not her real name, Moll Cutpurse, but her canting name, as she admitted to me. I wonder who she really is. Truly, 'tis a different world these people live in, what with their own made-up names and manners of speech, even their own society, with its own rules."

"One might say the same of the queen's own court," said Shakespeare. "Save that with the thieves guild, we have less pomp and more circumstance. Did you think to ask our Molly what she was doing abroad with such a wolf's head?"

"How could I? Then she would know that I had followed her."

"And are you ashamed of that? Were your motives less than honorable in that regard?"

"Surely, Will, you know me better! Besides, you know that my affections are already spoken for."

"Aye, indeed, I do know that, my friend. But when it comes to women, men oft' do such addle-pated things as to defy and mystify all those who know and love them. Although, once all is said and done, Molly is a much more suitable object for the affections of a player than your Elizabeth, who stands well beyond your humble reach, as I have told you more than once."

"Indeed, you have," said Smythe, "but I assure you nonetheless that any affection that I have for Molly are the affections of a friend and not a lover."

"Then why are you afraid to tell her that you followed her tonight?"

"Why? Well, because . . . because she might not understand my motives."

"Which were concern for her safety and well-being, purely as a friend, of course."

"Just so, precisely."

"Just so, my rump and bollocks," Shakespeare said. "You followed her for no other reason than that you were curious to see who it was that she was meeting and what would transpire between them."

"Not so," Smythe replied. "I went out to take a walk, so as not to disturb you at your work, and when I saw Molly come out all alone, why, I was going to offer to escort her home, as the streets are not safe at night—"

"And on how many previous nights had you offered to escort her home, out of concern for her safety and well-being, as you put it?" Shakespeare asked. "Or was tonight merely the first time that the notion of her safety and well-being alit upon your chivalrous young brain? How long has she been working at the Toad and Badger, hmm? She has been in service here ever since we came to London, and yet you never once before evinced an interest in her safety!"

"Well . . . I . . . I suppose it simply never before occurred to me. . . ."

"Nay, it did not, Tuck, which is just my point. You followed the girl out of simple curiosity and nothing more. You followed her because you, my friend, are as curious as a marten sniffing round a henhouse. 'Tis a thing we have in common, so do not attempt to tell me that your motives were any loftier than that. And 'tis why you are afraid to tell Molly that you followed her, because that is the truth of it, and if you tell her any different, then she will think there is a stronger reason for your interest and you know it!"

Smythe simply lay there for a moment, without speaking. Then he sighed. "Very well, then. I suppose 'tis true. I followed her more for the sake of curiosity than for any other reason. And if I told her that, then she might be offended, or else she might misconstrue my motives. Either way, you see my dilemma. I cannot tell her that I followed her, and so I cannot ask what she was doing with a brigand like Moll Cutpurse. So . . . where does that leave us?"

"Us? How did I become involved in this?"

"Because you are now as curious as I. Admit it."

"Oh, I suppose I am," Shakespeare conceded, grudgingly. "But I do not intend to lose my sleep over this conundrum. I suspect it shall resolve itself upon the morrow."

"How so?"

"Because even if you do not tell Molly that you followed her, there is a very good chance that your new friend, Moll Cutpurse, will," said Shakespeare. "And I must admit that I am curious to know how she shall respond to that. You will be sure to tell me, won't you?" He smiled and blew out the candle. "Good night."

4

AT BREAKFAST THE NEXT MORNING, Molly said nothing as she served them their ordinaries, but Smythe did not find that surprising. In all likelihood, Moll Cutpurse would not have had a chance to speak with her, and so Molly would have no way of knowing yet about the events of the previous night. For that matter, Smythe had no way of knowing when or even if she might be seeing the notorious female thief again. He debated following Molly once again when she went home at the end of the day, but then decided that doing so could only bring him trouble. He did not wish to risk another encounter with Moll Cutpurse and her henchmen on a dark and foggy street at night. The next time might not go so well. And even if he avoided any such encounter, if Molly became angry upon learning that he had followed her last night, as she very well might, then doing so a second time would make matters even worse. Nevertheless, he was still nagged by curiosity. What connection could Molly the tavern wench have with Moll the thief?

After breakfast, he went back up to his room and took from his chest one of Greene's cony-catching pamphlets that he had purchased at the bookstalls in St. Paul's. It had an illustration depicting Moll Cutpurse dressed in men's clothing and wearing a sword. The drawing was rather crude and did not even remotely do her justice. One would certainly never recognize the real woman from the rudimentary illustration. In all likelihood, the illustrator had never even seen his subject. But then, that was not the point. The point was to convey the idea of a woman living in a man's world, dressing as a man and acting in a manner contrary to all the natural inclinations of her sex. And certainly, Moll Cutpurse would never have sat for any sort of much more lifelike portrait, such as those of the queen or other well-known aristocrats that were commonly sold at the bookstalls. Having her likeness so widely distributed and well known would doubt-less have been a detriment to one in her profession!

According to what Greene wrote, Moll Cutpurse was not only a thief, but a dealer in stolen goods, or a "brogger" in the canting tongue of London's underworld. She was also supposed to be a leading figure in the Thieves Guild, which struck Smythe as one of the true ironies of London society, for while thievery itself was unlawful, there was no actual law against thieves having a guild, and so such a guild did, indeed, exist and apparently met at regular intervals in one or another of the city's taverns. If Moll Cutpurse was one of the leaders of this guild, as Robert Greene claimed, then it should be no surprise that she could quickly summon up a band of surly henchmen to do her bidding. But whatever could Molly O'Flannery be doing associating with such a person?

Smythe tucked the pamphlet away inside his doublet, took his cloak, and went outside. Shakespeare had already left, without saying where he was going, but they knew they would be meet-ing later on that afternoon to rehearse with the rest of the Queen's Men at the Theatre. The playhouses might still be closed, but with the news that they might be reopening soon, it was best to be prepared to greet their returning audiences with a well-staged and polished production. Always assuming, of course, that there would *be* returning audiences, Smythe thought, rather glumly.

There was, unfortunately, no denying that the future of the Queen's Men seemed anything but bright. Even before they had their recent unsuccessful tour, they had suffered two devastating setbacks. Dick Tarleton, their popular clown, had succumbed and passed away after a long illness and the thundering Ned Alleyn, star of their company and the undisputed leading actor on the English stage, had defected to the Lord Admiral's Men. Alleyn had left in part because the Rose was a much better playhouse than the Burbage Theatre and in part because its owner, Philip Henslowe, had a pretty, buxom daughter and no sons to inherit his fortune.

It was, on a smaller and much lower scale, not unlike an alliance of nations, Smythe reflected wryly. Henslowe offered up his young daughter in marriage, in return for which he got England's finest and most popular actor to play upon his stage and draw larger audiences to his theatre. Alleyn got a better playhouse in which to showcase his talents, a brilliant young poet to write new plays for him, a pretty young wife, and upon his father-in-law's death, he stood to inherit a small fortune in business interests, including the Rose Theatre and a chain of brothels.

For Alleyn, it had been a smart decision and an excellent investment in his future. Sadly, the result of this strategic theatrical alliance did not bode well for the Queen's Men. With the combination of a better playhouse, the country's finest actor, and brilliantly innovative new plays produced by their flamboyant young resident poet, Christopher Marlowe, the Lord Admiral's Men had quickly started to draw audiences away from the Burbage Theatre. The new life that Shakespeare had breathed into their old repertoire had given them something of a respite, but some of the more seasoned players in their company now believed that it was merely postponing the inevitable. At one time the leading players in the land, the Queen's Men had been reduced to second-raters and, given the sorry state of their finances and the closure of the playhouses, there was serious doubt as to whether or not they could survive.

Smythe did not know what the answer was. Some of the hired men had already given up and found other employment, which was in itself no easy task these days. The city was teeming with people from the country, desperate for work of any kind, and with the shortage of jobs and housing, crime was on the increase. Ministers were preaching sermons from their pulpits in which they not only spoke out against the evils of crime, but also sought to advise the members of their congregations how to avoid being victimized. And if Robert Greene was no longer able to write plays successfully, or even sell his poetry, he was finding a new and thriving market for his cautionary pamphleteering. Even Shakespeare, whose passion for writing plays burned more brightly than the candle flames with which he illuminated his dogged efforts late into the night, was making his money elsewhere, selling laudatory poems to foppish noblemen. He was not too proud. He had a family in Stratford to support, not to mention helping out his fellow players.

For his own part, Smythe knew that his connection to the theatrical world was rather tenuous, at best. He had no illusions about what he could offer to the Queen's Men. Much as he was loath to admit it, he had no talent as an actor. It was a constant struggle to remember the few lines he was given, and though he felt that he was making some slight improvements in that regard, those few lines were doled out grudgingly and more and more sparingly as time went on. More often than not, he was nothing more than a mere spear carrier. His value to the company was primarily for the strength of his limbs and his skills as a blacksmith and farrier. He was constantly repairing things, or else lifting heavy objects, or ejecting troublemakers and seeing to the horses and making sure the ostlers did their jobs properly during the performances. He had been promoted, in a sense, from a mere ostler to a sort of general, all-around hired man, a sort of apprentice stage manager, but his acting responsibilities were still slight compared to all the others. To some extent, he provided a visual appeal that Shakespeare had termed "stage-dressing." Will had told him, trying to be reassuring and supportive, that it was always good to have some good-looking bodies on the stage and, regretably, there were few good-looking bodies left among the Queen's Men. Somehow, Smythe had not felt very reassured to know that he was valued more for his brawn than for his brains.

On the other hand, Liam Bailey believed he had a future as a craftsman. While not quite openly contemptuous of his job with the Queen's Men, Liam merely shook his head anytime Smythe mentioned it. The burly old smith was not unsympathetic. He understood, at least, what it meant to have a dream. In that, he reminded Smythe of his beloved Uncle Thomas.

The two men had much in common, Smythe thought, as he made his way to Liam Bailey's smithy. They were both simple and plainspoken men, honest and direct, who enjoyed their work and believed in doing it well and charging for it fairly. But where Thomas Smythe supported his nephew and urged him to follow his dream if that was what he truly wanted, Liam Bailey had no such avuncular disposition and believed in simply saying what he thought. And what he thought was that Smythe was wasting his time working as a player when he could make an honest, useful living as a smith.

Liam Bailey was already busy working at his forge when Smythe arrived. Though it was a cool morning, he was shirtless, wearing only breeches and his well-worn brown leather apron, which was covered with dark singe marks. His torso glistened with a sheen of honest sweat. The curly hairs on his chest and arms were gray and white, giving him something of a bearish aspect, and his grizzled hair was cropped close to his skull, as usual. Few men wore their hair so short, unless they were completely bald, in which case they usually wore wigs, but Liam found long hair both a hazard and a distraction in his work and so he kept it shorn. For an old man, he was in remarkable condition, with a strong, thick chest and big, heavily muscled arms that easily swung sledgehammers that a lot of men would have difficulty even lifting.

He had never even once been to a complete performance at a playhouse, which was a point of pride with him. He understood what plays were all about, of course, and had a general idea of what it was like to see one in a playhouse, for on several occasions he had been called upon to do some work at inns were plays were being performed. He came away with little regard for what he called "the silly posturings and prating noise" of players.

"Aye, not for me, lad," he said, when Smythe brought up the question as they worked together at the forge. "Never have I been to a gaming house, nor a bawdy house, neither. I see no purpose in such things. I work hard for my money, so why risk it in a foolish game of chance? Especially when chance plays so little part in it these days. Those gaming houses are all full o' cheats an' tricksters just waitin' for a nice, fat cony to come along that they can skin. An' as for bawdy houses, even if you do not come away poxed or lice-ridden from some doxy, or knocked over the head and get all your money taken away for bein' a damn fool, a moment's pleasure is scarce worth hours' work, if you ask me. An' for that matter, why sup from an unwashed trencher that's already fed dozens more afore you?"

"And what of other entertainments?" Smythe had asked him with a smile, as he worked the bellows.

"Such as what? Baiting bears or bulls or apes, you mean, as

they do down at the Paris Garden? Now what offense did a bear or bull or ape ever do to me that I should revel in the torture of the poor, dumb beast? Or go to a good execution, perhaps, eh? Now there's a splendid evening's entertainment! Watching some poor and misbegotten wretch have his guts pulled out, or else witness a hanging, or perhaps a whipping? One could always go and abuse some poor sod stuck in the pillory, that might be a pleasant way to pass the afternoon." He snorted with derision. "Such diversions hold little interest for me."

"There are other, less violent ways to entertain oneself, you know," said Smythe. "Have you never gone to Paul's and bought a book? Or just taken in the sights?"

"Aye, once."

"Only once? 'Twasn't to your liking, then?"

Liam Bailey's jaw muscles tightened. "A church is a place for prayin', not for sellin' things. If the Lord Jesus were to come back and pay a visit to St. Paul's, why he would drive the black-guards out as he drove out the moneylenders from the temple! An' he would call back the crowd that wished to stone the harlot and have them bury all the bastards in a rain of rocks. 'Tis a disgrace what they have brought that goodly cathedral to, if you ask me. 'Tis supposed to be the house of God, and yet, all manner of sin is found transacted there each day."

"Have a care, Liam. You are sounding just a wee bit like a Papist," Smythe said, with a chuckle.

"It need not take a Roman Pope to see that churches in this land have fallen to a sorry state," the grizzled old smith replied. "Far be it from me to claim that I could know God or understand His will, but I cannot believe that havin' whores sellin' themselves in church was what He had in mind."

"Well, I suppose Paul's Walk is out, then. What about music and dancing, then? Do you enjoy that?"

"I am Irish. Of course I enjoy music. And I might indulge in a jig or two every now and then, but I am not much of a dancer. Too big and clumsy. And too old."

"Oh, I do not believe that for a moment," said Smythe, with a chuckle. "I would bet that you could dance long after most men half your age have dropped from weariness. And singing. I have heard you sing a time or two, whilst you are working. You have a fine, baritone voice."

"If a man likes his work, why should he not sing? Good, hard work is its own song, if you ask me. But why all this sudden interest in my taste in entertainments?"

"I was simply curious, is all," said Smythe, with a shrug. "You love what you do. It makes you want to sing. Well, that is how working at the Theatre often makes me feel, although I do not have a voice as fine as yours. When I sing, I fear it sounds like geese farting in the wind. But I do it, so long as it does not greatly grate upon the ears of those nearby."

"Aye, well, if it makes you happy, then that is all that truly matters, I suppose," said Bailey, "though for the life of me, I cannot see why a fine, strong lad like you would wish to waste his time with a mincing flock of poppinjays. Here, hand me those tongs. . . ."

The quenching fire hissed and steamed as the red-hot iron was plunged into it.

"Now you take something like a piece of steel," said Bailey. "It has substance, value, worth. 'Tis useful, and when made right, by a good craftsman, it can be a thing of beauty. You have that gift, boy. This knife you made for me . . ."

He took the blade out of its sheath and gazed at it fondly. "A simple thing, really, no embellishments, no fancy decorations or engraving, no wire wrapping, just simple staghorn for the hilt. . . . 'Tis a good, honest, working man's knife. And yet, you have made of it a thing of beauty."

"I merely made it as my Uncle Thomas taught me," Smythe said, though he was pleased by the compliment, coming from a man who knew his steel.

"Do you know that I have had nearly a dozen requests already for ones just like it?" Bailey asked.

"You have?" Smythe said, with surprise. "From who?"

"From my customers," said Bailey. "Each one of them a craftsman in his own right, mind, men who know good work when they see it. And even though you are still unseasoned, yours is more than merely good. 'Tis fine work, indeed. Any man who knows can see that."

"Well . . ." Smythe said, somewhat sheepishly. He was a bit taken aback. "I do not quite know what to say to that."

"Say that you shall make them, and I shall take the orders," Bailey said. He drew the quenched steel from the fire. "You can start with this. I am not saying you should leave your mincing players," he added, wryly, "but as you know only too well, the playhouses are still closed, and I know you need the money."

"There is word that they may reopen again soon," said Smythe.

"And then again, they may not. If so, then you will have some honest work that honest men may then appreciate. And if the playhouses do reopen, why then, you may work here on the knives whenever you can find the time. My customers shall wait. They know that good work is worth waiting for."

Smythe looked at him. "I see what you are trying to do, Liam."

The smith looked back at him directly. "I am trying to please my customers and make us both some money in the bargain. If you prefer to act out silly daydreams on the stage, that is your business and none o' my concern. To each his own, I say. But I can offer you no work as a player, Tuck. *This* is the work I have. You either want it, or you do not. The choice is yours."

"I do need the work, Liam," Smythe replied. "And I did not intend to sound ungrateful. Forgive me. You have been naught but kind to me and 'tis not my place to go putting on airs."

"Aah, I would never say you had done that," said Bailey. "You're a good lad, Tuck, an' you have a place here anytime you wish. Now, you get to working on those knives, eh? That should keep you busy for a while."

Later on that afternoon, just as Smythe was getting ready to leave Liam Bailey's smithy for the playhouse, Ben Dickens stopped by.

"Why, Ben! I did not expect to see you here," said Smythe. "What errand brings you?"

"I was coming to see you," Dickens replied. "I recalled you spoke of picking up some work here and, since 'twas on my way, I thought I might stop by on my way to the Theatre and walk with you. That is, of course, if you do not spurn my company?"

"Not at all," said Smythe. "You are most welcome, Ben. Liam, do you know Ben Dickens?"

"Dickens . . ." Bailey furrowed his brow thoughtfully, staring at him with a vague glimmer of recognition. "You look famil-iar . . ."

"I was once apprentice to Master Moryson, the armorer," said Dickens. "You may remember me, sir."

"Ah. Indeed, I do remember you," Bailey said gruffly, with a frown. "You gave up a perfectly good trade to go off and be a soldier. Damned foolishness."

"Aye, well, perhaps, but it seemed like a good idea at the time," said Dickens, lightly.

"So now yer back, then?"

"So 'twould seem."

"For how long this time?" the old smith asked, sourly.

"For good, I hope," said Dickens. "That is, for good or ill, I have returned to England, but 'tis my hope that 'twill be for good."

Bailey frowned and grunted, then turned his back upon them and resumed his work.

"Come on, Ben," Smythe said, taking off his apron and hanging it up on its hook, anxious to be off before Dickens irritated Bailey any further. "Good night to you, Liam. I shall return upon the morn."

"Suit yourself," said the smith, without turning around.

Dickens chuckled as they left. "Sour as a green apple, is he not?" he said as they stepped out into the street.

" 'Tis just his way," said Smythe. "Liam Bailey is a good man. He is honest and good-hearted."

"I know he is," Dickens replied. "My old master would never have had aught to do with him else. But unlike a green apple, Bailey sours even further as he ripens. He does not approve of me, I fear."

"He seems like that to everyone," Smythe replied. "Besides, methinks he does not truly know you."

"Nay, he knows all he needs to know, or else thinks he needs to know," said Dickens, good-naturedly, "and that is that I left a good apprenticeship to become a mercenary soldier. And for that sort of 'damned foolishness,' as he called it himself, I do not think that Liam Bailey could ever forgive anyone, least of all an ungrateful apprentice who left the service of a friend of his."

"I have never heard him speak of your Master Moryson," said Smythe. "What became of him? Does he still pursue his craft?"

"He died," said Dickens. The joviality left his tone. "He fell to the sweating sickness the year after I left."

"I am sorry," Smythe said.

"So am I," said Dickens. "He was a good man, and a fair master. He taught me much. Bailey was right, you know. 'Twas ungrateful of me to have left him."

"You did what you felt you had to do," said Smythe. "You wanted adventure, and you knew that you would never find it working in an armorer's shop."

"True," Dickens agreed. "I did want adventure. Very much so. And I found it. Very much so. And now, looking back on it all, I am sorry that I ever left."

"Was it so bad then?"

Dickens shrugged. " 'Twas all very different from what I had expected. But then, enough of that. I should not wish to have you thinking 'tis my wont to wallow in melancholy. As I have said before, had I known then what I now know, methinks I would have made some different choices, but there is little to be served in regreting what is past."

"Indeed," said Smythe. "There is much to be said for looking forward."

Dickens smiled. "And to what do you look forward, Tuck?"

"At the moment, I merely look forward to the playhouses opening once more," said Smythe. "S'trewth, we all desperately need the money. And not all the players are able to find other work, as I have been fortunate to do."

"I doubt that fortune has very much to do with it," said Dickens. "I saw what you were doing there. You seem to know what you are about."

"My Uncle Thomas was a smith. He taught me," Smythe replied.

"I would say he taught you well," said Dickens. "And I daresay he was more than just a smith. You were not forging horseshoes back there. You were working on a blade."

" 'Twas his true passion," Smythe replied, adding with pride, "and in the craftsmanship of blades, I never saw him have an equal. Truly, I would put his blades against the finest of Toledo."

"Indeed? Thomas Smythe, you say? Mind you, now, I intend no offense toward you nor toward your uncle, but if his blades are truly of such superior craftsmanship, how is it I have never head of him?"

Smythe saw that the question came from curiosity, rather than from skepticism of his claim, so he did not take umbrage. "Our village was a small one," he replied, "and no main thoroughfare ran through it. 'Twas tucked away upon the boundary of a wood, and we received few visitors. When the players came through on tour once in my youth, 'twas a momentous event. The arrival of each itinerant peddlar was regarded as a great occasion." He smiled. "I recall how I used to dream of going to the city to become a player. Naught else did I desire. But not Uncle Thomas. He liked his quiet life. He is a simple man who keeps his own company and keeps it well. He works for the love of the craft, and the pride he takes in it, not for wealth nor fame. And if he had those things, why, I do not believe that he would quite know what to do with them."

"Well, I should much like to see one of your uncle's blades someday," said Dickens.

"You might be disappointed," Smthe replied. "They are rather plain and ordinary looking, not at all showy in appearance . . . but then again, as a soldier and one who was an armorer's apprentice . . . Well, here then . . ." He unsheathed his simple knife. "He made this for me years ago, when I was just a boy. It bears his maker's mark."

Dickens took the knife and examined it. "It balances exceedingly well, and the design, while simple, looks quite strong." He lightly tested the blade. "It holds a fine edge, too. Very fine, indeed." He held it hilt downwards, point up alongside his inner forearm, as if concealing it, and then flipped it around in his grasp, blade held outward, ready to stab or throw. He turned it back around once more, holding his arm down by his side, to try the maneuver once again. It was, thought Smythe, a good way to carry a knife openly, yet unobtrusively, in the event that one expected trouble. Trust a mercenary, he thought, to know that sort of clever trick.

"'Allo, Ben," said Jack Darnley, suddenly stepping out in front of them from a side street. His fellow apprentice, Bruce McEnery, was right behind him.

"'Allo, Jack," said Dickens, coming to a halt. "I see you brought your ill-humored shadow with you," he added, smirking at McEnery's perpetual sneer.

"And I see you brought yours," Darnley replied, with a smile. "Tuck is your friend's name, if I recall aright."

"It is," said Smythe. "Tuck Smythe, at your service."

"Fancy running into you again so soon, Jack," Dickens said casually. "One might almost think 'twas more than happenstance."

"As well one might," said Darnley. "We have been keeping an eye on you, you know."

"Have you, now? And what would be the reason for such concern, I wonder?"

As Ben spoke, Smythe became aware of movement behind him. He glanced over his shoulder to see half a dozen apprentices spread out behind them. He groaned inwardly. What pernicious fortune had befallen him that it was the second time in as many days he was being accosted by a street gang? People around them in the street, seeing the congregation, gave them a wide berth, crossing over to the other side and hurrying past without a backward glance.

"We only wanted to make certain that you were all right, Ben," Darnley replied.

"How very kind of you and the boys, Jack. And tell me, what made you think that I might not be?"

"The city has changed whilst you have been away, Ben," Darnley said. "London is very different now. 'Tis no longer the same place you remember from the old days."

"Indeed? How very odd," said Dickens. "Why, it still looks much the same to me. S'trewth, and it smells the same as I remember, too," he added, wrinkling his nose. "The heady perfume of Fleet Ditch on the breeze is just as I recall it. Or mayhap 'tis just the fragrance of unwashed 'prentices upon the wind. What think you?"

"You may jest, Ben, but that does not change the truth of what I tell you," Darnley said. "London is now in many ways a different city than the one you left, and few of the changes have been for the better."

"I have an intimation that you intend to educate me as to those changes, Jack," said Dickens, with a smile.

"Indeed, methinks there is a need for it. You see, you left us, Ben, to go off adventuring and seek your fortune in some foreign land, whilst we all stayed here in London to make the best of things, because this is our home. *Our* home," he repeated, thumping his chest for emphasis. "*Our* city." He swept out his arm in an expansive gesture, encompassing all their surroundings. "*Our* streets. And yet, with each and every passing day, we have found our home invaded, as much as any conquering army might invade a country it has vanquished. Only *this* foreign army marched in piecemeal, coming in dribs and drabs . . . a few Flemish craftsmen here, some Italian merchants there, German traders, Egyptian fortune-tellers and the like, til now you can scarce spit on a street in London without hitting some damned foreigner. Take a look around you, Ben. On any day, a man can see countless good English working men and women out begging in the streets, desperate for a job, a warm place to sleep, a meager crust of bread with which to stave off hunger, and amongst them all go aloof Italian merchants in their silks, snobbish Flemish craftsmen in their three-piled velvet finery, arrogant German shopkeepers stuffed fat with ale and sausages, shifty gypsy moonmen ever ready to cozen some poor and honest working man out of the few brass farthings he has left. 'Tis not the same city that you left at all, Ben. 'Tis a city that the bloody damned foreigners are taking over. And someone has to stop it."

"And that someone would be you?" said Dickens. "You and the Steady Boys, of course."

"Who better?" Darnley asked. "They are driving our people out into the streets, Ben, leaving them homeless, starving, desperate. These damned foreigners should all go right back to where they came from!"

"And if they do not wish to go, why then, you shall drive them out, is that it?" Dickens said.

"Bloody right I will! Me and the boys. And what is more, the other 'prentice gangs are all getting behind us in this venture!"

"Indeed? Well, then really I must congratulate you, Jack," said Dickens. "You seem to haven taken a disorganized bunch of rakehell roaring boys who have all been at one another's throats and given them a common enemy against whom to unite in opposition. 'Tis an astonishing achievement, truly. And to think that I went abroad to learn the trade of soldiering whilst here you were all of this time, turning yourself into a general completely on your own. I doff my cap to you, Jack. I must say, I am full of admiration at what you have accomplished. Truly, I could not even imagine what a man of your inestimable abilities would ever want from me."

"I want you to join us, Ben," said Darnley, either ignoring Dickens's sarcasm or else missing it completely. " 'Twould be just like the old days once again! You and me, leading the Steady Boys at the forefront of it all. . . . Think of it! We could rouse all the 'prentices in concert and clean out the vermin from this city! And you, as well, Tuck. You can be a part of it. The Steady Boys will always have a place for a strapping, big brawler like youself. Come and join us!"

"I thank you kindly for the offer," Smythe replied, "but I always try my best to avoid brawls whenever possible."

"You mean to say that rather than stand up and be counted for your fellow countrymen, you would prefer to let all these foreigners ruin the livelihoods of honest Englishmen?" said Darnley, with challenge in his voice.

"Tuck has no quarrel with you, Jack," Dickens said.

"Nay, in truth, I do not," Smythe agreed, "but I daresay I have a quarrel with his report. For the truth of the matter is that 'tis not the foreigners in London who are to blame for all the poverty. If the blame should rest with anyone, then it should rest with English landowners who enclose their lands for raising sheep, for as many of my fellow countrymen know all too well, wool is much more profitable in these times than produce. Only as the landed gentry fence in all their lands for grazing sheep instead of tillage, they dispossess their tenant farmers, who are thus left with no work and homeless. And so, not knowing what else they can do, they make the journey to London, desperate and seeking work, only to discover that so many more like them have come that work is difficult to find. But 'tis not the Flemish silversmiths who take the jobs that would have gone to them, as you ought well to know, since you are an apprentice and know something of the crafts. Nor do the Italian merchants compete with them for work, nor the German shopkeepers and craftsmen, for that matter, for a simple country farmer knows nothing of such things. He knows and understands his husbandry, but for the most part, that is the compass of his world, beyond which he sails in ignorance. I suppose 'tis possible that the occasional gypsy here or there may swindle someone, but methinks that they are much more likely to cozen a wealthy Fleming or a prosperous Italian merchant than some poor old sod begging on the street. 'Twould be little profit there. In truth, one should think that quite the contrary to what you claim, each foreign craftsman or merchant who comes to London and opens up a shop creates an opportunity for Englishmen with no ready skills at trade or craft, for every merchant has need of assistants in his shop and every craftsman has need of apprentices."

"I told you 'twould be a waste of time with these two," said McEnery, with a sneer. "An' what with the way that this one speaks, it sounds to me more like he champions these stinking foreigners than stands up for his fellow countrymen!"

"Nay, I beg to differ," Dickens said. "He speaks truly and I, for one, can find no fault in his discourse. If you were to venture out beyond the city walls, then you would soon find that what Tuck says is true. 'Tis not the foreigner who dispossesses English farmers of their homes and livelihoods, but the gentleman who encloses his estate to turn his crop fields into pastureland for greater profit. These enclosures are a plague upon our poor, swelling their ranks as they fatten the purses of the gentry, and in the long run, all shall suffer from it. 'Tis an easy thing to point your finger at the foreigners, Jack, and claim they are to blame, but 'tis not so. You may make a scapegoat of the blameless for-eigner, but 'twill not solve the problem. On the other hand, it does give you a cry with which to rally others to your standard, does it not?" Dickens smiled mirthlessly. "You always did want to be the leader, Jack. Well, 'twould seem you have your wish, at last. You have no need of me. And for my part, I have no need of causing pain or trouble to those who have done nothing to offend me. S'trewth, I have done enough of that already. My battlefields are left behind me. Count me out. And as for Tuck, I believe he has already given you his answer."

Darnley compressed his lips tightly and gazed at him with cold rage in his eyes. Dickens returned that baleful look without regard for its intensity, meeting Darnley's fury with his own in-souciance. And although he tried, Darnley found that he could not stare him down.

"You players were always apt with pretty speeches," he said contemptuously, "but try as you might, you still cannot muddy up the truth with mere words. We know who belongs here and who does not. We have eyes, and we can all see for ourselves how the foreigner prospers at the Englishman's expense. The time has come for all good Englishmen to take a stand, and you are either with us, Ben, or else you are against us."

"Take whatever stand you wish, Jack, for I am neither with you *nor* against you," Dickens said. "What you and your friends do matters not to me, one way or another. So then, 'twould seem that we have settled our discussion. Now Tuck and I have an appointment at the Theatre that we must keep."

He started forward, but McEnery stood in his way defiantly, sneering at him, chin jutting forward in a challenge.

"Stand aside, Bruce," Dickens said, softly.

"And if I should refuse? What then, eh?" McEnergy replied, finding courage in his fellow Steady Boys around him. "Do you think that you can best us all?"

Moving with smooth, deceptive speed, Dickens took Smythe's knife, which he had held blade up, concealed alongside his inner forearm all the while, and before the startled apprentice could react, he flipped it around quickly and thrust it, edge upwards, high between McEnery's legs. With his free hand, he seized McEnery by his belt and held him close, while pressing upwards with the knife, causing McEnery to emit a high-pitched squeak of alarm.

"You know, you may be right, Bruce. Doubtless, I would not prevail 'gainst you all," said Dickens, in an even tone, "but I could do for *you* right proper. If your lads so much as take one step toward either me or Tuck here, St. Paul's Boys will have themselves a new soprano for their choir."

Darnley looked as if he were about to speak, but before he could say or do anything, Smythe reached out and spun him by the shoulder, then seized him from behind with his left arm around his neck and his right hand behind his head. When Darnley tried to struggle, he simply tightened his grip and, with a choking sound, the apprentice gave up all resistance. Smythe turned him around to face the other apprentices, who had been confident of their superiority and were now all taken by surprise at how quickly the tables had been turned.

"Be so good as to throw your clubs and dirks down in the street," said Smythe. "And then walk away. You can return to pick them up again after we have gone."

When the boys hesitated, Smythe once more tightened his grip.

"Do as he says!" croaked Darnley.

The clubs and knives fell to the cobbles with a clatter.

"Right. Off you go then," Smythe said.

Slowly, truculently, the apprentices moved off.

Dickens then released McEnery. "You can go and join them, Bruce," he said. "But mark me well now, for I give you fair warning . . . you come after us and I shall run you through ahead of all the others. Now run along, like a good lad."

He waved him away and McEnery shot him a venemous look, then trotted off after his companions.

"You can go with him," Smythe said, releasing Darnley and giving him a shove that almost sent him sprawling. Darnley stumbled, then regained his footing and turned back to gaze at Smythe with a look of intense hatred.

He inhaled raggedly and rubbed his throat. "I shan't forget this," he said, his voice rasping slightly. "We shall finish this another time, when you shall not have the advantage of surprise."

"Indeed?" said Smythe. "S'trewth, I could have sworn 'twas you who had the advantage of surprise . . . and numbers, come to think of it."

Darnley spat on the street, then turned and walked away.

"I fear that you have made an enemy on my account," said Dickens.

" 'Twasn't on your account," said Smythe. "I never liked him from the start. Not him nor his sneering shadow."

"Well, you are a stout enough fellow, to be sure," said Dickens, "but just the same . . . watch your back. Jack Darnley is not one to forget a slight, and you embarrassed him in front of all his boys. He shall do much more than merely look to even up the score. He shall want your guts for garters."

"He shall have to come and try to take them, then," said Smythe.

"Try he shall, you may count on it," Dickens replied. He handed Smythe's knife back to him. "My thanks. It served me well, as it turns out. Let us hope it serves you equally. Keep it close by."

"I always do," said Smythe.

"And if you do not scorn my counsel, I would consider strapping on a rapier," Dickens added. "The Steady Boys were never great believers in fair fighting. Under Jack's leadership, I should think they are much less so now."

Smythe sighed. "You are not the first to give me that good counsel, Ben. And for the life of me, I cannot say why 'tis so difficult to follow. I simply cannot seem to get into the habit of wearing a sword everywhere I go. I am likely to trip over it, although I must admit, there have been a few times when the habit of carrying a rapier would have served me well."

"Then I do earnestly beseech you to cultivate it," Dickens said.

5

THE REHEARSAL BURBAGE HAD CALLED for that afternoon mustered somewhat less than half the normal full complement of the Queen's Men. A number of their hired men who had been fortunate enough to find other employment in these trying times had already left the company, while others were still out looking for work and it was anybody's guess as to whether or not they would return when the theatre reopened. That they would reopen was not really in question; plague seasons had seen the closing of the city's playhouses before and would doubtless do so again. They always reopened once again when the worst of it was over. This time, however, Smythe knew, as they all did, that the question was not whether or not they would reopen, but whether or not they would be capable of mounting a production that anyone would wish to see.

They had lost nearly half the members of their company, including Alleyn. In retrospect, Smythe realized that Alleyn must have seen the writing on the wall. The time was right for him to leave not only because the opportunity was ripe, but because the company was going stale. Their beloved comedian, Dick Tarleton, was dead and Will Kemp, who had long dreamed of the chance to take his place as lead clown for the company, had fallen

prey to the worst condition that could befall a comic actor . . .
he had missed his timing.

Kemp was past it, although he would be the last one to admit
it. He had never bothered much about memorizing lines, trusting
instead to his ability to improvise or else caper his way out of an
awkward situation with a pratfall. Now, he simply could not
memorize his lines, even if he wanted. He absolutely refused to
admit it, insisting that memorizing lines was not the way he
worked, but the truth, as everyone could plainly see, was that his
memory was going and with it, his once brilliant ability at im-
provisation, a talent that required quickness of thought, which
was a skill that Kemp no longer had at his command. Quite aside
from that, even if he could still play the Kemp of old, the audiences had outgrown him.

Gone were the days when audiences howled with laughter at
simple physical highjinks on the stage, at jigs and pratfalls, clever
comments broadly spoken to the crowd with broad leers and expansive gestures, song and dance routines interspersed with juggling and a cartwheel thrown in here and there. The fashion now
was for much more realistic fare, involving strong characters and a
cohesive story. The juggling, the tumbling, the clowning and the
morris dancing could now be found on any street corner and in
every marketplace. The fashions of the stage were moving on,
but Will Kemp was not moving with them.

As for the other players, John Fleming was getting on in
years, and while Bobby Speed was still as clever a performer as
he ever was, more and more he seemed to need the fuel of drink
to pull it off, and if there was one thing that all performers knew,
it was that playing in one's cups rarely produced one's best performances and was, at best, a rather dicey proposition. Discussing
it with Speed, however, seemed completely hopeless. He would
either laugh it off as of no consequence, or else promise to do

better next time. The trouble was, there always was a next time, and a time after that, and after that, and after that. And each time, the influence of drink became more telling.

Will was of more value to the company as a poet than an actor. He knew full well his shortcomings in that regard, and although he was reasonably competent as a player, he knew he lacked the gifts to be inspiring, and an inspired actor was the one thing that the Queen's Men desperately needed. Dick Burbage, though young, had good potential, but he was still no Edward Alleyn, and while all of his performances were good, none was truly memorable, as Alleyn's were. As for the rest, himself included, Smythe knew that they were merely an agglomeration of young men with little talent or experience, not one among them capable of dazzling an audience and leaving them breathless to come back for more.

To make matters even worse, the Burbage Theatre was dilapidated and much in need of repair. The thatch was old; the galleries were creaking and there were more than a few cracked and splintered boards among the seats up in the boxes. The stage was in a state of disrepair and needed rotten boards replaced and hangings mended. Even the penants drooped with all the listlessness of an old beggar woman's breasts. The Burbage Theatre was a tired and weary old maiden, and merely slapping on some paint would not cover up all of the wrinkles and the blemishes of age.

Nevertheless, it was still *their* theatre, and to all of them who remained, it was much more their home than where they ate and slept. And as their decimated company gathered for rehearsal, despite all of their ill fortune and dim prospects, there was nevertheless a strong sense of cameraderie and *joi de vivre*. This was where they truly came alive, a sentiment that Shakespeare had expressed to Smythe quite often.

"Aye, this is where it matters, Tuck," he had said again, moments after he came up to greet them. As he stood beside them just inside the entrance, he looked out with them over the yard, up at the stage, then back round to the galleries. "This is where their laughing faces fill our hearts with joy or where their catcalls plunge us all into despair. This is where the smell of unwashed bodies and fresh rushes mingles with the smells of greasepaint and the vendors' offerings to create a heady perfume that intoxicates each player's soul. This is where we stage our plays and play the dramas of our lives, where shadow becomes substance and substance masquerades as shadow. This . . ." he held out his hands, palms up, as if presenting some great work, ". . . *this* is our world. And you, prodigal Ben Dickens, are welcome to it once again."

Dickens grinned. "It feels somewhat strange to be back again after all this time," he said. "And yet, despite that, it also feels most welcome and familiar. It has been only a few years, and yet so much seems to have happened in that time. Can it have been so long since last I trod the boards in women's clothing, declaiming in my high and squeaky, boyish voice the lines that I had worked so hard to drill into my memory, dreaming of the day when I could at last cast off my girlish gowns and walk out like a young knight in doubtlet, cape and hose, and carrying a sword?"

"That day has come," said Shakespeare.

"Aye," said Smythe, with a chuckle, "and a good thing, too, for you would make a most unnatural woman now with that deep voice, those broad shoulders, and that beard."

"Well, we could shave off the beard," said Shakespeare, as if contemplating the idea. "The face would look comely enough with a bit of paint upon it, but there would be no hiding that breadth of arm or depth of chest. S'trewth, Tuck, he is a strapping youth, indeed, almost as big as you."

"We could always cast him as a horse," said Smythe.

"Soft now, keep your voice down, else Kemp may hear and wish to ride him," Shakespeare replied, with a wink.

"*Ben*!" Fleming called out, as he spied him from the stage. He threw his arms out as if to hug him from up there. "*Welcome! Welcome*! Well met and welcome once again! Look, everyone, look! Ben has come! Ben Dickens has come back to join us!"

They all gathered round to greet him, Speed and Fleming, Burbage, Hemings, Pope and Phillips, Kemp and Bryan . . . all a motley looking crew, but still a happy lot, despite their tribulations. And as he saw them all together, Smythe thought of Liam Bailey's admonitions against wasting his time amongst the players and realized that for all his good intentions, Liam Bailey simply did not understand. How could he?

They were a family, much more of a family than he had ever known. Symington Smythe had never truly been a father to him in anything save name, for all that they had shared that name. That patronymic bond was one of the reasons he now preferred to be called Tuck. That grasping woman that his father married, whom Tuck did not even care to think of as his stepmother, had never wanted to be bothered with having a child underfoot, so to appease her and free his father of a burdensome responsibility at the same time, he had been packed off to his uncle's. And much as he would always love his uncle, Thomas Smythe was a quiet man by nature and by disposition, reserved and not given to boistrous demonstrations of his thoughts and feelings. Uncle Thomas gave him what he could, and did as well by him as he knew how, but Tuck had always felt that there was something missing. Now he knew that he had found it.

These simple players wore their hearts upon their sleeves and everything they did was boistrous and demonstrative, done not only with feeling, but frequently with an overabundance of it. Smythe found it impossible to be around them without his spirits

soon being raised. They gave an honest, open boon companion-
ship that was worth more to him than all the money he could
make working as a journeyman in Liam Bailey's shop or elsewhere.

It was something that his father had never understood, nor
did Smythe hope to ever make him understand it. The world his
father lived in now seemed as far removed from him as the life
that he had left behind. And good riddance, too, he thought. He
had walked away from it without a backward glance the day that
he had started on the road to London. What did chasing dreams
of wealth, social position, and respectability ever do for his father? He had managed, with diligence and perseverence—and
more than a little bribery—to make himself a gentleman at last,
and to give him his due, it was an achievement of no small scope
for a man of his beginnings. Nevertheless, it proved not to be
enough. No sooner had he hung up his newly won escutcheon
than he began to covet spurs. And where had it all left him? In
debt, and nearly penniless, dependent on his brother's charity to
help keep him out of prison. Surely, there was a lesson to be
learned in that.

Meanwhile, Tuck had come to London without anything at
all save the clothes upon his back and a friend that he had made
upon his journey, and now, for all that times were difficult, he
felt richer by far than he had ever been. He had a place to live,
where many shivered on the streets at night. He had work that
helped to feed and clothe him, where many went hungry every
day. He had a trade, of sorts, that admitedly he was not much
good at, but it gave him pleasure and he felt that he was learning
how to be a better player every day . . . or at the very least, he
tried his best to learn. While his father, who had accused him of
being a wastrel, had wasted his own life, Tuck had built a life in
which not one moment felt wasted. The thought of losing this

life and these friends was more than he could bear. Somehow, despite their difficulties, he felt certain they would manage. Somehow, he knew that they would see it through.

They began rehearsing one of their old standards, *The Wastrel and the Maid*, a comedy about a rogue who sought to woo and bed a virtuous maiden, and it seemed only natural for Ben to play the rogue, because he was by far the most handsome among them and the most suited to the part. Burbage took the demanding part of the young maiden's much beleagured father, once played to great acclaim by Edward Alleyn, and Kemp took the part he always played, that of the rogue's hapless, comic henchman. George Bryan, as the youngest and the slightest of them, was assigned to play the maiden. Sadly, they had lost both their juveniles, one of whom had sickened and died at the beginning of the plague season and the other, doubtless frightened by the fate which had befallen his young companion, ran away to parts unknown. They had not yet managed to find suitable replacements, but for that matter, they had not looked very hard, either. Any juvenile apprentices that the company took on would have to be housed and fed by the players, and without being certain where their own next meals were coming from, none of them wished to take on such an additional expense.

The play was old enough that Dickens was able to remember some of it, having played the part of the maiden when he was a boy. Needless to say, he did not have any of the same lines, some of which had been changed in the intervening years in any case, but it all came to him quickly, the way a familiar task comes to one who has not practiced it in a while, but has never entirely forgotten. They all worked with prompting from Will Shakespeare, who as book holder gave them their lines if they could not remember — Kemp, of course, being the chief offender save for Dickens, who had to learn almost everything anew — and if some line or bit of business did not seem quite right, they experimented with changes on the spot.

They all knew that they had a great deal of work to do in order to be ready for their reopening, especially with the strength of their company reduced. Most of them would have to play several parts, which would involve rapid costume changes, but then that was nothing they had not done before. There would simply be more of them doing it this time, crowding the tiring room with rapid changes, necessitating careful planning as to who would stand exactly where and how in order to avoid confusion backstage. This did not concern them greatly; they had dealt with worse. Many times, while on the road, their stage had been nothing more than planks hammered together and placed across barrels and their tiring rooms nothing more than narrow curtains hung from poles. A player had to learn to improvise amidst adversity. One way or another, the show always went on.

This would be only the first of the plays they would rehearse in preparation for reopening, for staging just one play would never do. One of the things that had both surprised and dismayed Smythe after he had joined the Queen's Men was the discovery that no company ever staged the same play two days in a row, unless a particular production became unusually popular and there was great demand for it, though that was rare. Audiences were easily jaded and they demanded variety. Generally, the selection of the plays was somewhat random, and it was not at all uncommon for a player to arrive for a performance only to discover that, at the last minute, there had been a change and a different play was being staged. Thus, one of the requirements of the actor's trade was the ability to "con" or learn a new play very quickly, something Smythe could never do, for which reason he was always relegated to to playing nonspeaking parts or else to roles which had only one or two lines, at most. Ben Dickens,

on the other hand, proved every bit up to the challenge of con-
ning a new role quickly.

Dickens required at most a little bit of stage direction and a
quick reading of the line that he was to deliver before playing
the scene and doing it almost flawlessly. Shakespeare would make
a small correction here, a helpful prompt there, and Dickens
would seem to absorb it all like a sponge and just continue on.

" 'Tis like he had never even left us," Fleming said proudly,
watching from the wings with Smythe as Ben worked through a
scene with Kemp and Bryan. Tuck had learned that it had been
John Fleming who had housed young Dickens when he had apprenticed with the company as a juvenile and so, strictly speaking,
Ben had been Fleming's apprentice, even though all the players
generally regarded the juveniles as their apprentices in common.
Fleming was married, but he and his wife were childless and no
longer young. They had both taken to Dickens as if he were their
own. Now, he looked for all the world like a proud and beaming
father as he watched his grown "son" rehearsing on the stage.

"He is very good and a quick study," Smythe observed. "Was
he this good as a juvenile?"

"Aye, he always had the gift, I thought," Fleming replied,
nodding his silver-maned head emphatically. "Methinks that he
could be another Ned Alleyn if he set his mind to it."

"Indeed?" said Smythe, with admiration. "That is high praise,
coming from another player."

Fleming nodded. "I saw it in him even when he was just a
boy. He has the ability to become the role he plays, to believe it
so that it no longer seems like acting, but more like *being*. In that
respect, however, he is not at all the same as Alleyn. Ned was
always Ned, at heart. He never lost sight of being Ned, because
he was very fond of Ned, you see. Whenever Ned Alleyn stepped
out upon the stage, 'twas Ned Alleyn that the audience was seeing, Ned Alleyn playing a part, and often playing it brilliantly,

mind you, but nevertheless, one could never quite lose sight of that."

"What do you mean?" asked Smythe, not quite following him.

"I mean that when you see Ned Alleyn playing a part, you always remain aware that you are watching Ned Alleyn playing a part. You never quite forget that 'tis Ned Alleyn, the great actor, you are seeing." He purposely broke up the word 'actor' into two syllables, accentuating each one pointedly. "The very nature of his performance demands that you remember it." To illustrate, Fleming took a dramatic pose, standing bolt upright with his right hand upon his chest, his chin up aristocratically, his left arm held out before him as if he were Caesar speaking to his troops. And when he spoke, his voice performed a very credible imitation of Ned Alleyn's ringing and bombastic stage cry. " 'Lo!" he intoned, " 'tis I, the great Ned Alleyn, playing this part! Behold how brilliantly I act! Revel in the very wonder of me!"

Smythe laughed. "He would kill you if he saw that, you know."

"Oh, I have no doubt," Fleming replied offhandedly, in his normal voice. "He would squash me like a beetle, the great oaf. But still, it changes nothing." He shrugged. "That is how he acts."

"Perhaps, but if we are truly going to be honest with ourselves, John, is that not how all players act?" asked Smythe.

"Aye, most of us do, I suppose," Fleming agreed, nonchalantly. "If, as you say, Tuck, we are truly to be honest with ourselves, then perforce we must admit that once all the trappings of our craft are stripped away, we are all nothing more than great infants in want of much attention. We live or die at the whim of the groundlings; we fatten our pride on their applause. But not Ben. Ben is something else entirely."

"What makes him different?" Smythe asked curiously, as he watched him rehearse out on the stage.

"For Ben, 'tis not the applause that truly matters. For him, the play's the thing. And not really the play so much as the playing. In that, I perceive he has not changed."

Smythe frowned. " 'Twould seem to me that playing matters neither more nor less to him than to any of the others. Or do my eyes see things less keenly than do yours?"

Fleming smiled. "The flaw lies not so much in your observation as in your knowledge, Tuck. I have known Ben since he was but a boy, whilst you have only met him recently. And the truth is that there is rather more to Ben than the eye can plainly see. Ben did not much like his life, and so he went off to make himself another. And now he has come back, because the life he went in search of doubtless proved a disappointment, and so once again he seeks to make himself another."

Fondness seemed to mingle with a sort of wistful regret in John Fleming's exression as he watched Ben Dickens on the stage. He sighed and continued while Smythe listened with great interest.

"There is a sort of magic to our Ben," Fleming said. "For all that he is a grown man now, there is still the child within him, a fey child, a changling who possesses the ability to believe in things the way only a child can believe. I first saw it within him when he came to us as an apprentice player and I see it still. When you and I go out upon that stage, Tuck, we take the parts we are to play and play them as best as we are able, do we not?"

"Well, I fear my best is not to be compared with yours on equal footing," Smythe said, somewhat sheepishly.

"Nevertheless," the older man replied, gently patting him on the shoulder, "you put forth your best effort each and every time, for which you are to be commended, and you strive always to improve. But that is not the point. 'Tis this: when the rest of us step out upon the stage, we are but playing parts, pretending to be something we are not. Yet when Ben steps out upon the stage, what he does is rather different. He *becomes* something he is not. That is his gift, you see, his special magic, and perhaps, his curse, as well. He has the ability to so completely throw himself into a role that he becomes that role during the time he plays it . . . for howsoever long that time may be. I first saw him start to do it on the stage and I did marvel at it. I thought that he had the potential to be better than merely good; I thought he could be great. And I still think so. But when I later saw him do the same thing in his life, offstage, then I became truly concerned for him. It frightened me."

"In what way were you frightened?" Smythe asked.

"Do you recall those two thoroughly unpleasant ruffians who came into the Toad and Badger that day when Ben returned?"

"Aye," Smythe said, with a grimace. "Jack Darnley and Bruce McEnery were their names."

"They are the very ones," said Fleming, nodding emphatically. "After Ben had been with us for a few years, he met those two somehow. I do not know where precisely, perhaps here at the theatre, perhaps in town somewhere . . . in truth, it matters not. What matters is that he fell in with them and began to spend his free time roaming the streets with that unruly lot of theirs —"

"The Steady Boys," said Smythe.

"Aye, steady on the road to ruin, if you ask me. I watched him begin to change before my own two eyes, become *another* Ben . . . a Ben that I no longer knew, in many ways. And yet, in other respects, he still seemed much the same. When he was with us, he was the Ben that we had always known and loved. But then there were times when it seemed as if he were a changling, as if the faeries came whilst he had slept and stolen him away, leaving in his place some evil creature that merely had his aspect. It puzzled me at first, until at last I understood what was afoot.

It always used to happen when he was returning from keeping company with those troublesome apprentices. There was something about those roaring boys that very much appealed to Ben, you see."

"I cannot imagine what it may have been," said Smythe.

"Nor could I," said Fleming, with a grimace of distaste. "But methinks perhaps that what he saw in them in the beginning was something of what he wished to be himself, a sort of adventurer, a man of action and determination, a young gallant . . . not that they were any of those things, in truth, but I suppose that they believed they were, and spoke as if they were, and so Ben believed it, also. I attempted to dissuade him from their company, to convince him that they were a bad influence upon him and would bring him naught but trouble, yet 'twas all to no avail, of course. When did youth ever credit the wisdom of their elders?"

"I do not recall that I ever did, myself," said Smythe. "Well, save for my Uncle Thomas, to whom I always listened with respect. But for the most part, when I was younger, I did not find that my elders seemed to possess very much wisdom."

"Amusing, is it not, how the older one becomes, the wiser one's elders seem to grow?" said Fleming, with a smile. "Well, as you might imagine, the more I prevailed upon him to abandon this bad company, the more he sought it out. In the end, he drifted away from us. He found a position as apprentice to an armorer, which was just the sort of manly thing for a young gallant to be, I suppose, but then, he soon drifted away from that, as well. The rest you know. He saw how his friends paled in comparison to the genuine adventurers he met at his new master's shop and 'twas not long before he left them behind, as well, to make himself yet another life."

"I do not believe they liked that very much," said Smythe.

"Aye, that sort never would," agreed Fleming. "When one

leaves that sort of company, 'tis often perceived as weakening the others, for they find their strength in numbers. But much more than their strength, methinks, they find their very identity in numbers. And so when someone leaves them, they feel threatened and betrayed."

"I realize that they do, but I am not sure that I understand why they should," said Smythe.

"Consider who they are and how they live," said Fleming. "They are young and working class, though not yet old enough or, in most cases, skilled enough to work in their own right as journeymen or master craftsmen. Yet at the same time, they are old enough to consider themselves full grown, though again, in most cases, they have not yet acquired the wisdom of adulthood. And so they find themselves in service as apprentices, at the bidding of their masters and unable to achieve their independence until such time as their masters deem them worthy. They have no ability to determine the course of their own lives, no true feeling of worth, and no power of their own. In their masters' shops, they labor hard and long and must do as they are told. But when they go out on their own and band together with others like themselves, why then they find within that company a strength of purpose and a sense of belonging to something that gives them worth and a feeling of respect. One becomes more than merely a lowly young apprentice; one becomes a Steady Boy, or a Bishopsgate Brawler, or a Fleet Street Clubman, or whatever other colorful appellation these gangs of apprentices choose for themselves. And this company thus becomes a band of brothers, in one sense a family, in another sense an army . . . not unlike your highland clans. And if you are a member of this clan, then you are someone worthy of respect, someone to be feared . . . for when one is young, fear and respect seem much like the same thing. If you should become the leader of such a band, why then you have importance, power, and position, all of which is yours by virtue of the men you lead. The more men, the more power; the more power, the more prestige."

"So that if one of the men you lead chooses to leave your command, then 'tis very like a mutiny," said Smythe.

"Exactly so," replied Fleming, nodding. "I could not have said it better."

"Now I understand what transpired earlier today," said Smythe.

Fleming looked at him. "What happened?" he asked, and briefly Smythe described their encounter with the Steady Boys while he and Dickens were on their way to the theatre.

"I just knew those two would be trouble," Fleming said, when he had finished. "And now, regretably, you have become mixed up in it. You would do well to avoid them, if you can."

"Did you expect me to run off and leave Ben to face them by himself?" asked Smythe.

"Of course not," Fleming replied hastily. "I know you better than that, Tuck. But just the same, I wish you had not become involved. Ben knows what they are like, and he knows what to expect of them. And not meaning to slight your abilities in any way, Ben is also a trained soldier who has been to war. He knows well how to take care of himself."

"Well, 'tis not an army we are talking about, after all, John," said Smythe, "just a few young malcontents and troublemakers."

"Just the same, they can be dangerous," insisted Fleming. "If you do not wish to give me credence, then go ask your black-smith friend, Liam Bailey, whose former apprentice was killed in one of their street brawls. Do not underestimate them merely because they are young, Tuck. Aside from which, those two, Darnley and McEnery, are of an age with you, or very nearly so. Some of the others might be younger, but put enough of them together and they can be trouble enough, believe me. They might forgive Ben, in consideration of the past, but they have no reason to grant you any such consideration."

Smythe nodded. "I shall keep that in mind, John. But 'tis not in my nature to run away from trouble."

"Just see that you do not run toward it," Fleming said. " 'Allo, what have we here?" he added, looking out past the stage into the yard. " 'Twould seem that Master James has brought us visitors."

The rehearsal stopped as the players came down off the stage into the yard to greet James Burbage, Richard's father and the owner of the Burbage Theatre, who had arrived with a party among whom were Henry Darcie, one of the investors, his daughter, Elizabeth, Ben's friend, Corwin, and another gentleman, dark and foreign looking, richly dressed in silks, who came in company with a beautiful young woman whose pale skin was a striking contrast to her jet black hair. Even before they were introduced, Smythe had already guessed that this was Master Leonardo, the wealthy Genoan merchant trader, and his lovely daughter, Hera, who had so captivated Corwin.

There was yet another gentleman who came along with them, a man Smythe did not know. He was large, heavy, and robust-looking, with a florid face and a thick, bushy gray beard. Shoulder-length gray hair came down from beneath a soft, dove-gray velvet cap, which matched the three-quarter length cloak and short, soft gray leather boots that set off his burgundy hose and quilted black doublet shot through with silver thread. They must have come in carriages, thought Smythe, for otherwise those new, expensive clothes would have been filthy from the mud outside.

The red-faced gentleman turned out to be Master William Peters, the goldsmith to whom Corwin had been apprenticed and in whose shop he now worked as a journeyman, well on his way to establishing a successful reputation as a craftsman in his own right. James Burbage made the introductions, pointing out the individual players to his guests. Henry Darcie and Elizabeth, of course, already knew them all, but this was apparently the first time that Master Leonardo and his daughter had ever seen the Burbage Theatre. Master Peters had attended several of their productions in the past, but he was apparently not a regular. He came, primarily, to act as an intermediary for Master Leonardo with James Burbage and Henry Darcie. And doubtless he also came for Corwin's sake, for it was clear from the way his eyes never left Hera for an instant that the young journeyman was very much in love.

"Well met, good players, well met all!" said Master Peters in a jovial tone, after Burbage had completed the introductions. "I beg you, do not allow our merry company to interfere with your busy preparations. We have merely come to visit and observe. My friend, Master Leonardo, late of Genoa and newly arrived upon these shores, is in the mind of considering new ventures here in London and, in that regard, was curious to learn something about the business of a company of players. Thus, upon learning of his interest, I could think of nothing better than to introduce him to my old friend, Henry Darcie, whom I knew to be an investor in your theatre. Therefore, 'tis my great pleasure to introduce Master Leonardo, and his fair young daughter, Hera, and the rest here, I believe you all already know."

"Indeed, we do, good Master Peters," the younger Burbage said, speaking for them all, "and you are all most welcome to the Theatre. Sad to say, we cannot regale you with a play, for as you doubtless know, by order of the council, the playhouses of the city are all closed til further notice and we are thus enjoined from performing for you."

"Indeed," said Master Leonardo, speaking excellent English, albeit with a pronounced Italian accent, "I was aware of the decree, though 'tis a pity, for I had hoped to learn something of your work and, at the same time, perhaps provide some amuse-ment for my daughter, who has never seen an English company perform."

"Well, good Master Leonardo," Shakespeare said, "we cannot disobey the council's edicts, as you know. But while the council did close down the playhouses to prohibit our performing, fear-ing that the plague could breed among the crowds, they did not prohibit our explaining to a prospective investor in our theatre how a play is staged. And so, as we were in rehearsal for one of our productions when you arrived, you might find it both di-verting and enlightening if we were to explain to you how such a production is prepared for a performance."

"Methinks a Papist could not have split a hair more finely," Kemp said wryly, and then grunted as Speed gave him an elbow in the ribs.

"The man's a Roman, you bloody great buffoon," he said, under his breath.

"Please, come this way," said Smythe, beckoning to them. "We shall set up some benches on the stage for you so that you may see how our company prepares for the performance of a play."

The guests climbed up upon the stage and took their seats at the side while the company resumed rehearsing. James Burbage explained the process to them as the Queen's Men went through the play, stopping at intervals to correct or change a line, or else to adjust their movements on the stage and fine tune their en-trances and exits.

While Master Peters played the part of genial host, asking questions or else calling out encouragement to the players, Mas-ter Leonardo watched with interest, and with a critical, discern-ing eye it seemed, as James Burbage explained what they were doing and Henry Darcie offered the occasional supplementary remark. Watching from the wings, Smythe could see that Hera was thoroughly enjoying it all, watching with bright eyes and laughing at their antics, for despite the fact that it was only a rehearsal, the players, being players, could not resist joking around and clowning for their audience. Elizabeth, who might have greeted Smythe more warmly were it not for the presence of her father, sat next to Hera and they spoke often to each other and laughed together like good friends. The two of them made a very comely sight. Smythe noticed that just as Hera scarcely took her eyes off what was happening before her on the stage, so Corwin scarcely took his eyes off her. But then he also noticed that just as Corwin scarcely took his eyes off Hera, so Elizabeth scarcely took her eyes off Ben.

A number of times during the rehearsal, Smythe sought to catch her gaze, but all to no avail. It was as if he wasn't even there. When she was not speaking to her new friend, Hera, Elizabeth kept staring straight at Ben, and with what seemed to him more than a little interest.

" 'Twould seem you have yourself some competition," Kemp said slyly, as he sidled up to Smythe backstage.

"Stuff it, Kemp," Smythe replied in a surly tone, irritated both at Kemp's remark and at the fact that Elizabeth's interest was obvious enough for him to have noticed.

"Oh, my, my," said Kemp, with a soft, delighted chuckle. "We *are* prickly today! But then, 'twould seem a simple enough thing to understand. After all, he is quite handsome, our young Ben, a veritable Greek god, the very personification of Mars! Aye, he would be Mars himself, since he has been to war and thus has the glamor of a warrior."

"Mars was a Roman god, you ignorant poltroon," replied Smythe, irritably. "The Greek god of war was Ares, which you might have known if you troubled to read a book once in a while. But then 'twould be unreasonable to expect a man to read a book when he can scarcely even read his lines."

Kemp's nostrils flared and his eyes shot Smythe a look of pure venom, but his voice remained mellifluously smooth as he replied, "A touch, by God! And from a hired man, no less. One would not have thought you capable of so telling a riposte. Bravo, Smythe. Well done. Well done, indeed."

Smythe sighed, regretting his words. "Forgive me, Kemp," he said. " 'Twas rude and intemperate of me to make such a remark."

"Oh, now, do not dilute the vinegar with oil," Kemp said, with a grimace. " 'Tis most unseemly. If you are going to be a proper bitch, my dear, then 'tis best not to lick after you bite."

"Kemp . . ." But the older man had already turned smartly on his heel and walked away.

For Smythe, it was a thoroughly miserable afternoon. Everyone else seemed to have an absolutely splendid time and when their guests departed at the end of the rehearsal, just as the shadows were beginning to lengthen in the early evening, everyone seemed quite full of good cheer, almost as if they had actually given a successful performance to a packed house. Smythe alone felt glum, in part because he had allowed Kemp to get his goat, but mostly because Elizabeth had completely ignored him throughout the entire rehearsal.

As for Ben Dickens, Smythe could not see how he could have failed to notice the way Elizabeth had watched him. In fact, he thought that Ben had made a point of flirting with her a little during the rehearsal, not that he could blame him. It was not Ben's fault. Elizabeth Darcie was a breathtakingly beautiful young woman and Ben had absolutely no way of knowing how Smythe felt about her, a feeling he had thought, up til that point, had been reciprocated, if not in the same degree, then at least to *some* degree. Now, it seemed as if Elizabeth no longer felt anything for him at all. How could she? She had not even looked at him once.

Smythe watched morosely as they left, heading back toward their carriages, then he turned and set about helping to put everything away after the rehearsal. It was not until a short while later that he noticed there was still someone standing in the yard, toward the back, near the entrance. It was a man, and the man appeared to be watching him.

Shakespeare came up beside him. "Anyone you know?" he asked, casually.

Smythe frowned. And then he caught his breath. "Good God!" he said.

"What is wrong? Who is it?" Shakespeare asked.

"The last man I ever expected to see here," said Smythe.

"*Who?*"

"My father," Smythe replied.

6

"OUR FATHER?" SHAKESPEARE SAID, STARING at Smythe with surprise. "You mean that man there? But I thought you said that he threatened to disown you if you became a player."

"He did," said Smythe, "and so he would have, I believe, if he had anything left of which he could disown me when I set out for London with nothing save the clothes upon my back. And even had I stayed, I doubt 'twould have made much difference to him, one way or the other. From the time he sent me off to live with my uncle, we scarcely even saw each other. For all that he is my father, there never has been any love between us. When I left home, I felt certain that I would never set eyes on him again."

"And yet there he stands," said Shakespeare.

"Aye. There he stands."

Shakespeare glanced at him. "You are quite certain 'tis your father?"

"Aye, 'tis he."

"There can be no mistake?"

"I should think that I would know my own father, Will."

"Aye . . . well . . . perhaps, but . . ."

"What?"

Shakespeare bit his lower lip. "Well . . . meaning no offense, you understand, but, ah . . . you told me that your father was a gentleman and that man there does not look much like a gentleman."

"He never was," said Smythe, with a shrug, "save in his name and his attire. The name he kept. The attire he appears to have lost, along with his fortune."

As they stood there, looking out across the yard at him, Symington Smythe II stood there, looking back, dressed in a coarse green woolen cloak and cap, a plain brown doublet, homespun breeches, and worn boots. He carried a walking staff and little else. He did not even seem to have a sword. It was a far cry from the rich apparel that he once habitually wore, although no matter what he wore, how costly or well-tailored, clothes had never seemed to sit well on him. Thomas Smythe had once remarked that for all the money his older brother spent on his varied and expensive wardrobe, it was like trying to caparison a dray horse. Those words came back to Tuck as he stood there, staring at his father, thinking that he now looked more like a bedraggled tenant farmer than a man with his own family coat of arms. Indeed, he thought, as Will had observed, he did not look much like a gentleman. But then, he had never really acted like one, either.

"Do you not think that you should go and greet him?" Shakespeare asked, raising his eyebrows.

"I was hoping to find some excuse to avoid it," Smythe replied, with a sigh. "However, I suppose 'twould be the proper thing for a dutiful son to do."

"Do you want me to come with you?"

Smythe moistened his lips as he thought about it for a moment. Finally, he made up his mind. "I am grateful for your offer of support, Will, but methinks that this is something I had best see to myself," he replied.

"Would you like me to wait for you?" Shakespeare asked.

"Nay, Will, go on. S'trewth, I am not sure what he could

want with me, and if there is an argument, I should not wish for you to witness it. I shall see you when I get back."

"If that is what you wish."

"I do. Go on. I shall go and speak with him."

"Will you be all right?"

"Aye, Will." Smythe clapped him on the shoulder. "Thanks. Go on. I will follow before long."

Most of the others had already left. A few were still lingering, putting things in order or else talking amongst themselves. Smythe watched Shakespeare walk away. He looked back and called out, "I will see you anon, Tuck," then continued on his way. Tuck's father glanced at him as Will passed him, and Will gave him a polite nod of greeting, but they did not speak. Tuck stood there watching his father for a few moments. Then he smiled to himself. His father would not come to him. He was expected to make the approach, as always. He took a deep breath and let it out in a heavy sigh. "Very well then," he said to himself. "On with it."

He walked across the yard to meet his father. As he approached, he saw that his father looked thinner and there was more white in his hair than before. The dark hair was now liberally streaked. The crow's feet around his eyes looked more pronounced than he remembered, and his features seemed a bit more gaunt. Clearly, he had not been eating as well as was his wont. But in a curious way, the loss of weight seemed to agree with him. He looked older and leaner, but more fit for it. As his son approached, Symington Smythe II drew himself up to stand erect and proud, his chin high, his gaze aloof. It was his "knight's demeanor," as Tuck had always thought of it. Well, the knighthood had eluded him, and though he had somehow managed to cozen his way to an escutcheon, everything else he had now seemed lost to him as well. But the proud "knight's demeanor" still remained, even though it did not go with the clothes.

" 'Allo, Father," Tuck said, as he came up to him.

"Son," his father said, curtly. He looked him up and down. "You look well. Seem fit, as always."

"Did you expect me not to be?"

"Well . . . with the indolent life these players lead, I scarcely expected you to look as hale and hearty as you did when you were at your uncle's forge. Hard work always agreed with you."

"It still does, Father. My life is not quite so indolent as you might imagine it to be. There is much hard work to be done at a playhouse, and I still keep my hand in at a forge. There is a blacksmith here in London who is good enough to give me work anytime I need it."

His father raised his eyebrows. "So? You are a journeyman blacksmith, then?"

"Nothing quite so respectable, I fear," Tuck replied. "Liam Bailey lost an apprentice not too long ago, and I fill in for him, after a fashion, every now and then. He pays me. Not a great deal, but 'tis a fair wage."

The corners of his father's mouth turned down slightly. "I see. And this . . ." he waved his hand in a sort of desultory fashion, taking in the yard and the theatre all around them, ". . . this is where you . . . what is the word? Perform?" He said it with distaste.

"Aye, among other things," said Smythe. "But then, you already knew that, Father, else you would not be here. I take it Uncle Thomas told you that you could find me here."

His father pursed his lips and nodded as he glanced around with the air of a courtier who had somehow wandered by mistake into a pigsty. "Aye. You saw fit, it seems, to write to your uncle, but not to me."

"You had made it plain on more than one occasion that I would be disowned if I decided to go to London and become a player," Tuck replied. "I merely took you at your word."

His father sniffed. "And you had made it plain when you left home that being disowned meant nothing to you, since I had nothing left to leave you."

"So . . . what? That makes us even? Your bankruptcy cancels out my disobedience, is that it?"

"Do not be insolent. I do not need you to throw my ill fortune into my face. I am quite aware of it, thank you."

" 'Twas not my intention to be insolent, Father, or to dwell upon your ill fortune, as you call it. I intended no offense."

His father merely grunted in reply. "I heard your friend call you by some other name," he said. "Is my name no longer good enough for you?"

Tuck sighed. "My name is still the same as yours," he said. "Tuck is merely what my friends call me. 'Tis a sort of nickname. I rather like it, actually."

His father sniffed again. "Suit yourself. 'Tis your life. You may choose to call yourself anything you wish, I suppose."

"Did you come all the way to London merely to find further fault with me, Father, as you always did, or was there something that you wished of me? I shall not be coming home, if that was what you came to ask of me. I have my own life now."

"You presume I came to London merely to ask you to return?" his father said. "Do you suppose it makes a difference to me what you choose to do?"

"I would have thought not," Tuck replied. "But if you did not come for me, why *did* you come?"

" 'Tis possible, is it not, that I came for myself? To make a new beginning? To rebuild my fortune? Or do all things have to be concerned only with you?"

Tuck frowned. "You mean . . . you have come here to live?" He shook his head, puzzled. "What of your wife?"

His father looked away. "She ran off."

"Ah. Well . . . I am sorry."

"No need. I do not require your pity. I could have gone after her, I suppose. Taken a cane to her, as she deserved. But then I thought, why bother? What need have I of an ungrateful and disloyal wench? 'Tis just as well she left. Good riddance to her, I say. Aye, good riddance, indeed."

"Indeed," Tuck said.

There was an awkward silent moment that seemed to stretch uncomfortably. It seemed as if neither one of them quite knew what to say next.

"Have you found a place to stay?" asked Tuck, finally. He dreaded hearing the reply. He could not imagine having to share quarters with his father. There was barely enough room for him and Will. And inflicting his father upon Will would be cruel beyond all measure. But, still, he *was* his father, after all. "It can be difficult finding a place to stay in London these days," he added, "what with so many people arriving from the country. Rooms are often scarce and—"

"Oh, I have accommodations," his father replied, with a dismissive wave. "I may have fallen upon hard times, but I am still not without some influence in London, you know. You need not concern yourself on my account. Besides, I have no intention of staying in some hovel of a tavern, sleeping on some flea-infested mattress, next to some unwashed mountebank." He curled his lip in a sneer. "Nay, you need not worry. I was quite capable of securing my own lodgings."

"I am glad to hear it," Tuck replied, meaning every word. He avoided rising to the bait. He would not have wished to have his father stay at the Toad and Badger, in any case. He did not imagine that Symington Smythe II and his airs would go over very well with Courtney Stackpole. "Well, then, if there is anything else that I can do to help, then you will please be sure to let me know."

"As it happens, there is," his father replied. "The move to

London, the journey, and finding lodgings and all that, has left me a bit out at the elbows, so to speak. Purely a temporary situation, I assure you, and one that I intend to remedy as soon as possible, but in the meantime, if you could see your way clear to granting me a small loan of a few pounds, I would be grateful."

"Of course," said Tuck, reaching for his purse. "How much will you need?"

"Oh, that should be sufficient, I should think," his father replied, taking the purse out of his hand. "No need to trouble yourself further. I am sure I can manage with this."

A bit taken aback, Tuck did not quite know what to say.

"Oh, and by the by, your uncle asked me to give you this," his father added, handing him a letter. "He sends his warmest affections and all that sort of thing. Well, I am grateful for this, son. I shall try to repay it at the earliest opportunity. No need to trouble yourself further on my account. I can find my own way back. I have a carriage waiting."

"A *carriage*?" Tuck said.

"Aye. Astonishing what these fellows charge. Bloody brigands. But one simply cannot go about slogging through the mud, now can one? Well, I shall be seeing you, I suppose. Good luck and all that sort of thing."

He turned and walked away without a backward glance.

"A carriage," Tuck said to himself, shaking his head in disbelief. "He asks me for a loan, takes *all* my money, and then drives off in a bloody carriage!"

He glanced down at the letter in his hand. He recognized his uncle's handwriting. For all that Thomas Smythe was just a simple craftsman, his chancery hand was every bit as fine as that of any London scribe. He eagerly opened the letter and read:

My dear boy,

 I trust this letter finds you well. Your father has promised that he would deliver this to you at the Burbage Theatre, where I told him you could most easily be found. Doubtless, you shall be surprised to see him, and some word of explanation is most likely in order, since I do not expect him to enlighten you, or else if he does, at least to some extent, explain himself, then I would wish for you to hear my side of it.

In short, I have given him the boot. For all that he is still my brother, I could not bear his insufferable presence in my house one moment longer. I never did begrudge him his inheritance, and although he never once saw fit to share any of it with me, as I continue to believe our father wished for him to do, I bore him no ill will. When, through his own profligate intemperance and uncontrolled ambition, he had squandered nearly the last penny he had left, I took him in, for he was still my family, and I believed that perhaps his fall might have taught him some humility. His wife ran off with some itinerant peddlar, as I understand it, though that is Symington's version of events and, as such, the details are suspect. Still, there is no question that the woman left him when the money was at last all gone, so mayhap there is truth to how he says it came to pass. Either way, it makes little difference. He had no one to take care of him, and no means to do it on his own, and so, somewhat reluctantly, I must confess, I took him in.

I had forgotten just how difficult a person he could be, and how trying was his temper, and how utterly selfish and ungrateful he was, and always had been. I shall not recite the entire litany of offenses that he gave to me, nor regale you at length with how, in his foolish thoughtlessness, he had nearly managed to burn down my home. I gave him money every time he asked, and for all I gave him, he ever asked for more. Much of it, I know, he spent on drink. As for the rest, he squandered it in gambling or else in madcap schemes with the intent of somehow making back his fortune. Do not, I pray you, give him any money, for he shall only waste it in some foolishness. I have given him enough to see him through upon his journey and to find some lodgings once he reaches London, as well as to sustain him for some time, until he can find a job and make some sort of life for himself. What he does after that is none of my concern, for after all of the indignities and hardships he has visited upon me, I have washed my hands of him.

Do not, I pray, allow him to presume upon your sympathies. You have a good heart and a kind nature, neither of which you have inherited from him, to be sure, and I do fear that he may try to take advantage of you. Thus, I caution you to keep a firm hand on your purse strings and exercise sound judgement in whatever he may ask of you. Remember that he had sent you away because he found a son to be too much of a burden. Be wary now should the father prove too much of a burden to the son. Write soon and God keep you.

Your loving uncle,
Thomas Smythe

Tuck shook his head and gave a small snort as he put away the letter. "Sound advice, Uncle, if a bit too late. Small wonder he did not give me the letter first." He sighed. "Well, let us hope that Will has some money left from those sonnets he had sold, else I shall not be eating supper on this night."

He wrapped his cloak around him and set off back toward the Toad and Badger on foot, thinking all the while about his father traveling in a carriage that he was going to pay for with money he had borrowed from his son. Not that Tuck truly expected the "loan" to be repaid. He knew his father far too well for that. Even his own brother, who was as patient as his father was arrogant, had finally reached the limit of that patience. And now the problem would be his. Well, thought Smythe, he would take his uncle's advice to heart. He would not allow his father to presume upon their relationship only to take advantage of him. He would give him what help he could, within reason, but he would not suffer himself to be cozened. He was no longer quite so naïve.

It was already dark as he drew near the Toad and Badger and due to the lateness of the hour, the streets were for the most part deserted. On occasion, a coach or carriage would drive past, clattering along the cobblestones, but there were few pedestrians. Smythe was still preoccupied with his brief reunion with his father as he walked, and the conflicting emotions the meeting had brought up, and so he failed to note that anything was amiss until he heard the sound of running footsteps very close behind him.

As he turned, the club that would have struck him squarely on top of the head came down instead on his shoulder with a numbing impact. He cried out with pain and brought his arm up to ward off the next blow that came whistling toward him. The shock of it nearly broke his arm. The next blow came so quickly that he couldn't block it. The club struck him in the side of the head, grazing his skull, and he saw stars.

There were several of them, he could not tell how many, and they were all around him, raining down blows. He couldn't even draw his knife. He was too busy trying to ward off the blows that just kept coming. In desperation, he put his arms up over his head to protect himself, then lowered his head and charged, bellowing like a bull. He collided with one of his attackers and threw his arms around him, driving him backward until they struck a wall and the impact drove all the wind out of his assailant.

There were more of them, however, and they did not let up. Smythe felt blood running down the side of his head and he could not see straight. With an abrupt finality, it suddenly struck him that he might be killed. Somehow, he found the strength to fight back, absorbing the punishing blows as he wrested a club away from one of his assailants and started dealing out some of his own. Then he heard somebody yelling and a moment later realized that someone else had joined the battle on his side.

His vision swimming, he swung the captured club around in all directions, flailing away madly, and moments later, the attackers were on the run. He sank down to his knees in the street, unable to stand any longer. Everything was spinning.

"Tuck! *Tuck!*"

He thought he recognized the voice, but he could not be certain. There seemed to be a ringing in his ears. "Ben?"

"Hang on, Tuck. Hang on. I must try to stop the bleeding."

"Are they gone?"

"Aye, they ran off, the bloody bastards. But not before I drew some blood. I ran one through and slashed another pretty badly. After that, the rest all ran."

"Well done. I am much obliged to you."

"Do not try to speak, Tuck. Save your strength. I will—"

But that was the last thing Smythe heard as he lost consciousness and collapsed to the street.

He awoke to the worst headache he had ever experienced. He groaned, involuntarily, and brought his hands up to his head, only to find that it was bandaged.

"Lie still," Will said, bending over him, his face full of concern. "Do not try to sit up."

"Where am I?"

"You are back at home, in our room at the Toad and Badger," Shakespeare replied. "Ben brought you here. Do you recall what happened?"

Smythe touched his bandaged head gingerly. "I was attacked . . ."

"You remember?"

"Aye."

"Good. Ben was afraid that you might not. He says that is often a sign of severe injury."

"God, my head . . ."

"You took quite a drubbing, my friend. When we saw all the blood, we were afraid that they had split your skull, but 'twould seem your head is a good deal harder than we had thought. 'Twas only a flesh wound that bled a great deal, thank God. But aside from that, you are a symphony of bruises, though there do not appear to be any broken bones, thanks to your large frame. A lesser man would have been positively splintered. Doubtless, you shall be sore for quite a while."

"Well, if this is anything akin to those hangovers you have from time to time, then I want no part of them, believe me. Lord! It feels as if my head is being squeezed between two millstones."

"Is he awake?" asked Stackpole, from the doorway.

"Aye, after a fashion," Shakespeare replied. "He is a bit confused and says his head hurts."

"I shouldn't wonder," Stackpole said. "Poor lad was very nearly clubbed to death. I brought some chicken broth for him."

"Good of you, Courtney, thank you," Shakespeare said.

"Aye, thank you," Smythe added. " 'Tis good of you, indeed."

"Thank Molly," Stackpole said. "She made it. She said 'twas her mother's recipe for when someone in the family fell ill. She asked if she could come up and look in on you when you felt up to it."

"Of course," said Smythe. "Anytime she likes." He tried to sit up, winced with pain, and fell back into bed again.

"I *told* you not to sit up," said Shakespeare. "You never listen to me. When you are fetched such a mighty clout upon the head, you truly need to rest awhile. If you move too quickly, then you will grow faint and dizzy and you may fall and do yourself an injury."

"I have already *had* my share of injuries," said Smythe, dryly. "I doubt that falling on the floor would make matters much worse."

"Suit yourself," said Shakespeare, with a shrug. "But if you should fall and break your nose or else knock out a few teeth, do not come crying to me. You are a fine looking young man, Tuck, but you would not look quite so handsome were you toothless. And considering your lack of talent as an actor, you might want to hold onto being handsome for as long as possible."

"Right. I shall stay in bed, then."

"And while we are on the subject of your various shortcomings," Shakespeare continued, "this may not be the best time to bring it up, but you might recall that both Sir William and I, as well as others I could mention, have advised you on more than one occasion to start carrying a sword. Sir William even gave you one of his." He glanced pointedly over to the corner of the room, where the sword Sir William gave to Smythe leaned against the wall in its scabbard and belt. "Of course, it does not do you a great deal of good over *there*, although I must admit that ever since you put it there, no one has yet attacked that corner of the room."

Smythe sighed and winced again. He touched his bandaged head gingerly. "Point well taken," he said. "Methinks from now on, I shall not only wear it everywhere I go, except to bed, but I shall resume my long-neglected fencing practice, also."

"Considering how often people try to kill you, that does seem an excellent idea," Shakespeare said. "You do seem to attract more than your share of peril. One might almost think that you were cursed."

"What o'clock is it?" asked Smythe, noticing the shutters closed. There did not seem to be any daylight seeping through the cracks.

"Past ten of the clock, according to the bellman who went by outside a little while ago," Shakespeare replied. "You have been senseless for nearly two hours since Ben brought you back. We feared that you might not reawaken."

"Where is Ben?"

"He has gone to escort Granny Meg back home," Shakespeare replied.

"Granny Meg was here?"

"Aye. Ben and I went to fetch her while Molly stayed here to look after you. Granny Meg removed the bandage Ben tore from his shirt and replaced it with one of her own that she brought with her. She placed a poultice underneath it to draw out the bad humors and left very strict instructions that 'twas not to be removed until she herself removed it and once more looked at your wound. She assured us that your head was more or less intact, although she did caution us that you might not remember things if the blow was strong enough." Shakespeare shrugged. "I asked her how we might possibly be able to tell the difference, since you could not seem to remember things before the blow was struck."

"Very amusing."

"She seemed to think so. In any event, she said that if you could not recall your name, then it could be a bad sign."

"But you did not ask me my name when I awoke."

"I was going to see if your remembered. If not, then I was going to tell you 'twas Ned Alleyn, just to see if 'twould have any improvement upon your acting abilities. But . . . you remembered who you were, worse luck."

Despite the pain, Smythe smiled. " 'Twould seem that I owe Ben a debt of gratitude," he said. "Not to mention a new shirt." He frowned. "Wait a moment. You said that Molly stayed with me while you and Ben went for Granny Meg?"

"Aye, she did. And she was most concerned about you."

"And she is here still?"

"Aye. She would not go home until she knew that you were going to be all right. As Courtney said, she awaits downstairs, to see you and satisfy herself that you are in no grave danger."

Smythe felt a pang of guilt at her concern. "Please send her up, Will."

"I shall."

"Oh, and Will?"

"Aye?"

"Thanks."

Shakespeare smiled. "No need. You would have done no less for me. In fact, as I recall, you did save my life once."

"Then consider the score even."

Shakespeare held up his index finger. "Not quite yet. But I shall be sure to let you know."

A few moments later, Molly knocked and then looked in anxiously. "Will said that you were awake and feeling better."

"Well, I am not so sure that I feel better, but at least I am awake. Please come in, Molly."

"I am so very sorry, Tuck," she said, as she came in and sat down on a stool beside the bed. "Does it hurt very much?"

"Like the very Devil. But your broth helped. Thank you."

"You are most welcome. Did you see who did it?"

Smythe shook his head and at once regretted it. The room spun and he closed his eyes a moment, hoping that he would not retch. "Nay, I did not," he said, after a moment. "But Ben did. He said 'twas the Steady Boys. It appears that I shall have a score to settle with Jack Darnley and his lot."

"Granny Meg said 'twas likely that you would recover fully before long."

"I believe I shall," said Smythe. "For the most part, 'tis just my head that aches as if 'twill burst. From now on, methinks I shall be more careful about walking through the streets alone after it grows dark. Which reminds me, Molly. . . . I have a confession I must make to you. And I fear that it may make you angry with me."

"You are going to say you followed me?"

Smythe grimaced. "You already knew. She told you."

Molly nodded. "I am not angry with you, Tuck. I know you thought 'twas a man that I was with and you only followed me out of concern for my safety and welfare."

"She told you that?"

Molly smiled. "She did not need to. I know you, Tuck. You are not a scoundrel. There is no meanness in you. You have always been kind to me. You and all the other players have always treated me as if I were part of the family, and I have always been very grateful for that. You are all very nearly the only family I know."

"Well, I am relieved to hear you are not angry with me," Smythe told her. "And you have repaid my kindness with kindness of your own. But I still cannot help but wonder . . . What in the world have you to do with the likes of Moll Cutpurse?"

Molly glanced down at the floor. " 'Tis a private matter, Tuck, and I wish you would not ask me."

"Well, I know 'tis no concern of mine, but—"

"Just so, Tuck. 'Tis no concern of yours. And I would be grateful if you did not press me on the matter."

"But you do know who she is, Molly?"

"I know," she replied. "And I know you ask from motives that are good and well intended. But I promise you that I am in no danger, Tuck. I have nothing to fear from Moll Cutpurse.

Truly. What we have between us is a private matter, as I said. And I do not wish to discuss it further. As you are my friend, I ask your word that you shall not pursue it or discuss it with any of the others."

"Molly, I merely—"

"Your *word*, Tuck."

He sighed. "Very well. You have my word."

She smiled. "Thank you. And now you should try and get some sleep. Granny Meg said that you would need your rest to heal. And for that matter, I should get some sleep, myself. Master Stackpole has been kind enough to let me have a bed for the night. If you feel poorly and need anything tonight, call out. I am a light sleeper and shall hear." She leaned forward and kissed him on the forehead. "You can barely keep your eyes open. Go to sleep now. I shall look in on you tomorrow."

It was true. It was all that he could do to keep his eyes open. His head ached terribly, he felt dizzy and queasy, but most of all, he felt so tired that all he wanted to do was close his eyes and sleep. It seemed like a most excellent suggestion. He could not recall for certain later if he even said good night to her. He could not even recall seeing her leave. He seemed to recall hearing the door to his room close softly and that was the last thing he remembered. He slept a long, deep, and dreamless sleep. In fact, he slept all through the next day and the next night. And when he finally awoke, it was to discover that while he had slept, Master Leonardo had been murdered.

7

TUCK FOUND OUT WHAT HAD happened over breakfast downstairs in the tavern. Or at least, once he got past all the speculation, he found out as much as anybody knew, which was not a very great deal. When he came down in the morning, after sleeping fitfully through most of an entire day, everyone solicitously asked him how he felt. He replied with gratitude that he still hurt in at least a dozen places, yet in the main, he was very much improved. But despite their genuine concern about his welfare, it was nevertheless obvious that what had happened to him was no longer the primary topic of interest. Everyone seemed anxious to move on quickly past the question of how he felt in order to discuss the news of Master Leonardo's murder.

It did not take Smythe very long to piece together the details. From the general conversation in the tavern, he learned that sometime during the previous afternoon or evening, Master Leonardo, the wealthy Genoan merchant whom they had all met briefly only a day earlier, had been viciously murdered at his residence. His young and beautiful daughter, Hera, had not been at home, fortunately, but was away visiting her new friend, Elizabeth Darcie, who had taken the shy foreign girl under her wing and was helping her become acclimated to her new life in London. Regrettably, it had been Hera who had discovered her own father's body when she arrived back home that night.

"Dear God! The poor girl!" Smythe said. "How terrible for her!"

"Terrible is not the word," George Bryan replied. "Horrible would be more like. They say the man was sliced to ribbons. Slashed more deeply than a fop's silk shirt."

"Aye, there was blood everywhere," added Tom Pope, one of the newest members of their company, as he busily ladled porridge into his mouth.

"There is going to be porridge everywhere if you persist in trying to speak and gorge at the same time, you odiferous hog," said Kemp with contempt. "S'trewth, watching you eat is enough to put a starving beggar off his food. I know it puts me off mine."

"Well then, since I have put you off your food, 'tis only meet that I should put some food on you," retorted Pope, and with that, he flipped a generous ladleful of hot porridge right into Will Kemp's face.

"*Aaarghh!* You misbegotten Philistine!" roared Kemp, leaping to his feet as he wiped the porridge from his eyes. "How *dare* you!"

"Never say I gave you naught, Kemp," Pope replied with a grin, "for I daresay you have just had breakfast on me."

"Well then, allow me to return the kindness!" Kemp said through gritted teeth, and with that, he picked up his own bowl of steaming porridge and upended it over Pope's head.

"Gentlemen! Gentlemen! We were speaking of murder, for God's sake!" said Smythe.

"Aye, and that is just what I am going to do to that miserable, mincing old goat!" snarled Pope, wiping the dripping gobs of porridge from his face and shaking his hands off. The flung-off gobs of porridge made wet, smacking sounds as they landed on the wood-planked floor. Pope reached for the clay pitcher in the center of the table.

"Oh, no, Tom!" Speed cried out. "Not the beer!"

Too late.

Pope dashed the beer into Kemp's face, neatly rinsing off the porridge Kemp had not fully succeeded in wiping away.

Smythe rolled his eyes and gave up on them. He turned to Phillips. "The devil with those two. Tell me, what happened after Hera found her father?"

"Well, from what I hear, she very nearly lost her mind," Gus Phillips replied, as Kemp grabbed his ladle and launched himself at Pope, knocking him off his bench. They both fell backwards in a tangled, flailing heap. "I mean," continued Phillips, "can you imagine, walking into your own home and finding your own father sliced up like an Easter ham and lying on the floor in a spreading pool of his own blood?"

"You need not be quite so lurid," Smythe replied dryly, as Kemp shrieked and hammered away at Pope with his wooden ladle, while the latter desperately tried to dislodge the smaller man, who had clamped his legs around him like an octopus and hung on like grim death. "What about the servants?" Smythe continued.

"What about them?" Speed asked. "You do not think they did it, do you? You think they did the foreigner in for all his gold?"

"I honestly do not know," Smythe said, as Pope finally succeeded in dislodging Kemp, throwing him off, and then rolling over on top of him with his not inconsiderable bulk, squeezing the wind right out of him. "But I very much doubt that a canny merchant would have been careless enough to keep all of his gold inside his house," Smythe went on, ignoring the combatants. " 'Twas not what I intended to suggest, though I suppose 'tis possible. I meant to ask if Master Leonardo's servents had not heard anything amiss? After all, does it not seem odd to have a man killed in his own house, and in so violent a manner as you describe, and yet none of the servents knew of it, so that the body was not even found until the daughter arrived home that night?"

Phillips frowned. "Hmm. I must admit that thought never even occurred to me. An excellent question, Tuck. However, I must confess 'tis one I cannot answer."

"There were servants in the house, surely?" Smythe said.

"I assume so," Phillips replied, with a shrug, as Kemp tried in vain to escape from underneath Pope's bulk. He squirmed and yelped as the larger man took hold of his nose and began twisting it painfully.

"You mean you do not know for certain?" Smythe asked.

"How am I know a thing like that for certain?" Phillips asked. "I have never been in the man's house, now have I?"

"And yet you know that he was found all cut to ribbons, with blood spilled everywhere?" Smythe asked.

"Well, that was how I heard it," Phillips said.

"From *whom* did you hear this?"

"S'trewth, I cannot say for certain," replied Phillips, with a shrug. "Everyone has been talking about it, it seems."

"Amazing," Smythe said. "The man was only killed last night, and this morning, everyone in London seems to know all the details of the crime. If Sir Francis Walsingham had intelligence this good, then the Armada would have been destroyed before it ever even sailed from Spain."

"What are you picking on me for?" Phillips asked, with an aggrieved air. "I was merely telling you what I had heard. You *asked* me, after all!"

"*Aaaaaahhhhh! Let me go, you stinking pile of offal!*" Kemp wailed.

" 'Allo, 'allo, what's all this then?" Stackpole demanded, as he

came out from the kitchen, wiping his hands on his apron. "Get
off him, you great, slobbering dungheap!" He gave Pope a kick
that sent him sprawling with a yelp.

"Thank heavens, Stackpole!" Kemp said, clutching at his
chest. "The big oaf nearly crushed me! You are a godsend!"

"You'll not think so when I start mopping up all this mess
with your face," said Stackpole, grabbing him by the shirtfront
and glowering at him as he pulled him to his feet. "Who is going
to clean this up then?"

"He started it!" cried Kemp, pointing an accusatory finger at
Pope.

"I never did, you lying pustule!" protested Pope. "You be-
rated me!"

"Enough!" Stackpole thundered. "I have had my fill of you
both! Now clean up this mess or so help me I shall hang you
both from the rafters and have Molly beat you with a stick!"

"Have a care now, Stackpole, Kemp might like that," Bryan
said.

"And *you* be quiet, else I shall have you helping them!" said
Stackpole, glaring at him. "I shall have peace in my own house
or I shall have you all in pieces! *Players*! I would have done better
to open up my inn to a gang of wandering gypsies!"

The door opened at that moment and Shakespeare came bus-
tling in. "They have taken Corwin!" he announced. "He has been
arrested for the murder of Master Leonardo!"

"*What?*" said Smythe.

Immediately, everyone surrounded Shakespeare and began
peppering him with questions. "Patience! Patience!" Will cried
out, holding up his hands. "I shall answer one and all, to the
fullest extent of my knowledge, but I pray you, my friends, give
me room to breathe!"

They backed off and Stackpole pulled out a bench for him.
Molly came out, too, along with the cook and the scullery maid,

as everyone gathered around Shakespeare to hear the latest news. But before he spoke to that, Shakespeare turned to Smythe.

" 'Tis good to see you up and about, Tuck. How does your head feel?" he asked with concern.

"A bit sore, still, and the poultice itches, but otherwise, I am feeling better," Smythe replied. "Never mind about me, however. Tell us what happened, Will, and begin at the beginning. But first of all, does Ben know about what has transpired?"

"Aye," said Shakespeare, nodding. "I have just left him with Master Peters, where I had gone upon an errand. The gentleman who has been good enough to buy my sonnets and then have them bound for distribution to his friends has been a boon not only to me, but his generosity has helped us all in these difficult times, and so I had thought, what with Ben now being one of us and Corwin being his friend and ours, perhaps I might presume on that acquaintaince to have Corwin craft some small piece of jewelry at a price I could afford, as a token of my appreciation to our patron, as it were. I had arranged with Ben to meet at Master Peters's shop and Ben was to ask him the favor for me, but even as we arrived, the sheriff's men were taking Corwin away."

"Do you mean to say 'twas Corwin who killed Master Leonado?" Molly asked, wide-eyed.

"He was crying out, protesting his innocence as they took him away," Shakespeare replied, "but then 'tis said that killers oft' protest their innocence, even to the gallows."

"But why would he kill the father of the girl he wished to marry?" Molly asked.

"Perhaps because the father would not give his consent," ventured Gus Phillips. "Think you 'twas the reason for the crime, Will?"

"Nay, the consent to wed was given freely," Shakespeare said. "Stay your questions for a while, my friends, and I shall tell you all the tale as I know it. As most of you must surely know by now, Cupid's arrow did strike Corwin from the moment that he first laid eyes on Hera, Master Leonardo's daughter, whereupon he had resolved to end his bachelor days and marry. To this end, he asked his friend and ours, Ben Dickens, to speak on his behalf to Master Leonardo, whom Ben knew well from having traveled aboard ship with him to England. Ben did speak with Master Leonardo, and the latter did readily consent to the proposed match, as Ben's word bore weight with him and, quite aside from that, he perceived the advantages to both his daughter and himself in Hera's marriage to a successful young journeyman well on his way to becoming a prosperous master goldsmith."

"I wonder if anyone troubled to ask Hera what she thought of the idea," Molly said.

"One assumes that in Genoa, dutiful daughters obey their fathers' wishes in such things," Shakespeare replied. "However, as to what Hera herself thought of this, 'twould seem that she was not averse to Corwin, for he had started paying court to her and it appeared she was receptive to him. Yesterday afternoon, however, whilst you Tuck, slept, and recovered from your injuries, Corwin came to the Theatre, seeking Ben. And he was in a most agitated state."

"Aye, he seemed very troubled," Bryan said. "And he did not long remain. He left before Ben arrived, as I recall."

"Indeed," said Kemp, his contretemps with Pope forgotten for the moment as he became caught up in the news. "He rushed off right after he spoke with you, Will. But you would not tell us what the matter was."

Shakespeare shook his head. "I saw no need to dwell upon it," he replied. "'Twas the sort of matter that could bring an innocent young girl to grief if it became bruited about and was made the subject of malicious gossip. Already, trouble was afoot, and I had no wish to add to it."

"What was this troubling matter, Will?" Smythe asked with a frown. "Whatever it may be, a greater trouble has now befallen Corwin, and it may have a bearing on his fate."

"I fear it shall," said Shakespeare. "As I have told you, Corwin was in a most perturbed state, and so I did not have all the details of the matter from him, but 'twould seem he had somehow discovered that Hera had deceived him and was not, in fact, a virtuous young woman."

"How does he know this?" Molly asked. "Does he have proof?"

"I do not know," Shakespeare replied. "As I have told you, he was hot and very agitated. He could not or else would not wait for Ben. He left word with me to tell Ben when he arrived that he was going to Master Leonardo's house to break off the engagement."

"Without even giving her a chance to speak in her own defense?" said Molly.

"Again," said Shakespeare, shaking his head, "you are asking questions of me that I simply cannot answer. I do not know whether or not he intended to accuse her and hear her answer to the charge. Nor do I know what sort of proof he had, if any. In any event, he certainly seemed convinced. He was in quite a state, I tell you, and his words were tumbling over one another. Aside from that, 'tis not as if the woman were *my* daughter, thus I did not truly feel entitled to press him on the matter."

"What happened then?" asked Smythe.

"Well, Corwin departed, and then you all started to arrive, and there was talk of Tuck and how he fared after the cowardly attack upon him, and then Ben came and also asked after you, Tuck—"

"Never mind about me," said Smythe, impatiently. "Go on. What about Corwin?"

"Well, I gave Ben my report, relaying to him Corwin's words

as best I could, and as I spoke, his eyes grew wide and he appeared most disconcerted. He bade me tell him how much time had passed since Corwin left for Master Leonardo's house and, in truth, I was not certain." Shakespeare spread his hands out. "I told him 'twas scarce an hour or so, perhaps less, perhaps more. . . . I could not be more precise. At this, he seemed somewhat torn and confessed to me that he felt his duty was to remain and rehearse with the company, for his was the key role in the play, and yet, he was moved to rush straight off to Master Leonardo's home, but knew 'twas already too late to prevent Corwin from speaking to him. The damage, he decided, had doubtless already been done. If Corwin had gone to Master Leonardo in a fit of temper and denounced his daughter as a whore, then there would be no possibility of any intercession. An Englishman, he said, would never forgive a man who so besmirched his daughter's honor; a Genoan would very likely kill him."

"Prophetic words," said Phillips, "save only 'twas the Genoan who was killed."

"Indeed," said Shakespeare. "I said to him then, 'Ben, if blood is likely to be spilt, then to the devil with the play! You must go and try to stop it!' And he considered, then replied that knowing Master Leonardo as he did, 'twas little chance that he would drink hot blood and allow rage to drive him into violence. Without a doubt, he thought, Master Leonardo would insist upon satisfaction and seek it in the honorable, formal manner of the *code duello*."

"What did they do? Fight a duel right there in his home?" asked Pope.

"Of course not, you cretin!" Kemp said. "One fights a duel at sunrise, according to the code, with seconds and all the forms properly observed!"

"Don't you go calling me a cretin, you sheeptupper!" Pope

replied, rounding on Kemp, but a low growl from Stackpole silenced them both.

"Never mind them," said Smythe, with a grimace. "Go on, Will. Then what happened? I cannot believe I slept through all of this!"

"You would have slept through the flood," said Shakespeare. "You awoke every now and then, but only for a moment or two, and never quite completely. I began to grow concerned, but Granny Meg assured me that—"

"Aye, never mind him, either; he survived, get *on* with it!" said Kemp.

"Thank you, Kemp, your concern touches me deeply," Smythe said, dryly.

"Stuff it!" Kemp replied. "Go on, Will."

"Where was I?" Shakespeare asked with a frown.

"They were going to fight a duel," Molly prompted him. "Or at least Ben thought they would."

"Aye, just so," said Shakespeare. "Say, Stackpole, this is thirsty work. A man could use a drink."

Stackpole scowled. "Right. Just one, mind! And then you pay."

"You are a prince among men, Courtney," Shakespeare said expansively.

"And you are a bloody sot among lushes," Stackpole retorted, irately. "Get on with your story, then!"

"And so I shall. Ben decided that the thing to do would be to let both men have their air, and then speak to each of them the following day, for there could be no opportunity for them to fight a duel the very next morning. Seconds would have to be found first, and then second, those seconds would need to meet and appoint a time and place, and thirdly, weapons would need to be chosen, and so forth."

"They would need to choose weapons fourth?" said Pope. "Why not chose weapons first?"

Shakespeare shook his head. "Nay, they would need to chose weapons *and so forth* . . . I suppose there is no reason why they could not choose weapons first."

"Well, if they chose weapons first, then what would they choose fourth?" persisted Pope.

"He said that they would choose weapons *thirdly*," said Phillips.

"He just said that they would choose them first!"

"Nay, he said they would choose them *fourth*," said Bryan.

"I said they needed to choose weapons *and . . . so . . .* forth," said Shakespeare.

"So fourth what?" asked Pope. "They would meet?"

"Nay, they needed to *meet* first," replied Phillips.

"I thought they needed to meet second," Pope said, frowning.

"*First*, the seconds need to be appointed," Shakespeare explained, patiently. "*Second*, the seconds have to meet."

"Aye, 'tis why they call them seconds, you buffoon," said Phillips, tossing a lump of bread at Pope.

"Oh, for heavens sake!" said Shakespeare, getting exasperated. "They do not call them seconds because they must *meet* second; they call them seconds because they *are* seconds!"

"So then who is called first?" asked Pope.

"*No one* is called first!" said Shakespeare, clenching both hands into fists.

"Well, that makes no bloody sense!" said Pope, irritably. "Why would you call someone second if there is no first?"

"*Right!*" said Shakespeare, leaning forward and fixing him with a direct gaze. "The *duelists* are called firsts, and the *seconds* are called seconds. *Got it?*"

"Second at what?" asked Pope.

Shakespeare rolled his eyes. "At *dueling*. They shall be second at *dueling*."

"The seconds duel?"

"The seconds duel."

"What for?"

Shakespeare took a deep breath. "Because that is how the thing is done," he said, struggling to maintain a level tone.

"So the seconds duel second, and the duelists duel first?"

Shakespeare nodded with finality. "Aye, that is it, exactly."

"So then who comes third?"

Shakespeare's eyes narrowed into slits. "Nobody comes third," he said, softly.

"And so nobody is fourth, then?"

"Right. You have it, Pope. Nobody is fourth."

"So then when do they choose the weapons?"

"Whenever they bloody well want to."

"Are you quite finished?" Smythe asked.

Shakespeare turned and pointed a finger at him. "Don't *you* start with me."

"Wouldn't dream of it," said Smythe. "But if you write your plays the way you tell your stories, then 'tis no wonder you never get any of them finished."

"Zounds! Where is my sword?" said Shakespeare, looking around. "I am going to kill him."

"You do not have a sword," said Smythe.

"A *sword*!" cried Shakespeare, leaping to his feet and stabbing his forefinger into the air. "A *sword*! *My kingdom for a sword!*"

"Oh, here we go . . ." sighed Smythe, rolling his eyes.

"Friends! Colleagues! Countrymen! Who shall lend me a weapon with which to run this rascal through?"

"Sit down, you silly goose," said Smythe, reaching out and

taking hold of him by the hips, then yanking him abruptly back down to the bench. Shakespeare sat down so hard his teeth clicked together.

"Sweet merciful God!" he said. "You've broken my arse!"

"I shall break a good deal more than that if you do not cease this skylarking at once and get back to the point," said Smythe, impatiently. "What happened next? What did Ben do after the rehearsal?"

"Why, he went home, I should imagine," Shakespeare replied.

"What do you mean, he went home?"

"I mean . . . he went home," Shakespeare repeated, with a shrug. "What other meaning can there be to that?"

"His closest friend went to confront his intended's father so that he could break off his engagement and so doubtless be challenged to a duel, and Ben stayed at the Theatre to rehearse and then went *home*?" Smythe asked, frowning.

"Aye," said Shakespeare. "He had decided 'twould be best to let Corwin sleep off his distemper, then go and see him in the morning and find out what had transpired. We had agreed to go together, although, as Ben had told me, if Master Leonardo had already challenged Corwin, then 'twas doubtful that there was aught that he could do to stop it."

"Well, 'tis possible that a challenge could be withdrawn, is it not?" asked Smythe.

"I suppose so," Shakespeare replied. "But then Ben told me that once Master Leonardo had made up his mind, heaven and earth could not dissuade him. In any event, the point is certainly now moot. Master Leonardo has been killed, and Corwin has been arrested for the murder."

"Aye, I can well see how it must have gone," said Kemp. "Corwin went to see the Genoan and doubtless in his anger at having been deceived, he said things to him that could not be borne by any gentleman, whether English or foreign. And so the Genoan then and there flung down his gage and, in a fury, Corwin slayed him, right there in his own home."

"Do you suppose that was how it happened?" George Bryan asked of no one in particular.

"It could well be," said Gus Phillips. "Do you recall how Corwin acted on the day that we first met him, right here in this very tavern, when he came in company with Ben? All he could seem to think of was that Italian girl, the merchant's daughter, Hera. He seemed obsessed with her."

"I can see how any man would be," Bryan replied.

"Aye, but to the point of wanting to take her to wife? After seeing her only once?" countered Phillips. "That bespeaks a certain hotness of the blood, do you not think?"

"A man so quick to love would likely be as quick to kill, is that your meaning then?" Smythe asked, raising an eyebrow.

"Does it not follow that hot blood would beget hot blood?" asked Phillips.

Shakespeare smiled. "Methinks what Tuck means, Augustine," he said, "is that he himself was smitten with a girl upon first sight, and thus far at least, he has not yet murdered anyone."

"Ah. Well . . ." Phillips cleared his throat uncomfortably. "No offense there, Tuck, old boy."

"None taken, Gus," Smythe replied. "But 'twould do us all well to remember that if being quick to love also meant that one was just as quick to kill, then most of us would probably be murderers."

"You know, that was not too bad," said Shakespeare. "Not bad at all. 'Twas a decent line, Tuck. Perhaps if I fiddled round with it a bit . . ."

"For instance, if Pope were to suddenly turn up dead," continued Smythe, "then we would all think you had done it, Kemp, for every one of us saw you flinging porridge at him and trying to beat his brains out with the ladle. Well, after all . . . what more proof do you need?"

Kemp folded his arms and harrumphed.

"In all of this debate, there is one thing you all seem to have forgotten," Molly said. "The unfortunate Master Leonardo's murder has now left his daughter orphaned in a strange land, friendless, and with her reputation sullied. What about poor Hera? Whatever shall become of her?"

They all fell silent for a moment, thinking of the shy, beautiful young Genoan girl.

" 'Tis a hard thing to be left without a family to care for you," said Molly, quietly. "Harder still when one is in a foreign land."

"Well, orphaned she may be," said Smythe, "but neither alone nor friendless, not if I know Elizabeth. She had given the girl her friendship, and Elizabeth is not one to abandon a friend in need."

"But what about Corwin's need?" asked Shakespeare. "Surely, his situation is more dire. Neither Ben nor Master Peters can believe that he is guilty of the murder. They both insist that he would not be capable of such a thing."

"Any man is capable of murder," Smythe said. "Any man can lose his head and give in to his baser impulses."

"You, for instance?" Shakespeare asked.

"I am no different, Will," Smythe replied. "Under the right circumstances, or given enough provocation, I believe that any man could kill. Even you."

"Perhaps," said Shakespeare, "but that still does not mean Corwin did the deed."

"But if not him, who else?" said Kemp. "He came to the theatre in an agitated state, as you said yourself, Will. 'He was hot,' you said. Those were your very words. And he was so incensed that he could not wait for Ben; he had to leave at once for Master Leonardo's house. And sometime between then and the time the Genoan girl came home that night to find her father slain, the deed was done. Who else could have done it? Who else had the opportunity? And the motive?"

Shakespeare grimaced. "Aye. Who else, indeed?"

"Perhaps we should find that out, Will," Smythe said. "For if Corwin did not do it, then an innocent man shall be taken to the gallows, and a murderer shall go free."

8

Henry Darcie's four-story, lead-roofed townhouse built of rough-cut gray stone bore stately testimony to his success in business. As with many homes built so close together in the crowded environment of London, the upper floors jutted out over the cobblestoned street, so as to take the maximum advantage of space, and expensive glass windows not only afforded plenty of light to the upper floors, but also showed all passersby that the owner of the house was wealthy enough to afford such luxuries. The servant who opened the door glanced at them as if they were curious insects, heard their names without a word, and closed the door again while he went to announce them to the master of the house. Moments later, Henry Darcie came to the door himself to greet them.

"Ah, Shakespeare, Smythe," he said, nodding to them curtly. "Come in. I assume that you have come about the news of Leonardo."

"Indeed, we have, sir," Smythe replied. "We had hoped to speak with Hera, unless, that is, she is too grief-stricken to entertain a visit at this time."

"Aye, 'tis a terrible thing, terrible," Darcie replied, shaking his head. "Here we were, on the verge of acquiring a prosperous new investor for the Theatre. 'Twould have neatly taken care of all of the needed refurbishing at once, too. Ah, well. Such a pity. Still, one learns to accept these sort of reverses if one is to survive in business. Such is the nature of things. Life goes on." And then he added, almost as an afterthought, "Poor Hera is upstairs with Elizabeth."

As they went through the entry hall and toward the stairs, Shakespeare gawked at their surroundings. The planked floors were covered not with rushes, but with rush mats woven in intricate patterns and handsomely colored. The walls were panelled with wood and hung with tapestries, not the cheaper painted cloths that were used by all except the very rich. The furnishings were carved and inlaid with ivory or pearl, many pieces draped with patterned carpets, and some of the chairs were actually upholstered. There was not a boarded stool or chest in sight.

"Actually, sir, with your permission, before speaking with Elizabeth and Master Leonardo's daughter, I should like to ask you a question or two, if I may," said Smythe.

Darcie turned toward him and raised his eyebrows. "Concerning what?"

"Concerning the very matter that you just now mentioned, sir," Smythe replied. "I merely wanted to make certain that my understanding was correct. Had Master Leonardo already made a firm commitment to you and Master Burbage concerning an investment in the Theatre?"

"Indeed, he had," Darcie replied, nodding emphatically. "And he was most anxious to proceed. Unlike most people, he did not hesitate to make decisions. I saw that quality in him and was encouraged by it. He would weigh an opportunity, assess the potential advantages and risks, and then proceed without wasting any time. As I have said, 'tis a great pity that things turned out the way they did. We had discussed the possibility of partnership in several ventures." He shook his head again, in resignation. "He was excited to be making a new start in London, anxious to take advantage of the opportunity to be a partner in the Theatre, and to explore other avenues, as well. Now, all his hopes and dreams have been snuffed out, just like that." He snapped his fingers.

"Do you know if Master Leonardo had planned any other business ventures, that is to say, other than those he had discussed as possibilities of partnership with you?" Smythe asked.

"I suppose 'tis entirely possible he may have had such plans, but if so, he did not mention them to me," said Darcie. "He did not strike me as the sort of man to limit himself. His interests seemed varied and diverse." He frowned. "Why, what the devil are you getting at, Smythe?"

"Well, sir, I was merely wondering if he might have been involved with anyone in some venture that might have gone amiss in some way," Smythe replied. "Something of that sort could possibly have been a motive in his murder."

"Whatever do you mean? I was under the impression that the murderer had already been placed under arrest," said Darcie, frowning. " 'Twas that young goldsmith who had desired to marry Hera, was it not?"

"Corwin was, indeed, arrested this morning, as you have already heard," Shakespeare said, "but he did protest his innocence most strenuously. And he has friends who believe firmly in his innocence, as well, among them Master Peters, whom you know."

Darcie grunted. "Aye, well, the lad was his apprentice, after all, and a valued journeyman in his shop. A skilled artisan, by all accounts, whose work was in considerable demand."

"Are you suggesting that Master Peters may have a selfish motive for his stated belief in Corwin's innocence?" asked Shakespeare.

"Why, does that not seem possible to you?" asked Darcie.

"Well, I suppose 'tis possible," Shakespeare replied. "Master Peters does seem quite fond of Corwin."

"Well, there you have it, then," Darcie said, with a shrug. "The young man wanted the daughter; the father disapproved; tempers ran hot—these Italians often get that way, I under-stand—and the next thing you know, blades are drawn and blood is spilt."

"You say the father disapproved of him?" asked Smythe, with some surprise.

"Fathers do not always approve of the young men their daughters choose," said Darcie, wryly, with a glance at Smythe.

Smythe ignored both the well-placed barb and the pointed look. "How very curious," he said. "I was under the impression that Master Leonardo had not only approved of Corwin, but had already given his consent to the match," he said.

Darcie raised his eyebrows. "Indeed? Where did you hear that?"

Smythe turned to Shakespeare. "Where did we hear that?"

"We have it on the word of Master Peters," Shakespeare said.

"Is that so?" said Darcie. "Hmm. I had not known that."

"Betimes, fathers do approve their daughters' choices," Smythe said with a straight face, unable to resist.

"Well, then I cannot imagine why the young fool would have killed him."

" 'Twould seem that there was some sort of accusation con-cerning the young lady's virtue," Shakespeare said. "When he came to the theatre, looking for Ben Dickens, Corwin had in-formed me that he was going to Master Leonardo's house to break off the engagement."

"Odd's blood!" said Darcie. "I had heard none of this at all! I had not even known that there was a formal engagement, much less any question concerning Hera's virtue!"

"Had she said nothing to you about the matter?" Smythe asked, frowning.

"I should say not!" Darcie said. "S'trewth, the girl scarcely speaks at all. She speaks only to Elizabeth and keeps her eyes so downcast, 'tis a wonder she can see where she is going. Not that I can fault her for her modesty. 'Tis a manner most demure and most becoming in a woman. I would not find it amiss if some of it should rub off on Elizabeth. Why, the very thought of such a girl having her virtue brought into question . . ." He snorted with derision. " 'Tis an absurdity! I simply cannot credit it."

"Yet 'twould seem that Corwin could," said Shakespeare.

"If so, then his love for her was fickle," Darcie said.

"Perhaps. Or else so overwhelming that it overcame his reason," Smythe said.

"Aye, friendship is constant in all other things save in the office and affairs of love," mused Shakespeare.

"Yet one more argument in favor of marriages being arranged, as by tradition," Darcie said with a sniff, as he led the way up the stairs, past portraits of the queen and her most celebrated courtiers. The portraits all looked fairly new, and among them were no relatives, thought Smythe. The mark of the new man was that he had no illustrious antecedents with which to grace his walls. "This peculiar notion of allowing young people to make their own choices in marriage, as if they were no better than working class," continued Darcie, "is arrant nonsense, if you ask me. Such foolish, bardic sentiments are best left to romantic balladeers and poets. Marriage is much too serious a matter to be cluttered up with feelings."

"I do not know that I could argue with you there," said Shakespeare, wryly. Smythe gave him a look.

"And how is poor Hera bearing up under this woeful tragedy?" asked Smythe. Thus far, Darcie had said nothing whatever of her state.

"As well as could be expected, one supposes," Darcie replied, with a shrug. "She is a quiet girl, and does not seem given to any loud displays of lamentations. Her comportment has been the very model of decorum and restraint. Elizabeth seems more upset about it all than she does."

"How very strange," said Shakespeare. "I should think that if my own father were killed, I would be a very torrent of emotions . . . grief, rage, melancholy, the desire for vengeance, each feeling battling with the other for supremacy."

"Not all children have so strong an attachment to their parents," Smythe replied. "And not all parents engender such affection."

They reached the third floor and proceeded down a short corridor to an open sitting room where they found Elizabeth keeping company with Hera. Both women sat quietly near the windows. Elizabeth was doing some embroidery, while Hera simply sat staring out the window.

"Elizabeth, we have visitors," her father said, as she looked up when they entered. To Smythe and Shakespeare, he added in a low tone, "Mark you, do not over-tax the girl with questions, especially concerning the conduct of her father's business. Make the appropriate expressions of sympathy and so forth, offer condolences and whatever help she may require. Allow her to know that the company shall stand behind her in her hour of need, so that she will know that her fortune is tied to yours and yours to hers. But do not overstate the case. She will need some time, no doubt, to recover from her grief, and then she shall remember who her friends were when she had need of them. I'll leave you now. Elizabeth can show you out when you are done."

Smythe and Shakespeare exchanged glances of disbelief at Darcie's callousness, but there was no opportunity to discuss it, as Elizabeth was already approaching them.

"Will! Tuck! So good of you to come!" she said, holding out

her hands to them both. Her eyes widened at the sight of the bandage on Smythe's head. "Goodness, Tuck! Were you injured? What happened?"

"Nothing truly worth discussing," he replied, dismissively, "certainly not in comparison with what happened yesterday."

"What a dreadful thing," Elizabeth replied. "And just when things had looked so promising for everyone!"

"You know they have arrested Corwin?" Smythe said.

She nodded. "Aye, like an ill wind, bad news travels quickly," she replied. "They were crying the news out in the streets before, and thus Hera heard it, whilst sitting at the window and dwelling upon her father's tragic fate." She glanced toward the dark-haired girl, who still sat looking out the window. She had not even glanced around when they came in.

"How long has she been thus?" asked Smythe, glancing from Hera to Elizabeth.

Elizabeth shook her head sadly. "Ever since this morning," she replied. "She simply sits there, saying naught and doing naught in her melancholy humor. I have tried to draw her out, but now she will not even speak to me. 'Tis as if a veil has been drawn betwixt her and the world. I cannot even tell if she knows that we are here."

"Has the poor girl lost her reason?" Shakespeare asked with concern.

Elizabeth bit her lower lip. "I pray not," she replied. "I fear for her. Father says that 'tis a melancholy that will pass. I wanted to send for Granny Meg, but he does not wish to hear of it. He says there is no need for witches, and that God shall heal her in time." She sighed and gazed at Hera anxiously. "I do so want to believe that, but I cannot help feeling afraid for her."

"How did she come here?" Smythe asked.

"She came last night, on foot," Elizabeth replied.

"On *foot*?" said Smythe. "At night? *Alone*?"

"One of the servants came after her," Elizabeth said. " 'Twas not that he came with her to escort her so much as he followed her, out of concern for her safety. After she had found her father, she cried out and then went running from the house, he said. She came straight here." Elizabeth sighed. "Indeed, where else would she go? I am her only friend in London."

"She had been with you earlier that day?" asked Smythe.

Elizabeth nodded. "And what a happy time we had." She smiled at the memory. "We spoke of English weddings. She wanted to know all about our marriage customs. She was so full of happy expectation . . . Such a marked contrast to her present, mournful humor."

"She was happy about the engagement, then?" said Smythe. "Her father had approved?"

Elizabeth nodded. " 'Twas all settled save for the setting of the date and the arrangements for the wedding," she said.

"Were they not Catholic?" Shakespeare asked. "Would that not have posed some impediment to the marriage?"

"I had thought the same," Elizabeth replied, "but it seems not to have presented any difficulty. Hera had told me that her father said to her, 'We are in England now, and we shall do things as the English do.' He was, I believe, content to provide the dowry and leave all the arrangements for the wedding to Corwin and Master Peters."

"I see," said Smythe, gazing at the Genoan girl. "But your father seemed to think that Master Leonardo may not have approved of Corwin."

Elizabeth glanced at Smythe with surprise. "Whatever gave him that idea?"

"Did he have reason to think otherwise?" Smythe asked.

Elizabeth frowned. "I do not know. I have no idea why he would have thought so. I know that he and Master Leonardo spoke at length that day when we came to the Theatre, but I think that they discussed matters of business. I do not recall if they spoke of anything else. I do not know that anything at all was said of Hera and Corwin, one way or the other."

"Corwin seemed smitten with her," said Shakespeare. "Was she in love with him?"

Elizabeth glanced at him. "She seemed excited at the prospect of the marriage," she replied.

"Aye, but was she in love with him?" Shakespeare asked again.

"Do you doubt that she was?"

Shakespeare shrugged. "I do not know. That is why I asked. She scarcely knew him."

"He knew her no better," Elizabeth replied. "Have you never heard of two people falling in love upon first sight?"

Smythe glanced at her sharply, but she did not look at him. Almost as if she were carefully avoiding it, he thought.

"I am a poet," Shakespeare replied. "Of course I know that people can fall in love upon first sight. The question is, was she one of those people?"

Elizabeth did not seem to have an answer.

Shakespeare tried another tack. "Did she know that Corwin had gone to her house to see her father and break off the engagement?" he asked, softly.

Elizabeth gasped and her eyes grew wide. "Is this true?" she asked with astonishment.

"He told me so himself," Shakespeare replied.

"But . . . *why?*"

"It seems he believed she had deceived him about her virtue," he replied.

"*What!*" Elizabeth said, with disbelief.

"I do not know precisely what Corwin had heard, or from whom," Shakespeare said, "for he was in a fever of outrage and indignation when he came to the Theatre, but it seems that some-one had convinced him that Hera was not . . . chaste."

Elizabeth brought her hands up to her face. "Who would do such a vile thing?"

"We do not know," said Shakespeare. "But we intend to do our utmost to find out."

"She sits there as if she does not even hear us," Smythe said, staring at Hera where she sat by the window on the other side of the room. "I know that we are speaking softly, so perhaps she cannot tell what we are saying from over there, but just the same, you would think that she would respond to our presence in some way, at least."

Elizabeth's eyes were glistening with tears. "I have tried speaking to her," she said, "but she simply does not answer."

"Let me try," said Smythe.

"Be gentle with her," said Elizabeth.

He crossed the room and knelt on the floor by her side. She did not respond to his approach. "Hera . . ." he said, softly.

She did not respond.

"Hera?"

She kept on staring out the window, as if she hadn't heard him.

"*Hera*," he said, more firmly and emphatically, though with-out raising his voice. He reached out and gently placed two fin-gers on her cheek, carefully turning her face toward his.

He was not certain if she really saw him, although she seemed to. Her gaze met his and, for a moment, it was as if she were looking *through* him. Then her eyes focused on his. He wanted to say something to her, but suddenly, he could not seem to find the words. The look in her eyes was one of unbearable pain and sadness, a grief that ran so deep it went down to her very soul. She blinked, and a single tear trickled down her cheek.

❋   ❋   ❋

"What did you see when you gazed into her eyes?" asked Shakespeare, as they left the Darcie house.

"Unutterable sadness," Smythe replied. "A grief so deep and
all-encompassing that there was no room within her for aught
else. It filled her to the very brim."

They walked side-by-side along the cobblestoned street, keeping near the buildings so as to avoid all the muck that drained
down into the declivity at the center. Traffic flowed by in a constant stream, horses and pedestrians, two-wheeled carts and four-
wheeled open carriages, coaches and caroches with their curved
roofs and ostentatious, plumed ornaments, all creating a caco-
phany of jingling and creaking, clopping and splashing, shouting
and neighing that filled the air with constant noise during the
daylight hours.

"Do you suppose she could have known that Corwin was
going to break off the engagement?" Smythe asked.

Shakespeare shook his head. "I do not see how she could
have known," he said. "I suppose the only possibility would be
if perhaps one of the servants overhead whatever had transpired
between Corwin and her father, and then mentioned it to her
when she came home, but that seems very unlikely."

"Why do you say that?"

"Well, for several reasons," Shakespeare replied. "Servants
who eavesdrop on their masters and then gossip about what they
had overheard are certainly not rare, but then they usually gossip
amongst one another, certainly not with the daughter of the master of the house."

"Good point," said Smythe, nodding.

"And for another matter," continued Shakespeare, "if any of
the servants *had* overheard whatever passed between Corwin and
Master Leonardo, then one would think they surely would have

known that something was amiss. One would think they would at least have looked in on their master when Corwin left the house. However, we are told 'twas Hera who had found her father's body, and not any of the servants. Either the murder had occurred without any of the servants being alerted, or else they all turned a deaf ear and ignored it. Does that seem very likely to you?"

"It does not," said Smythe.

"Nor does it to me," said Shakespeare, emphatically. "What we know thus far about the murder only raises further questions. If Corwin had gone to Master Leonardo's house to kill him, then surely he would not have stopped first at the Theatre to tell us he was going there. 'Twould be absurd. So then if Corwin is truly guilty of the crime, then 'twould only seem reasonable to suppose that he did not go there with the intent of killing Master Leonardo, and that what happened came about in a spontaneous manner. They argued, perhaps a blow was struck, then blades were drawn —"

"Or at least *one* blade," Smythe said. "Master Leonardo may have been unarmed for all we know."

"Quite so," said Shakespeare. "We must find that out, as well. If he was unarmed, then 'twas clearly murder. If not, then Corwin could have merely been trying to defend himself. Either way, if the two men fought, then it seems unlikely that there would have been no noise. How could the servants have failed to hear the sounds of such a struggle?"

" 'Tis a question we must try to answer," Smythe replied, "for unless we can find someone who was there to witness it or even hear what happened, the only one who knows the truth of it is Corwin. And I do not know if we shall be permitted to put the question to him."

"Aye, and even if we could be allowed to speak with him, how would we know if what he told us were the truth?" asked

Shakespeare. "Neither of us truly knows him well. If he is guilty of the crime, he could dissemble with us, and if he is a practiced liar, then we would never be the wiser."

"One thing is for certain," Smythe said, "we are not going to discover what occurred by questioning Hera any further. For the present, at least, the girl is much too grief-stricken to be of any use. We shall have to seek out Master Leonardo's servants to see what we can learn."

"I agree," said Shakespeare, nodding. "That is the very next thing we must do. And there is one more thing we must discover. Who told Corwin that Hera was not chaste?"

"Who in London could know her well enough to say such a thing and make Corwin believe it?" Smythe asked.

"We are proceeding, then, on the assumption that the tale is a lie?" said Shakespeare.

"Do you doubt it even for a moment?" Smythe asked, with surprise.

"Does it seem impossible there could be truth in it?" Shakespeare countered.

"How can you say such a thing? You have met the girl!"

"Aye, and I have had no words with her other than to give her greeting when we were introduced the other day. To all outward appearances, she seems modest and demure, as Henry Darcie said, but what do we truly know of her?"

"Will! I am surprised at you!" said Smythe.

"Why?" asked Shakespeare, puzzled. "Does the question not seem reasonable to you? And if not, then why not?"

"Oft' it seems to me that you have little love for women," Smythe replied. "Perhaps your own marriage was not everything you hoped 'twould be—"

"My marriage has naught to do with it," Shakespeare said, irritably. "If we are to pursue the truth, Tuck, then we must not presume. Regardless what we think, we must find things out for certain, so that we know them to be true beyond any shadow of a doubt. You are moved to sympathy for Hera, perhaps because of your own feelings for Elizabeth. You know that Henry Darcie only tolerates your friendship with her because he owes you a debt of gratitude, and because he trusts that you would do nothing to dishonor her, nor would she do aught to bring dishonor to herself or to her family. You look at Hera, and what I suspect you see is Elizabeth in a similar situation. You look at Corwin, and I suspect that in some ways, you see yourself. 'Tis a bad situation altogether, Tuck. You must divest yourself of prejudice and sympathy if you intend to find the truth. What do you *truly* know of Hera?"

"I know that when I look into her eyes, I see an innocent," said Smythe with conviction.

Shakespeare stopped and turned to face him. "When I look into *your* eyes, I see a bloody innocent," he said. "You, my lad, are a great, hulking, soft-hearted, and besotted fool and if you do not season your romantic notions about women with a pinch of caution and a dash of doubt, then someday some sweet and pretty face is going to ruin you and leave you gutted like a dressed-out stag."

"Oh, that was rather nicely put," Smythe said. "You must be a poet."

"You know, if you did not have that bandage on your head, I would slap you."

"Very well, then," Smythe replied. "You look for the worst in people and I shall seek the best. That way, betwixt the two of us, we should cover all the ground."

"You can be a wearisome bastard, you know that?" Shakespeare said. He clapped Smythe on the shoulder and they resumed walking. "Very well. Let us assume, for the sake of argument if naught else, that the fair Hera is as goodly and godly as her name implies. She was accused unjustly and maliciously. So . . . who is to profit from such an accusation?"

"I cannot see how there could be any profit in it," Smythe replied, with a frown.

"A child lies for attention or amusement," Shakespeare said. "A villain lies for profit, of one sort or another. There must be something in this to benefit someone."

"But who could benefit from the ruin of Hera's reputation?" Smythe asked. "She scarcely even knows anyone in London."

"I do not think that the ruin of Hera's reputation was in itself the object," Shakespeare said. "And whilst I may play the Devil's advocate in an attempt to keep us honest, like you, Tuck, I believe the girl to be an innocent. All this has the odious scent of malice hanging over it like a miasma. Hera has suffered very greatly from it, nevertheless, I do not think that she was the intended victim. We need to look elsewhere, I believe. Let us dissect this plot to make our augery. We must consider who else, save Hera, has been harmed by this."

"Well, most immediately, her father, of course," said Smythe. "And then, after him, Corwin. Assuming he is innocent."

"Let us proceed on that assumption, for if he is not, then the guilty party is already apprehended and justice shall be done. But if he is innocent, then we must act swiftly to prevent a miscarriage of that justice. So . . .'tis entirely possible that Master Leonardo had made enemies and that one of them had followed him to England and then done away with him. If so, then perhaps vengeance is the profit that we seek. We must find out if anyone had compelling reason to wish Master Leonardo dead."

"How would we discover that?" asked Smythe.

"At the moment, I have not the slightest clue," said Shakespeare. "Even if she were in any state to speak with us, Hera might not know aught of her father's business dealings and what enemies he might have made. Mayhap Ben could be of some assistance to us, since he knew Master Leonardo best."

"Or perhaps one of the household servants?" Smythe said. "Surely, he must have had at least one servant, if not more, who had accompanied his daughter and himself from Genoa. Hera did not seem comfortable speaking English, though she seemed to speak it well. She must have had a maidservant, a governess, perhaps, who came to England with her."

"Of course," said Shakespeare. "That only stands to reason. So, once more then, we came back to the servants. Let us consider Corwin."

"He could have enemies, I suppose," said Smythe. "His rise from apprentice to successful journeyman was swift. He had already made something of a reputation for himself among the fashionable nobility. There may be someone who felt envious, another apprentice, perhaps, who believed that Corwin's place was rightly his."

"You are thinking of your friends, the Steady Boys, perhaps?" asked Shakespeare.

"I did not have to think too hard," said Smythe, touching his bandage. "They have impressed themselves upon my memory."

"Indeed," Shakespeare replied. "And I do not for one moment think that murder would be beyond them. They very nearly murdered you. And that aside, there seemed to be little love betwixt Corwin and that Darnley fellow and his sneering friend."

"Bruce McEnery," said Smythe. "I'll not forget either of those names anytime soon."

"I did not expect you would. Nor shall I, for that matter. I do not have so many friends that I can afford to lose any of them. We both have a score to settle with those two and their misbegotten Steady Boys. But let us not allow our outrage to blind us to our course. They may not have been the culprits."

"And yet, I could easily see them spreading vile rumors about Hera," Smythe replied.

"As could I. But then, why would Corwin give any credence to them, considering their source?"

Smythe grimaced. "I am still not ready to dismiss them from our consideration."

"Very well then, we shall not. But for the moment, let us put the Steady Boys aside, as well. Where does that leave us? Who else is affected by Master Leonardo's death?"

"We are," Smythe replied.

"We are?"

"I mean, the Queen's Men," Smythe said. "Master Burbage and his son, all of the shareholders and the hired men, even Henry Darcie, for that matter. He is a partner in the Theatre, in which Master Leonardo was going to invest."

"Very true," said Shakespeare, nodding. " 'Twould seem our list of suspects grows and grows."

"Oh, you cannot suspect any of the Queen's Men, surely!" Smythe said. "Or Henry Darcie, for that matter. He may be an insufferable old goat, but he is certainly no murderer."

"Methinks I am in agreement with you there," said Shakespeare, "else he would have had you murdered long since for making cow eyes at his daughter."

"Very funny," Smythe replied dryly, "but that still does not refute my point. Henry Darcie, for all that he is more full of himself than a baker's dozen of courtiers and finds me utterly unsuitable to pay court to Elizabeth, is nevertheless a good and decent man, and only stood to lose from Master Leonardo's death."

"Did he?" Shakespeare asked.

Smythe frowned. "What do you mean? Of course he did! Had Master Leonardo lived, he would have invested in the Theatre, and necessary refurbishments would have been made with his money. As things stand, those refurbishments must still be made, but now, instead of being paid for out of Master Leonardo's investment, the cost will fall upon Henry Darcie and the Burbages. His death was a great disadvantage to them."

"Ah, but was it?" Shakespeare said. "Consider this, Tuck: thus far, we have only Henry Darcie's word that Master Leonardo was eager to invest. 'Tis quite possible that after seeing the Theatre and then meeting with the company and considering all his options, Master Leonardo had some reservations, or else changed his mind entirely."

"But Burbage would have known that," Smythe said.

"Perhaps," Shakespeare replied. "Or perhaps not. Elizabeth had already taken Hera under her wing, as it were, and thus Henry Darcie had somewhat more to do with Leonardo than Burbage did. Most likely, they were spending more time together, especially since Leonardo had aspirations of advancing himself in London and Darcie would have been more helpful to him in that regard than the Burbages would be. So, if the late, lamented Master Leonardo had reservations about investing in the Theatre, or else had set his mind against it, 'tis possible that he might only have told Darcie. If so, then Henry Darcie would have been the only one to know that Leonardo was *not* going to invest."

"And so what then?" asked Smythe. "He killed him? Or else had him killed? How could he profit by that? Either way, there would be no investment money."

"Nay, not necessarily so," Shakespeare replied. "Leonardo had no male heirs, apparently. Hera was his only child. As such, she stands to inherit her father's wealth. Alone in a strange country, to whom would she turn for guidance if not to the father of her only friend in London?"

"God's mercy, Will! You cannot believe that, surely! 'Tis absolutely diabolical!"

"Aye, murder *is* diabolical, Tuck. I am not saying that I believe it came to pass that way, but I *am* saying that if we wish to find the truth, we *must* consider every possible alternative, else the truth, and the real murderer, may easily elude us. We must not allow our sympathies to blind us to *any* possibility. We must be crafty, canny hunters, you and I, carefully following each spoor that we find, else we shall lose the trail entirely."

Smythe nodded. "Aye, your argument is sound. And much as I dislike to say so, Henry Darcie did seem somewhat callous in regard to both Master Leonardo's death and Hera's grief. His main concern, now that I think of it, was for us to convince her that we were her friends and to make her understand that her fortune was now tied to ours and ours to hers."

"I thought you would remember that," said Shakespeare.

"Aye, but still, that merely shows that he is selfish," Smythe replied. "It does not mean he is a murderer."

"True," said Shakespeare, "it does not. Nor do I think he is. Yet I do see where he may nevertheless profit by the death. And that is the sort of thing that we must look for. So . . . who else profits by it?"

Smythe shook his head, puzzled. "I cannot imagine, unless he had unknown enemies in London and, if so, I do not now see how we may discover them. 'Tis easier by far to see who stands to lose by his death rather than who stands to profit."

"Very well. Let us try to view the situation from that vantage point," said Shakespeare. "Who stands to lose?"

"Most obviously, Hera," Smythe replied. "But I cannot believe that she had aught to do with it. Her misery is deep and clearly genuine."

"I am inclined to agree," Shakespeare said. "Who else?"

"Well . . . we stand to lose, that is, the company does if the investment is not made and the refurbishments cannot be done," said Smythe. "Without Master Leonardo's money, Darcie and the

Burbages may find the cost too dear and the work may not be done."

"And the result of that will be?" asked Shakespeare.

Smythe shrugged. "Audiences may well decide to attend productions at the Rose, instead. 'Tis a much newer playhouse and they boast Chris Marlowe and Ned Alleyn. So I suppose that could make Henslowe a suspect, but that would mean he would have to have known about the planned investment. How likely would that be?"

"At this point, we cannot say," Shakespeare replied. "My thought is that 'twould be somewhat unlikely, but not impossible. Leonardo was interested in making an investment in a playhouse. For all we know, he could have approached Philip Henslowe first."

"I suppose 'tis possible," said Smythe.

"Or else someone in our own company who plans to defect to the Lord Admiral's Men, as Alleyn did, could have told Henslowe about it."

"A long shot, even for an accomplished bowman, I would say," Smythe replied. "We have at present far more to fear from Henslowe than Henslowe has to fear from us. He has already taken our best actor. He has a better playhouse and he has—"

"If you say he has a better poet, I shall kick your arse," Shakespeare said.

"I was going to say he has more *money*," Smythe replied, with a grimace. "The Lord Admiral's Men are in the ascendancy whilst we are in decline. Thus, I do not think 'twould stand to reason that Henslowe would have aught to do with it. After all, why bother to kick a dying dog?"

"Well, we may be down, but we are not dead yet," said Shakespeare. "But do you know who very nearly is? Young Corwin. Whether he is innocent or guilty of the crime, he now stands to lose his life in either case."

"Aye, he does, indeed," said Smythe. "There is no question that he was obsessed with Hera. But was he obsessed enough to kill?" He shook his head. "Those who knew him best do not believe it, nor do I."

"Why not?" asked Shakespeare.

"I cannot give you a sound reason, Will," Smythe replied, with a helpless shrug. "I simply *feel* that he could not have done it. He did not strike me as the sort. He struck me as the sort who might stand on his affronted dignity and break off his engagement if he felt that he would be dishonored by the marriage, but he did not strike me as the sort to fly into a rage and cut a man to ribbons. That phrase sticks in my mind, Will. 'He was cut to ribbons.' Master Leonardo was the captain of a merchant ship. That is not a life for a soft, indolent, and doughy shopkeeper. Seamen are a hardy lot and it takes a hardy man to lead them. He was lean and weathered, erect in his carriage, and with a spring in his step. He carried a fine sword and had the look of a man who knew how to use it. Italians are well known for their schools of fencing. And Corwin was no duelist. He was an apprentice who but recently became a journeyman. A sword was never a tool of his trade. I cannot recall that he even wore one, can you?"

Shakespeare thought a moment. "I do not think so."

Smythe shook his head. "I do not believe he did. And even if he did, I find it hard to credit that he could prevail over a man like Master Leonardo, who must have had to deal with men a great deal rougher than Corwin in his time."

"He may have gained the advantage of surprise and so prevailed," said Shakespeare, "but I do not believe it, either. Betimes, a man must act upon his instinct, even if it seems to go against his reason. And whilst my reason tells me that Corwin may be guilty, my instinct tells me he is not."

"Then we are in complete agreement," Smythe said, emphatically. "We must find someone else who had good reason to see Master Leonardo murdered."

"Or else see Corwin blamed for it," said Shakespeare, thoughtfully. "Methinks that is another possibility we should consider. Master Leonardo's death may not have been in itself the end, but just the means."

"You mean that he could have been killed merely so that Corwin would be accused of his murder and thus destroyed?" said Smythe. "Odds blood! 'Tis a cold heart that could conceive of such a deed!"

"Aye, a cold heart," repeated Shakespeare, "with cold blood coursing through it, as opposed to hot. Mayhap 'twas not a crime of passion, after all, but of opportunity."

"We have much to do," said Smythe, grimly. "And little time in which to do it. The noose for Corwin's neck is being plaited even as we speak."

9

THE TOWNHOUSE WHERE MASTER LEONARDO had all too briefly lived was not nearly as ostentatious or as large as Henry Darcie's. Situated in a tidy row of houses near the Devil Tavern and the Thames, it was a modest-looking residence built of lathe and plaster, with nothing to set it apart from any of the other row houses on the street. It certainly did not look like the home of a wealthy man. Perhaps, thought Smythe, it might have been intended merely as a temporary residence, meant for use only until such time as Master Leonardo had established himself and found a better home or else had built one just outside the city, as some successful tradesmen were now doing. But on the other hand, he may have been a man of relatively simple tastes who did not require much out of a home that was not functional, comfortable, and practical, rather than elegant, ostentatious, and luxurious.

In a city where the members of the new, rising middle class were constantly competing to show off whose rise was faster, and where the nobles were always trying to outdo one another in elaborate displays of wealth and fashion, a frugal man who spent his money wisely on his business interests rather than on expensive homes or carriages or suits of clothes that he could change as many as three times a day could quietly build up his wealth and become a rich man without fanfare. And that seemed like just the sort of thing an unassuming, former seafaring man would do.

"This seems like the kind of place where a retired ship's captain would drop anchor," Shakespeare said, echoing Smythe's thoughts. "A nice, solid, comfortable place to live on dry land, within walking distance of the river, where he could stroll on the bankside and observe the wherrymen and the ships beyond the bridge. A man could do much worse."

"And many do," said Smythe.

"Someday, I shall have a fine house of my own in town," said Shakespeare. "You know, I could be well satisfied with something similar to this. I need no cut stone or brick to look like some archbishop's residence. A good, solid, English home of lathe and plaster will do me nicely, the sort of place befitting a gentleman, rather than a marquis or a viscount."

" 'Tis good to know that your ambitions are merely modest ones," said Smythe, with a straight face. " 'Twouldn't do at all for a humble poet to overreach himself."

"You think?" said Shakespeare.

"Aye. How many poems or plays, do you suppose, would one have to write in order to be able to afford a modest place like this?" asked Smythe, giving him a sidelong look.

"Do you mock me, you pernicious rascal?"

"What, I?" Smythe said, feigning surprise. "Nay, 'twas merely an idle question. Three or four score, do you think? Well, perhaps less, if you are made a shareholder. Aye, two score or so should do it. So long as they are all as popular as Marlowe's. That should not present too great a difficulty, not to a fellow as industrious and talented as yourself. How many have you written thus far?"

Shakespeare glowered at him.

Smythe blithely went on. "Well, let us see . . . there is that one about the drunken lout who falls asleep and is then found by a noble and taken to his house . . . oh, no, wait, you never finished that one, did you? Ah, but then there is the one about the war . . . no, you still have not got past the first act, have you? Oh, hold on, there was that idea you had about the twins, from the time we helped Elizabeth and encountered that fiendish foreign plot . . . did you ever actually *do* anything with that?"

"You cankerous, flea-infested, mocking dog! See who nurses you the next time you are brought home with a broken head, you ungrateful, prating wretch!"

"Ah, well, thus am I justly chastised," Smythe replied, hanging his head in mock shame. "Ungrateful wretch I am, indeed. I am a rude fellow. You may beat me. Here, let me find a stick . . ."

"Oh, cease your foolishness," Shakespeare said, with a snort. "Come along, let us go and question Master Leonardo's servants."

The household servant who opened the door to them had the look of a man whose future was uncertain. Tall, thin, and balding, with wisps of white hair sticking out in all directions, as if he habitually ran his hands through what little of it was left, he reminded Smythe of a horse that had been spooked.

"Dear me, *more* visitors and *more* inquiries," he said, anxiously. "I really do not know what I should do. The master of the house is cruelly slain, the mistress is not present and is grieving in seclusion, and it simply is not right to have people coming to the house and asking questions, searching through everything . . ."

"Your concern for your master's house and goods is very commendable," said Shakespeare. "We are here merely to ask some questions of you and the other servants on behalf of your mistress and your master's business associate, Henry Darcie. But tell us, first, who *else* has spoken with you? Someone has been here to search the house?"

"Aye, and he, too, claims to have had business dealings with poor Master Leonardo."

Smythe frowned. "Who was he? Did he give you his name? Can you describe him?"

"You may see him for yourself," the servant said. "He is within."

Shakespeare and Smythe exchanged glances, then quickly pushed past the distraught servant and entered the house. They saw two female servants in their aprons standing near the stairs, huddled together like frightened chickens in a corner of the coop, and at once they could hear the sounds of someone rummaging about upstairs. As they exchanged glances once again, they heard a loud crash, as if something heavy had been overturned.

"This time, I have brought my sword," said Smythe, drawing it from its scabbard.

"I shall be right behind you," Shakespeare said.

"With what, your *quill*?"

In response, Shakespeare pulled out a knife from inside his boot, a bone-handled stiletto with a six-inch blade.

"Good Lord!" said Smythe. "Where did you get that?"

"I brought it from the Theatre," Shakespeare said.

"Do you know how to use that thing?"

"I understand one pokes at people with it," Shakespeare replied, wryly. "I *have* done some fencing on the stage, you know."

"On the stage," repeated Smythe, rolling his eyes. "God help us. Just keep behind me."

"Precisely where I had intended to remain," Shakespeare replied.

They went up the steps cautiously, with Smythe leading the way. The rummaging noises grew louder as they drew closer. Someone was ransacking the house, and from the sound of it, being none too gentle about it.

"Be careful, Will," said Smythe, when they reached the top of the stairs.

"*You* be careful," Shakespeare replied. "If anything should happen to you, I would be next."

"Your concern for my safety is touching," Smythe said with a grimace. He reached out and placed his hand on a door that stood slightly ajar. The noise was coming from within. "Get ready . . ."

He shoved the door open hard, slamming it against the wall, and came into the room fast, his sword held out before him. The man ransacking the room spun around, immediately drawing his own blade.

"*Tuck*!"

Smythe's eyes grew wide. "*Ben*! What the devil are you doing here?"

Dickens lowered his sword, then sheathed it as he spoke. "I might well ask you the same thing," he replied. He glanced over Smythe's shoulder. "Is that you, Will?"

" 'Allo, Ben," said Shakespeare, coming into the room sheepishly after having peeked around the corner.

Smythe sheathed his blade, as well. "We came to question Master Leonardo's servants, to see what we could learn about what had transpired here the night that he was killed." He looked around. "God's body, Ben! You have bloody well torn the place apart! What in Heaven's name are you searching for?"

Dickens shook his head, looking around helplessly. " 'Twas not me, Tuck. I came to look for something . . . anything . . . that could help Corwin prove his innocence, but the house had already been ransacked when I got here."

"Did you find anything?" asked Shakespeare.

Dickens shook his head in frustration. "Nothing. Save only that there seems to be no money left anywhere in the house."

"He may have had it all cubbyholed away somewhere," said Smythe.

"If he did, then I cannot find it," Dickens replied. "And I have looked everywhere. But I tell you, there is not a tuppence nor a halfpenny in this house. Not anywhere. It must have all been stolen."

"Did you question the servants?" Smythe asked.

"Aye, I have already spoken with them. They swear that they did not ransack the house. They have no idea where Leonardo kept his money. They are worried. They say that they have not received their wages, but despite their claim that they have not even ventured upstairs since the crime, I suspect they have already looked through everything."

"You think they might have taken it?" asked Shakespeare.

Dickens shook his head. "I cannot say. I would have thought that if there was money in the house for them to take, they would have found it and absconded with it. Then they would be far away by now. Instead, they are still here; there is little in the larder, and they do not even seem to know where their next meal is going to come from." He shook his head again. "Methinks that there was nothing here for them to find."

"Perhaps he had his money deposited with some merchant banker," suggested Shakespeare.

Dickens shook his head again. "I had thought the same, but then there would have been letters of credit, or else bills of exchange, and I have discovered none. I thought perhaps that he might have devised some clever hiding place in which to store such things, but if so, then I have failed to nose it out." He sighed with exasperation as he looked around at the mess. " 'Tis a mystery to me, I tell you. Leonardo was a wealthy man, and yet, there is not one coin to be found in this entire house. If his money was not stolen, then where is it?"

Shakespeare scratched his chin. "A thought occurs to me," he said, "and yet, I hesitate to speak it for fear that it might give offense."

Dickens glanced at him. "Go on, Will. Be forthright. Say what is on your mind."

Shakespeare cleared his throat. "Well . . . if there were such documents as letters of credit or bills of exchange, do you suppose that Corwin could have taken them?"

For a moment, Dickens did not speak. The corners of his mouth drew tight. "After he murdered Leonardo, do you mean to say?"

Shakespeare cleared his throat once more. "To find the truth, must not one consider *all* the possibilities?"

Dickens stared him down.

"Ben," said Smythe, placatingly, "we know that Corwin is your friend and that you are loyal to him. But if we do not ask these questions, others shall. Corwin has already been arrested. Soon he shall be tried. He is in dire straits and your loyalty, however honorable or well-intentioned, cannot help him now. Only our diligence and perseverence in searching out the truth can be of any aid to him. And if he is truly innocent, then the truth shall set him free."

"Or else condemn him," Dickens said, tightly.

Smythe stared at him as comprehension suddenly dawned. "Odd's blood. You think he might have done it," he said, softly.

Dickens looked down at the floor and then savagely kicked out at a chest that had been overturned. "Aye, damn it, I think he may have done it. Beshrew me, a fine friend I have turned out to be to suspect him guilty of so vile a deed!" He kicked the chest again, splintering it. "Bloody hell! What keeps going through my mind again and then again is the thought that had I only followed him that night, then I may have arrived in time to prevent . . ." His voice trailed off.

"There may have been nothing to prevent, Ben," said Smythe, "at least insofar as Corwin is concerned. Had you followed him, then you may or may not have arrived in time to prevent him from breaking off his engagement, but if that was *all* he did that night, then you would doubtless have left the house together, and the murderer would have arrived after you had gone."

"Aye, but then at least I would have been able to swear to Corwin's innocence," said Dickens. "And as matters stand, I cannot say that I know in my heart that he could *not* have done it. Fie upon me for a false friend! Never would he have doubted me!"

"Perhaps not, but you cannot truly know that, Ben," said Smythe. "Were your roles reversed, Corwin might well be blaming himself even now for suspecting that *you* could be a murderer. Can any man truly know what another man may do when the blood runs hot and overwhelms his reason? Perhaps no man even knows what he may do himself in such a circumstance. Either way, it makes no difference. Suppose, just for the sake of argument, that you *had* followed him that night, and that when the two of you left here together, Master Leonardo was still alive. Then you could swear to that at Corwin's trial, of course. But everybody knows that for the price of only a few crowns, men can be bribed to bear false witness. They can be found in Paul's Walk every day, waiting to sell their honor for the price of a meal and a few drinks. And 'tis well known that you are Corwin's friend, and a mercenary, to boot. I mean you no offense, Ben, but 'tis doubtful that your word would bear much weight in his defense."

"The only thing that matters is that we find out what truly happened here that night," said Shakespeare. "You said that you have spoken with the servants?"

"Aye, and they could tell me nothing."

"But they *were* here that night?" said Shakeseare.

"They say so."

"And they saw *nothing*? They heard *nothing*?"

Dickens merely shrugged and shook his head.

"How is that possible?" asked Shakespeare, frowning. "Servants commonly know everything that goes on inside the house wherein they work. I would like to speak with them myself."

"Do as you wish," said Dickens. "If you discover aught, then I shall stand a ready listener."

They went back downstairs, where the servents waited anxiously, as if not knowing what else to do.

"Where are the other servants of the house?" asked Shakespeare, speaking to the wispy-haired man who'd let them in.

"We are all here, milord," the man said, glancing around nervously.

"What, just the three of you?" asked Shakespeare, frowning again. The two women stood close together, clutching their aprons anxiously.

"Aye, milord," the man replied. "We are all the servants in this house."

"What is your name?" Shakespeare asked him.

"I am called Edward Budge, milord."

"And the women?"

"This here is Mary Alastair, milord," he replied, indicating each with a gesture, "and this is Elaine Howard."

"You are both English," Shakespeare said.

"Aye, milord," they both replied nervously, almost but not quite in unison. They bobbed in a slight curtsy.

"Was there not a Genoan lady in this house?" asked Shakespeare. "A governess or maidservant for Master Leonardo's daughter?"

"Nay, milord, we was all there is," replied the one called Mary. "The mistress did for herself, she did."

"Aye, very good to us, she was, milord," added Elaine. "A

kind soul with a good heart is our Mistress Hera; never spoke a cross word to any of us. Never struck us, neither."

"Aye, she wouldn't ask us to do anything she wouldn't do herself," added Mary. As they spoke, they both kept glancing at Edward, as if for reassurance. He nodded in agreement.

"How very strange," said Shakespeare, puzzled. He looked at Ben. "You came to England aboard ship with Master Leonardo and his daughter, did you not?"

"Aye, I did," said Dickens.

"And did they bring no servants with them from Genoa at all?"

Dickens looked blank for a moment. "Now that you mention it, I do not recall there being any servants attending them aboard ship, although for most of the voyage Hera had remained below, struck with the sea sickness. I may have assumed that there was someone taking care of her, but in truth, I do not believe I ever gave the matter any thought, one way or the other."

"It never struck you as peculiar that a wealthy man such as Master Leonardo would be traveling without servants?" Shakespeare asked.

Dickens shook his head. "I suppose not. 'Twas his ship we sailed upon. Doubtless, with his crew, he had no need of servants on the voyage."

"That could be," admitted Shakespeare. "But it does strike me as peculiar that he would bring no one along to attend upon his daughter. And that he would maintain only three servants here in London."

"Perhaps, with a modest house like this, he did not require more," said Dickens.

"Aye, 'tis a modest enough house for a wealthy man," Shakespeare agreed. "We had been discussing that before. I suppose that I understand a man of means choosing to live in a home such as this if his needs were few and simple, or else if he had planned to purchase or build a better house at some point in the near future. Nevertheless, I still find it passing strange that he should choose to live so simply. After all, he had retired from his life at sea to live a more comfortable, settled life on land. And yet, observe these furnishings. Boarded stools and chests, likewise a cupboard, all pegged with wood or nailed . . . not a single piece of jointed furniture, not one carved or upholstered chair. That chest upstairs, which you had splintered with your boot . . .'tis the sort of simple, inexpensive, boarded chest that you or I might own. The one good, solid piece here was that old sea chest that was upended in the bedroom, with the clothes all tumbled out of it and strewn about. Everything else here is poor-man's furniture . . . made of common boarded oak, left plain, and stained with linseed oil."

"So what then?" asked Ben. "That only goes to show that Leonardo was a frugal man."

"Methinks I would say more than frugal," Shakespeare replied. "I would say he pinched his pennies so tightly that the queen winced."

"That is often how a man of modest means becomes a wealthy man," said Dickens. "And old habits die hard."

"Perhaps," said Smythe, as a new idea occurred to him. "Or else that is how a man of very little means makes himself out to *seem* a wealthy man."

"What, are you suggesting that Leonardo had no money?" Dickens said. "Nonsense! He was the master of his own merchant ship, which he had sold for a handsome profit upon coming to England!"

"Aye, and we may be standing in the midst of those profits," said Smythe, looking around at their surroundings. "And 'tis possible that they were not nearly so handsome as you think."

Shakespeare turned back to the servants. "Edward, tell us,

when you hired on with Master Leonardo, did he pay your wages in advance?"

"Aye, milord," the servent replied. "A week's wages for each of us."

"Only a week?"

"Aye," Edward replied. " 'Twas to be a trial period. We were to be paid a week's wages at a time until the master had decided we were suitable, and then we were promised that arrangements more to our advantage would be made."

"And your wages included room and board, of course?" asked Shakespeare.

"Well . . . they would, in a month's time," said Edward. "Once we had proved our suitability."

Smythe and Shakespeare exchanged glances. "So then you did *not* sleep here?" Smythe asked.

"Why . . . no, milord."

"Neither did you eat here?" Shakespeare asked.

"No, milord," Edward replied, a bit more tentatively. He suddenly looked uncomfortable.

Shakespeare immediately followed up, watching the man carefully. "Where *did* you dine?"

"Why . . . we all dined together at the nearby tavern," Edward said, glancing at them nervously, his eyes darting back and forth. "The ordinaries are very reasonable there."

"And the ale too, no doubt," said Smythe.

Before the man could reply, Shakespeare quickly asked, "How long were you gone to supper the night Master Leonardo was killed?"

They noticed that the women had gone very still. They both looked pale and Mary's lower lip had started trembling. They both looked frightened as they clutched each other's hands tightly. Edward did not look much better.

"Why . . . why, not long at all," stammered Edward. "No longer than usual, I am quite certain . . ."

"You were out drinking and carousing," said Smythe, fixing him with a hard look.

"Nay, milord, we were not!" protested Edward, blinking. "We only went to supper! Honest!"

"You are lying, Edward," Smythe said, stepping up close and looming over him. "You were out drinking."

"Nay, 'tisn't true! We only went to supper!" Edward protested, but he swallowed hard and retreated back against the wall, looking panicked.

"You were in the tavern, drinking and carousing," Shakespeare said, "all three of you." He turned to the women, who were now both trembling and crying. "We shall go to the Devil Tavern and inquire of the tavernkeeper. I am quite certain that he will recall what transpired that night, as everyone has heard of it by now. No doubt he will remember you. And then *you* three shall all be going to the devil!"

"We didn't kill him! We swear!" wailed Mary, sinking to her knees and clutching at Shakespeare's doublet. Elaine simply started blubbering.

"Shut up, you fools!" shouted Edward.

Smythe grabbed him by the front of his doubtlet and slammed him back against the wall, hard enough to stun him momentarily and silence him.

"We didn't do it! I swear we didn't!" Mary sobbed. "I swear, so help me God!"

"Please, sir! *Please*!" was all that Elaine was able to manage.

"Bloody hell!" said Dickens. " 'Twas the servants murdered him! They murdered him to get his money!"

"We never did! I *swear* we never did!" cried Mary, desperately.

"Nay," said Shakespeare, shaking his head as he looked down

at Mary, "they did not kill him. He was already dead when they returned."

She looked up at him with disbelief and awe, as if he were her guardian angel suddenly descended from on high. "Oh, God be praised, sir, 'tis true! 'Tis *true*! God bless you, sir, 'tis true, I swear it on my life!"

"You *are* swearing it on your life, you slattern," Dickens told her. "And 'tis a life that will be forfeit!" He looked at Shakespeare. "Surely, you do not *believe* this lying wench?"

"Aye, I do believe her," Shakespeare said, quietly, looking down at her with pity. "Think you that they would have remained within this house until Hera had returned, all the while knowing that their master was lying dead upstairs?"

Edward glanced from Smythe to Shakespeare and then back again. He had the look of a drowning man who had just been thrown a rope. " 'Twas just how it happened, milords, 'tis true! Honest! We never knew that he was dead! We never did!"

"And you became convinced you would be blamed," said Shakespeare, "unless you all swore to it that you were here when Corwin left the house."

"What strange mystery is this?" demanded Dickens. He glanced at Smythe. "What the devil is he talking about?"

"I see it now," said Smythe. "They have all lied out of fear to save themselves."

"You believe that they have lied before and yet they are not lying now?" asked Dickens. "What, am I the only one here who has not taken leave of his senses? I understand none of this!"

"Season your admiration for a while with an attentive ear, Ben," Shakespeare said, "and I shall deliver unto you the tale of what they did that night, and they shall stay my story and redirect me if I wander from the truth. Is that not right, Mary?"

She nodded several times as he gently helped her to her feet.

"Listen well and correct me if I stray," he told her, and then he looked at Ben. "A week's wages was what Master Leonardo paid them, by their own account," he said. "And week by week, they would be paid thus until they had proved their suitability, at which point, arrangements more to their advantage would be made. Such was the promise."

He glanced at Mary for confirmation and she nodded several times, emphatically. "Well," he continued, "for the first few days, they did endeavor to be most suitable, indeed. 'Tis not easy, after all, to get good work in London nowadays. But as the week drew near a close, and more wages looked to be forthcoming, they felt the need to celebrate. Their positions seemed secure and excellent. Their master did not seem to demand too much of them; likewise their mistress, who was kind to them and asked nothing of them that she would not do herself. A servant could certainly do a great deal worse.

"So then," he went on, "with the week drawing to a close, they decided, as was their custom of an evening, to go to their suppers in the tavern, where they lingered for a while to drink a toast or two or three to their good fortune. By now, after nearly a week, they had learned the regular habits of their master, who as a seafaring man for many years was no doubt an early riser so went early off to bed. They had also learned that Hera had found herself a friend, Elizabeth Darcie, with whom she often spent her evenings, and that these evenings went so pleasantly that Hera often stayed quite late, returning in a carriage that Henry Darcie had most likely provided for her use. Thus, there was no harm in staying out a little late to have their celebration. They had intended to be back before their mistress had returned."

All three of the servants were now staring at Shakespeare, speechless with disbelief, as if he were some sort of sorcerer, divining precisely what had happened on that night.

"They left the house just as Corwin was arriving," Shakespeare continued. "Thus did they know that he had been there.

They had, of course, seen him before, and so knew who he was, for he was courting Hera. They admitted him to see Master Leonardo, and told him that they were going off to supper. Doubtless, he told them that he would be letting himself out. Likely, he was glad that they were leaving, for he doubtless wished to speak privately with Leonardo, and thus avoid making a scene before the servants. And so, off they went to supper, and then stayed to celebrate a while. When they returned, the house was quiet, and so they naturally assumed their master had retired for the night. Before long, they knew, Hera would return, and then they would be able to go home. And so it was. Hera returned, then went upstairs to say good night to her father, as was her custom, and they heard her screams when she discovered him dead. The rest you know. She went running through the streets in a panic to the Darcie house, the carriage having already returned. Edward, fearful that some greater misfortune might befall her, followed.

"Thereafter," Shakespeare concluded, "it did not take him very long to realize how things stood. Clearly, he thought, after Corwin had arrived, he and Leonardo must have quarreled and then Corwin killed him. But they had not seen him depart, for they had not been present. When Hera came home later that night, they were there, having returned, unaware that Leonardo already lay dead upstairs. Corwin must have done it. Who else could it have been? Edward realized that they had to swear they saw Corwin leave the house, and that Leonardo had been alive when he arrived, else they themselves might be suspected of the murder. And therein lies the rub. They all swore that they saw Corwin leave the house, when they were never there to see it. And that means Master Leonardo could still have been alive when Corwin left, and that someone *else* came here to do the deed and leave unwitnessed."

"Oh, great merciful Heaven protect my soul, can this be

true?" said Edward, going deathly pale. "Have I borne false witness against an innocent man?"

"You have borne false witness, Edward, one way or the other," Shakespeare replied, "and there are penalties for that in both this life and the next which all three of you may now incur. Your only hope now to extricate yourselves from this terrible predicament is to tell us the entire truth."

"We shall do just as you say, milord," said Edward, meekly.

"We need to know *everything* that occurred that night," said Shakespeare, his gaze encompassing all three servants. "You must recount to us each thing you saw and did and heard, down to the most minute detail, from the time that you last saw your poor master alive to the time Hera came back and found him dead. And do not leave out *anything*, no matter how unimportant or insignificant it may seem to you, for somewhere in betwixt those times, the foul deed of murder was done, and we have much to do in order to ferret out the truth, and precious little time in which to do it."

10

THEY WALKED TOGETHER DOWN THE rain-slicked, cobbled street, heading toward the Devil Tavern. It had started to drizzle and the damp, chilly breeze coming in off the river made them draw their cloaks around themselves and pull their hats down low to avoid having them blown off. It was a gray and gloomy sort of day, an early herald of autumn's approach. However, despite the dismal weather, their spirits were unclouded. For the first time there was now a faint, tentative ray of hope beaming in on Corwin's fate.

"I was hoping to hear his version of what happened on that night," Dickens was saying, "but the prison warders would not allow me in to see him at the Marshalsea, where he is held, awaiting trial. And no one has said how soon that trial may be. For all we know, it could be on the morrow, or a month or more away. 'Twould seem that once a man's been thrown in prison, his fate is as chaff upon the wind. No one much cares what may become of him, save for his family and friends, and unless they have some influence, there is nothing much that they can do."

"Well, we may not be without some influence," said Smythe, "though I am loathe to use it prematurely. I would prefer to wait until it can truly do some good."

"You mean Sir William?" Shakespeare said.

Smythe nodded. "Aye. A word from him to his friend, Sir Francis Walsingham, would open nearly any door."

"Do you mean Sir William Worley?" Dickens asked, with surprise. "But he is one of the richest and most powerful men in England!"

"Indeed, he is," said Smythe. "For which reason I would hesitate to ask him any favors unless we were absolutely certain of our ground."

"Odd's blood! The master of the Sea Hawks, and an intimate of the queen, no less!" Dickens was taken aback. "Do you mean to say that you actually *know* him?"

"We found ourselves in a position to do him some small service a while ago," said Smythe, downplaying the relationship. "Since then, he has been kind enough to give me work at his estate upon occasion. He has a passion for well-crafted blades, and has a fine forge of his own at Green Oaks. As you know, I have some small skill in that regard. However, I would not wish to presume on Sir William's good graces unless we knew for certain that we could prove Corwin's innocence beyond any shadow of a doubt. I am sorry, Ben."

"Sorry?" Dickens said. "But this is wonderful news, my friends! It means that Corwin's fate is not nearly as bleak as it had appeared only this morning!"

"Well, I am very glad you see it that way," Smythe replied, "but I remind you that we are still a long way from our goal of finding out just what happened on that night."

"Aye, I know that," Dickens said, "nevertheless, this still means that there is hope. S'trewth, I had been half convinced myself that he had done it, shamed as I am by it. Now that I know the servants were not in the house that night, their testimony of what happened becomes absolutely meaningless. Why, they never even saw him leave! I wanted to seize that rascal

Budge right by his throat and throttle him for his base and cowardly lie!"

"He was afraid," said Shakespeare. "And he was absolutely
convinced that Corwin was the murderer. It had never even occurred to him that anyone else could have come to the house
after Corwin had left."

"That still does not excuse the foulness of his lie!" said Dickens, savagely.

"Indeed, it does not," Shakespeare agreed, "although it may
at least explain it. The poor man was stricken with remorse when
it dawned upon him that he may have condemned an innocent
man. And that is very fortunate, for it means he has a conscience.
We should be thankful for that, otherwise he would be packing
his things even as we speak and preparing to flee London."

"He may still do just that," said Smythe, "if he grows frightened enough. They may all run off once they have had time to
think about it."

Shakespeare shook his head. "I do not think so, Tuck. I think
you convinced them that 'twould look very bad for them indeed
if they fled London now, for with our testimony, *they* would then
become the chief suspects in the crime. Never fear, they shall not
be going anywhere. Guilt, remorse, and misery shall surely root
them to the spot as firmly as if we had put chains upon them."

"All the more so now that they know we shall be making
inquiries at the tavern to gather further proof of how long they
were there that night," said Dickens. "I am growing ever more
hopeful by the moment, my friends. Once we free Corwin from
prison, I shall be ever in your debt."

"Well, we have not freed him yet," said Shakespeare. "And
once again, Ben, I do not mean to cast gloom upon your spirits,
but simply knowing that Corwin had departed without the servants seeing him and that Leonardo was alone inside the house

for some period of time does not tell us that someone else came there and killed him. It only means that someone else *could* have done it."

"By Heaven, why do you persist in wanting to see only the worst, Will?" Dickens asked, irritably.

"Because I do not think 'tis wise to hold out any false hope," Shakespeare replied. "Nor do I think it prudent for us to assume things that we do not yet know. Also, in all fairness, I feel bound to remind you that while Corwin seemed to me an amiable young man of excellent character, you know him better than either of us do. You may well know in your heart that he could not have done this deed, but Tuck and I do not, for our acquantance with him is but slight."

"So then you *do* believe he did it!" Dickens said.

"Nay, I do not believe he did," Shakespeare replied, patiently. "But what I believe and what I *know* are not the same. I shall endeavor to find out the truth, Ben, but I may not find it if I only look in some places and turn a blind eye to others."

"And you did suspect yourself that Corwin may have done it," Smythe reminded Dickens gently. "You were so distraught at the possibility that he may truly have been guilty that now you have seized upon the mere possibility that he may be innocent. And 'tis only a possibility at this point, Ben. We do not yet know it for a certainty, although things do look brighter for him than they did this morning."

"The two of you seem very close," said Shakespeare.

"Aye, Corwin is, indeed, my very closest friend," said Dickens. "If he were my own brother, Will, we could not be closer. We have known each other since we were children. I had only just begun my apprenticeship with the Queen's Men and was living with the Flemings, as you know. Corwin was then apprenticed to Master Peters, who lived nearby. We often played together when we were not busy with our duties. In time, when my voice began to change and I could no longer play the female roles convincingly, 'twas Corwin who helped arrange my new apprenticeship by asking Master Peters to speak with Master Moryson the armorer on my behalf. I then asked to be released from my apprenticeship to the company and John Fleming let me go, although he said that he was loathe to do so, but he understood that I was young and chafed for something more, another sort of life, some manner of adventure similar to that which we portrayed upon the stage. Afterwards, for a while, I thought that I had found that sort of adventure with the Steady Boys, but once again, 'twas Corwin who came and convinced me of the folly of running with a bunch of wild, roaring boys who were just as likely to wind up in prison as they were to break one another's heads. I saw that he was right, but without the Steady Boys, I still felt a need for some adventure. I had met some soldiers of fortune through my work at Master Moryson's shop and they seemed to live the sort of life I yearned for. Once more, 'twas Corwin who tried to dissuade me, but my hunger for adventure was too strong. Afterwards, when I was gone, 'twas Corwin once again who . . ." And then his voice trailed off abruptly as he caught himself. He gave them a quick, sidelong glance. For a moment, he looked like a guilty boy caught stealing a steaming, fresh-baked pie from a windowsill where it was cooling.

"He kept an eye on Molly for you," Smythe said, "did he not?"

Dickens looked at him with astonishment. "However did you know?"

" 'Twas not very difficult to guess, Ben," Smythe told him, with a chuckle. "If the love you have for one another is a secret, then 'tis very poorly kept, indeed, for anyone can see how you two feel about each other. For all the verbal fencing the two of you engage in, for all the barbed remarks, the biting comments, and retorts, 'tis clear to one and all you are in love. What is not clear is why you ever left her. I do believe you broke the poor girl's heart."

"Is that what she believes?" asked Dickens. "That I had left her?"

"Have you ever given her any reason to believe aught else?" asked Shakespeare.

" 'Twas never so," protested Dickens. "I did not leave Molly. Instead, I left one life to make another. I had heard tales of mercenaries who had made their fortunes fighting in foreign wars, and how some had even gained rank and titles from grateful sovereigns. I had hopes that I, too, could make my fortune as a soldier and come back as a gentleman. Then I would have had the means to offer Molly a better life, the sort of life that she deserved. Alas, 'twas not to be. The glamour of a mercenary soldier's tale is only in the telling. The truth is that he does well if he loses neither life nor limb. I did well, I suppose, in that I did not come back a cripple. But I came back with nothing I could offer Molly."

Shakespeare sighed and shook his head. "Ah, Ben," he said, shaking his head. "Why is it that we men never learn? 'Tis not a better life that a good woman wants a man to give her; she only wants to share the life he has. A woman like Molly does not want your money. Faith, she only wants your heart."

"If you are so full of wisdom about women, Will, then where is the woman who shares your life and has your heart?" asked Dickens, irritably.

For a moment, Shakespeare looked stung, but he recovered quickly. "Alas, the one who had my heart was not, as it turned out, the one who shared my life, and shares it still, if only at a distance," he replied. "Had I not been such a fool . . . well, never mind, what's done is done. There is little to be served in dwelling in the past. 'Tis what lies ahead that matters."

The wooden sign that hung above the door of the Devil Tavern at a right angle to the street was painted with an image of St. Dunstan tweaking the Devil's nose, in homage to St. Dunstan's Church, which stood nearby. They opened the heavy, wood-planked door and went inside. The interior was not unlike that of the Toad and Badger in general appearance, but the place had a very different sort of atmosphere.

There were rushes strewn upon the wood-planked floor, but they were not fresh, which lent the place a stale sort of smell that Courtney Stackpole never would have tolerated. The furnishings, like those at the Toad and Badger, were much the same—heavy, wood-planked trestle tables, benches, and stools—but they were rough and cracked and stained with spills, not kept oiled and clean, as Stackpole always insisted at his place. The patrons were mainly working-class locals, with perhaps a few merchants and a craftsman or two here and there. The chief difference, however, was that the mood within the place was not nearly as lively as at the Toad and Badger.

The smell of tobacco smoke was heavy in the air as patrons sat and smoked their clay churchwardens while they drank their beer and ale out of pewter tankards or hard leather "black jacks" sealed with pitch. Some played hazard with their dice cups, others played primero, betting noisily on every hand. A few people glanced up at them as they came in, looking them over, but otherwise, no one paid them any particular attention.

They sat down at an empty table and a moment later one of the serving wenches came by to take their order. After conferring with her as to what she recommended, they decided upon a double-strength ale known as "Devil Dog," apparently a house specialty. It was brought to them in a large jug and they poured it themselves into heavy pewter tankards, discovering that it had a rich, strong, and heady, spicy flavor. They smacked their lips and nodded their approval.

"An excellent ale, my dear," said Shakespeare, "aye, excellent, indeed." He nodded to Smythe and Dickens, prompting them.

" 'Tis just the thing for a thirsty man at the end of a long day," said Smythe, thinking that he would actually prefer one of his herbal infusions brewed from rainwater to this thick and heady brew, for although there was no denying it was tasty, strong ale always left him feeling bloated and gassy. He noticed once again that he had never drank ale or beer until he came to London, where the water was undrinkable, and he had lately noticed that his midsection had started getting thicker from this recent addition to his diet.

"So tell me, my lovely, what is your name?" asked Dickens, flashing her a dazzling smile. It nearly undid the poor girl, who was not lovely by any stretch of the imagination, and was cursed with bad skin and a harelip that gave her a thick and pronounced lisp.

"Kate, m'lud," she replied, blushing and looking down while carefully avoiding the sibilance of "good sir" in her reply.

"Well, Kate," Dickens went on, charmingly, " 'tis a fine, rich brew that you have recommended, and we may have ourselves another jug or two just to see you bring it."

She gave him an awkward curtsy and a cautious underlook to see if he was making fun of her. Smythe began to worry that he was overdoing it, for what was the likelihood that any young man as handsome and dashing as Ben Dickens had ever paid attention to so homely and scrawny a girl? Surely, he thought, she could never believe he was in earnest. But in addition to his good looks, Dickens had apparently been gifted with a faery glamour, for within moments, he had completely captivated her with compliments that struck Smythe as rather heavy-handed and transparently insincere. Before long, he had her sitting on his knee and giggling as he laughed and joked with her.

"So do you work here every night, Kate?" Shakespeare asked.

"Well, if she does, then I may have to come back more often," Dickens said, with a wink. It brought forth another giggle from the girl as Smythe winced inwardly. It was almost embarrassing to watch.

"Aye, m'lud, I work here each day an' every night."

"Well, then you must know old Budge, who comes to have his suppers here, along with Mary and Elaine," said Shakespeare.

"Oh, aye, m'lud, I know them. Very kind, they are, never make fun o' me like what others often do. The way I talk, y'know." Her hand went to her mouth self-consciously and she looked away from Ben, as if suddenly remembering her deformity for the first time since they began their conversation.

"What of it?" Dickens said. "Methinks you have a charming voice."

"Aw, now, go on . . ." she said, giving him a poke, but at the same time, she beamed at him with childlike pleasure.

"They must have been here that night then, when that terrible thing happened at their master's house," Shakespeare said. "You have heard about that?"

Her eyes grew very wide. "Oooh, aye! What an awful thing! Poor Cap'n Leonardo!"

"You knew him, then?" asked Smythe.

"Aye, m'lud, he came in now and again," said Kate. "Nice gentleman, he was. Never had but one drink, an' off to home. 'A touch o' grog,' he called it. Poor man, to be murdered like that! What a terrible thing!"

"They stayed late that night, did they?" Shakespeare asked. "I mean, his servants?"

"Aye, they did," replied Kate. "I remember because they drank so much and got all tipply." She giggled again. "That old Budge! Who'd have thought it, the way he carried on with them two women! A man his age! And them laughing and encouraging him! Aye, they had a right grand old time, they did. An' they kept right at it, til I said 'twas time for them to leave."

"*You* said 'twas time for them to leave?" asked Smythe. "Were they so drunk and rowdy, then?"

"Oh, 'twasn't like that at all," she replied. "Old Budge asked me to tell him when it got near nine o'the clock, for 'twas when the mistress come back home in her carriage and they had to be back by then. He promised me a farthing if I would remind him. I mean, they was all tipply, but not no trouble, mind. Not like them roaring boys what come by being all mean an' horrible."

"Roaring boys?" said Shakespeare.

"Aye, all loud and full o'themselves," she said. "Puttin' on airs like they was young lords instead o' 'prentices. I didn't like them. Made fun o' me, they did. Not nice at all, like you good gentlemen."

"How many of these boys were there, Kate?" asked Dickens, casually, though Smythe noticed that his eyes had narrowed slightly as he watched her reply.

"Four or five, methinks. Nay, 'twas five. I remember now. One o' them tripped me an' made me fall an' drop two jugs! He had a mean laugh, he did, an' a cruel way o'mockin' me lip, makin' a face like a cony . . ." She demonstrated, twitching her lip like a rabbit. "An' him with his pockmarked face and his own lip all droopy and twisted like. Nasty, evil bugger."

Smythe and Dickens exchanged glances. "Bruce McEnery," said Smythe.

"Aye! 'Twas his name, all right! One o' the others called 'im Bruce!" In her agitation as she lisped the name, she doused both Smythe and Shakespeare with a spray of spittle.

"What was his name again?" asked Dickens, innocently.

"*Bruce! Bruce!*" She repeated, even more wetly and emphatically, making Smythe and Shakespeare recoil from the shower.

"Methinks the roof is leaking," Shakespeare said, wryly, wiping his face with his handkerchief.

Smythe leaned forward, took hold of Ben's hand, fixed him with a glare, and squeezed hard enough to make Dickens catch his breath. "We *got* the name, all right?" he said.

"Right," said Dickens, gritting his teeth against the pain. When Smythe released him, he took a deep breath and flexed his fingers experimentally, to see if any of them were broken.

"Ooh, you don't mean to tell me them horrible boys was friends o' yours!" said Kate, alarmed at possibly having said the wrong thing.

"Not by a long shot, Kate," Smythe replied. He removed his cap and touched the bandage on his head. "I have them to thank for this. I have a score to settle with that lot."

"Ooh, they did that?" Kate said, wide-eyed. "I knew they was no good!"

"And was one of them a handsome looking sort," asked Smythe, "tall, lean, with black hair and dark eyes, with a scar and a sort of smug, amused expression?"

"Aye, I remember him. I thought the others looked to him as if he was the leader," Kate said.

"Jack Darnley," Shakespeare said. "Stoats travel in pairs."

"And rats travel in packs," said Smythe, with a grimace of distaste. "It seems the Steady Boys were here that night."

"Let's have us another jug, my dear," said Dickens, bouncing her on his knee. "And hurry back, mind, so we can have more of your pleasant company!"

When she left to get another jug of ale, Dickens turned to Smythe and said, "Faith, Tuck, you have the strength of an ox! You damn near broke my hand!"

"You get her saying 'Bruce' again, and I shall," replied Smythe.

"Oh, I was just having a bit o' fun," said Dickens, with a grin.

"The same sort of fun those Steady Boys were having at her expense, no doubt," Smythe replied. "And if you ask me, 'tisn't very kind of you to lead her on so."

"Perhaps not," said Dickens, "but it did get us what we wanted, did it not?"

"Indeed," said Shakespeare. "And thanks to Ben's winsome ways, we now know not only that Budge and the two women never saw Corwin leave the house, but that they were gone for several hours, during which time a great deal could have happened."

"Aye," said Dickens, "and what I was thinking is that this tavern is a bit off the beaten track for the Steady Boys. Not their stalking ground at all. You shall find them on any given night down at the Broom and Garter, where the mood tends to be a bit more boisterous. This here is not their sort of place at all. 'Tis much too tame and quiet."

"So then what brought them here?" asked Smythe.

"I was thinking about that very thing," said Shakespeare. "Does it not seem interesting to you that they just happened to be here on the very night of Master Leonardo's murder?"

"I wonder how long they stayed?" asked Smythe, glancing at him and raising his eyebrows.

"That is, indeed, the question," Shakespeare replied. "And here comes young Kate, bringing us our jug and, with any luck, our answer."

"Ah, there we are!" Dickens exclaimed, as she set down the fresh jug of ale. "I am growing ever fonder of this Devil Dog, sweet Kate. Come, sit you down and have a drink with us!" He tapped his knee and she perched on it quite readily. He poured for all of them, then gave her the first sip from his mug.

"So tell us, Kate," said Shakespeare, "these boys that were so mean to you that night, do you happen to recall how long they stayed?"

"You mean the first time or the second?" she asked, wiping her mouth with the back of her hand.

Shakespeare frowned. "The first time or the second? I do not understand. Whatever do you mean?"

"Well now, the first time, they all come in together," she said, and Smythe noticed that except when she became excited, she had a way of avoiding the "th" and "s" sounds whenever possible, replacing them with "v's" and "z's" in order to minimize her lisp, so that the word 'first' came out 'furz' and 'together' came out 'togevver.' It was somehow endearing.

"The first time?" Shakespeare repeated. "You mean to say they left and then came back again, the very same night?"

"Aye. Well, all 'cept two o' them."

"You told us there were five of them in all," said Shakespeare. "Do you mean that three of them left the tavern and two stayed behind?"

"Aye, you got it," she said, nodding. "An' then a bit later, the other three come back and they all left together."

"Were Budge and the two women in here all during that time?" asked Smythe.

"Aye, they was," she replied, nodding as Dickens offered her another sip of ale. "I remember 'cause I kept bringing them more beer."

"So they drank small beer, then, and not ale?" Shakespeare said. Then he nodded to himself. " 'Twould make sense, of course. 'Tis a cheaper brew, and so they could drink more. And it sounds as if they drank rather a lot. So then while they were drinking and having themselves a fine old time, three of the Steady Boys left, while two remained behind."

"To act as lookouts, perhaps, and keep an eye on the servants?" asked Smythe.

Shakespeare nodded. "It could be. That way, if Budge and the women started back before the other three returned, then one of the two remaining would run to give his comrades warning, while the other lingered to delay them."

"The devil gnaw their bones!" Dickens exclaimed. "So *they* killed Leonardo!"

Kate gasped and her hand went to her mouth.

"We cannot yet say for certain," Shakespeare said, "but methinks something is rotten here."

The others frowned and sniffed at their clothing.

"I meant something smells fishy," Shakespeare said.

Smythe, Kate, and Dickens smelled their armpits.

"Oh, for God's sake! I meant it seems suspicious, too much of a coincidence!" exclaimed Shakespeare, in exasperation. "Odd's blood! I know that I am speaking English! Why is it so difficult to understand my meaning?"

"Not a word of this, Kate, you understand?" said Smythe. "Especially if you should see any of those boys again, although I rather doubt you will. Methinks they shall go out of their way to avoid this place for a good long while."

Her eyes were wide with fear as she nodded mutely and clung to Ben's arm for support, glancing around at all of them with alarm.

"Hola! You! Wench! Get yer skinny body over here!" called out one of the patrons at a table across the room.

Kate started to get up, but Dickens held her back. "Wait," he said.

"But, m'lud . . ."

"Wait, I said. You need not respond to such rudeness."

"Hola! Wench! You deaf? We need more ale, girl!"

She glanced at Dickens with consternation. "Stay," he said, calmly.

Shakespeare glanced over at the table where the shouting was coming from. "There *are* three of them," he said.

"And there are three of us," said Smythe.

"One of us with a bandage on his nearly broken head and another with but a dagger for his weapon," Shakespeare replied, dryly, "while all *three* of those gentlemen are wearing swords, in the event you have not noticed."

"*You there!*" one of the men called angrily to Dickens. "Stop mucking about with that skinny, harelipped wench and send her over here! She's here to work, not be your bloody doxy!"

"My friends," said Dickens, easing Kate gently off his knee, "allow me. I shall be but a moment."

"Right," said Smythe, with a sigh, as he started to get up, but Dickens stayed him with a hand upon his shoulder.

"Nay, Tuck, I beg you, keep your seat. This dance is mine."

With a scraping of stools, the three men got to their feet, reaching for their blades.

"Ben, do not be foolish," Smythe said. "There are three of them, for God's sake. And they have the look of men who know their business."

"Then that should make the odds just about even," Dickens replied, as he stepped forward and drew his sword.

"Why is it that this happens every time I go to some strange tavern?" Shakespeare asked, throwing up his hands. "And where are *you* going?" he asked Smythe as he started to get up.

"To help Ben, of course," Smythe said, putting his hand on his sword hilt.

"You were very nearly killed the other day," Shakespeare replied. "Have you not had enough? He said he did not *need* your help!"

Smythe opened his mouth to reply, then abruptly shut it and raised his eyebrows in surprise as Dickens engaged the first man with a quick circular parry to his lunge that sent his opponent's sword flying across the room. As patrons ducked their heads beneath their tables to avoid the flying blade, Dickens smashed the basket hilt of his rapier into his suddenly disarmed opponent's face, then pivoted to strike down the second's man blade, following that up with a brutal kick to the man's groin that made Smythe wince.

"Apparently," said Smythe, "he does not require any help."

The third man glanced at his two fallen comrades, swallowed hard, then turned and ran straight out the door.

"Well," said Dickens, turning around and shrugging. "That was rather disappointing."

Kate's eyes were shining with hero worship as she gazed at him, awestruck.

"If you gentlemen are finished with your drinks, then I would very much appreciate it if you left," the tavernkeeper told them.

Dickens turned toward him, still holding his sword at his side.

"However, I shall not insist," the tavernkeeper added, holding up his hands, palms out.

"Never mind," said Dickens. "We are leaving. Kate, my dear, when the Queen's Men stage their next production at the Burbage Theatre, you shall be my guest. Just tell them that Ben Dickens said so." He bowed to her with a flourish and then sheathed his blade. "My friends, shall we take our leave?"

"By all means," said Shakespeare, paying the awestruck girl for their ale. "Where to now?"

"Back to the Toad and Badger, I believe," said Smythe. "We must put our heads together and devise a plan to trap some rats."

11

✳

WHEN THEY RETURNED TO THE Toad and Badger, everyone was waiting for them. They had missed rehearsal, an offense which usually resulted in a fine among any company of players, for if one actor missed rehearsal, it placed a burden on the others that was directly proportional to the importance of that actor's role—or roles, since it was not uncommon for a player to have more than one. But for three of the company to have missed rehearsal was unheard of. As a result, the other members of the company were quite concerned, especially in light of the attack on Smythe. And they were not alone. Liam Bailey was also at the tavern, awaiting news. When they came in, they were at once surrounded and peppered with anxious questions.

"What happened? Where *were* you?" Hemings asked.

"Are you all right?" asked Fleming, with concern. "Where have you been?"

"You three had best have a good excuse for missing the rehearsal," Burbage said crossly, though it was clear that he, too, had been worried.

"I am so sorry, lad," said Liam Bailey, pushing his way through. "I only just heard about what happened. When ye did not come to the smithy yesterday, I had assumed the company had need of ye . . . I never knew that you were injured." He shook his head in self-recrimination.

"Stay your questions for a moment, everyone!" said Smythe, holding up his hands. "All shall be explained."

"Aye, just as soon as we have had ourselves a touch o' grog," said Shakespeare, as they made their way to a table.

Dickens stared at him. "Where the devil do you put it all?"

"Writing is thirsty work," the poet replied.

"But you have not been writing," Dickens said.

"That is because I have been thirsty," Shakespeare said. "Molly, my dear, a pitcher of your best Dragon's Blood stout, if you please."

The others all gathered around their table as Molly went off to bring the ale.

"What happened, Will?" asked Burbage, pulling up a stool. "We have all been terribly worried, thinking perhaps you had been set upon and left bleeding in some alleyway somewhere!"

"We have been making inquiries," Shakespeare replied, "first at Henry Darcie's home, then at Master Leonardo's house, and finally, we paid a visit to the Devil Tavern."

"The Devil Tavern!" Stackpole said, coming out from behind the bar. "Well, then, if this place does not seem good enough for the likes of you, then you can all three go to the Devil, for all I care!"

"Peace, my good Stackpole," Smythe said. "We went there out of necessity, to make inquiries, not out of any disloyalty to you, my friend. And thanks to Ben's charming a serving wench, we learned some things that may, with any luck, help to free young Corwin."

"Aye, well, Ben is an old, accomplished hand at charming serving wenches," Molly said laconically, as she set down their ale.

"Molly, let me explain . . ." Dickens began, but she did not allow him to continue.

"Nay, do not explain, Ben," she said, airily, "for there is no need. I know just how it went. You smiled at her with that special way you have, cocking your head over to one side and looking up at her . . ." she mimicked the gesture as she spoke, precisely capturing the way he did it, ". . . called her your 'lovely' and told her what a charming voice she had and how pretty her hands were and how you would simply have to have another drink, just to watch her bring it, and then you sat her down upon your knee and gave her a drink or two or three from your tankard—"

"Molly, 'twas not like that at all," Dickens protested.

"In truth, 'twas just like that, precisely," Shakespeare said. "I say, Molly, were you there?"

"*Will!*" Dickens exclaimed.

"Nay, Will, I was not, but I have seen that performance so many times before that I could play the role myself. What disappoints me is that in all this time, he has not changed it in the least. Any good player knows to make a few changes in his performance here and there, to keep it fresh."

"He did promise her that she could attend the next performance as his guest," said Smythe.

"*Tuck!*" Dickens said, turning toward him with a wounded expression.

"I am merely trying to be helpful," Smythe said.

"Well, I do not require your help, thank you very much!"

"Ah. Indeed," said Smythe, nodding. "You had said that before. I recall now that you prefer to fight against superior odds. Well, then, have at it. I shall not interfere."

"I thought you two were my friends!" said Dickens.

"Why, we are, Ben," Shakespeare replied, "but you know, it strikes me that 'tis a dangerous thing to be your friend. John

Fleming here was your friend, and you left him and his good wife after they had grown as fond of you as if you were their own son. Molly was your friend, and you went off and broke her heart. Corwin was your friend, and now he languishes in prison, awaiting execution. Master Leonardo was your friend, and now he is in his grave. Tuck here became your friend, and was very nearly beaten to death for his trouble. I shudder to think what fate may lie in wait for me."

Dickens stared at him with openmouthed astonishment. The others all fell silent, completely taken aback by his remarks. Only Smythe remained unsurprised. He had caught a certain look from Will that he had seen before, and his thoughts had already been running in a somewhat similar vein.

"Why, you scoundrel," Dickens said, quietly. "How dare you?"

"Truly, Will," said Fleming, "that was unconscionable! Wit is one thing, but this time you have stepped over the line!"

"Have I, John?" Shakespeare replied. He poured himself a tankard of ale. "A touch o' grog," he said, raising the tankard and looking at it contemplatively, then taking a drink from it. He smacked his lips. "Indeed. The very thing for a thirsty man. Was that not what our young Kate said back at the Devil Tavern, Tuck? Did she not tell us that Master Leonardo often came by for a 'touch o' grog'?"

"Aye," said Smythe, "she did say that."

"One drink and off to home he went, like a good abstemious soul. 'A touch o' grog,' he called it." Shakespeare furrowed his brow. "A most peculiar expression for a Genoan to use, would you not say?"

"Now that you mention it," said Smythe, "it does seem a bit peculiar."

"Of course, I suppose he might have heard it somewhere," Shakespeare continued. "Still . . . 'tis not the sort of thing that simply trips off an Italian tongue, eh? And now that I think on it, that serving wench never did refer to him as *Master* Leonardo. *Cap'n* Leonardo was what she said."

"What of it?" Dickens asked. "So she called him Cap'n Leonardo. What is the significance of that?"

"By itself, it has no great significance, perhaps," Shakespeare replied. "But when taken together with a few other things, a sort of significance does seem to emerge."

"What the devil are you talking about?" asked Dickens. "What other things?"

"Well, a gentleman who owns his own merchant ship would doubtless call himself 'Master' of that ship," said Shakespeare, "and so use it as his title, so to speak, as in 'Master Leonardo.' But a man who was *not* a proper gentleman of rank would call himself 'Captain' as opposed to 'Master,' I should think. He might shorten that somewhat as 'Cap'n' if he were English, but if he were a Genoan, I should think he would say '*Capitan*.' Of course, Kate might have head 'Capitan' and rendered it as 'Cap'n.' That could be. But then I also wonder at how we found no money anywhere in Leonardo's house.

"And again, 'twas not really the sort of house that one might expect a wealthy merchant from Genoa to buy," Shakespeare continued, taking another sip from his tankard. "We had discussed that, as you will recall. We had thought, perhaps, it may have been only a temporary residence, meant to serve until such time as he could build himself a better one, or mayhap 'twas only that he was a simple man who did not require much more than a simple house. That could be, as well. But why no coach or carriage? Why no Genoan governess for his lovely and eminently marriageable young daughter? Why only three servants? And why only engage those servants for one week at a time? Good servants are not that difficult to come by, and 'tis customary for the better classes to engage them for a month or more, at least. Should they not prove suitable, they can always be dismissed. There is no need to tell them that their initial period of employment is probationary; that sort of thing is taken as a matter of course. On the other hand, if a man does not have very much money, but wishes to appear as if he does, then he might well conceal his poverty 'neath the cloak of practical frugality. And he would drink beer or ale in the local tavern, as opposed to wine."

"None of this makes any sense to me," said Molly, looking confused. "What does Ben have to do with any of this?"

"Ben created Master Leonardo," Shakespeare said. "Or at least, he created him in the sense in which we knew him, as a wealthy merchant trader from Genoa who desired to retire from the sea and settle down in London with his riches. But 'twas all an elaborate scheme of cony-catching, a very clever and ambitious scheme, indeed. And it very nearly worked, save for one small problem. Along the way, somewhere a mistake was made. A mistake that, sadly, cost a man his life and may yet cost Corwin his, unless we are able to move swiftly. Ben, the time for dissembling is past. We need the truth, and we need it now if we are ever to help your friend, Corwin."

Dickens sighed and nodded. "Very well. There is no point in trying to hide it any longer. Leonardo was a Genoan only on his mother's side. His father was an Englishman and he was born in Bristol. I met him in the Netherlands, when I booked passage on his ship. As we grew to know each other, I discovered that he had grown tired of his life at sea. His ship was old and badly in need of repair and refitting, but he could not afford to have the work done. For several years, his luck had run poorly and he was nearly destitute. He had already decided to sell the ship for whatever he could get for it when we arrived in London and try to find some other trade with which to earn his living. And 'twas then the scheme occurred to me.

"I had made some money of my own while fighting in the

foreign wars," Dickens continued, as the others all hung on every word, "but not nearly as much as I had hoped, not nearly enough to serve my purposes. I desperately needed more. And so I proposed a scheme to Leonardo whereby we both might profit if we played our cards well and wind up wealthy men. All he needed to do when we arrived in England was to sell his ship, just as he had planned. We would then combine our resources and our efforts in an attempt to make our fortunes. The money from the sale of the ship would go to buy a house. Even if 'twere just a modest house, 'twould be enough, for he could always claim 'twas merely a temporary residence until his business interests in London were established and he could build a larger home. But 'twas here that Leonardo took the risk, for if he spent most of the proceeds from the sale of the ship upon a home, then he would have next to nothing left with which to set himself up in some trade. And indeed, thanks to the poor condition of his ship, that was just what happened.

"He had enough to buy the house," Dickens went on, "and hire a few servants and stock his larder for a week or so, but beyond that, his money would soon run out. And here was where I would share the risk. My money would go to help maintain the illusion of Master Leonardo. I purchased several suits of clothing for him, tailored in the height of fashion, bought him a new sword, a fine plumed hat, and paid for the carriages he hired. 'Twas my money he carried in his purse, to make himself look prosperous, and 'twas my money he had spent in entertaining the conys that we hoped to catch."

"You mean us?" asked Burgage. " 'Twas us you planned to fleece?"

"Nay, Dick, I never meant to cheat the Queen's Men. I hoped, instead, to become a shareholder in the company. And I had hoped to gain enough money from our scheme to set Corwin up in his own shop, with myself as an investor, for I knew how talented and skilled he was and had no doubt that he would be successful. Leonardo, too, would need to have more money to begin his life anew, and he would need to secure the future for his lovely daughter, Hera, for whom he did not even have a proper dowry. There, I had the answer, for if I knew my friend, then he would see Hera and quickly fall in love with her. And Corwin would not care much about a dowry. I would provide a token one for her, for appearances' sake, but I knew that I would quickly make it back in partnership with Corwin once his shop was thriving."

"But for all of this to work, you still needed more money," Smythe said. "And that was where Henry Darcie came in, was it not?"

"And Master Peters, of course," said Shakespeare.

"Aye," Dickens admitted. "Master Peters was to be our first cony, and as for Darcie, he practically begged to be spitted and placed over the fire. With Master Leonardo's 'shipping interests' and connections, there were great opportunities for them both to invest in trading voyages to the colonies and such, which money would, of course, be used by us to forward our own plans. And then, as happens on occasion when men invest in varied projects, things do not always turn out for the best. There are such things as storms at sea, and pirates. Ships are sometimes lost, and with them, all the capital that had financed their voyages. 'Twould be a shame, really, but nothing could be done. Any such investment carries certain risks."

"Did Corwin know about any of this?" Smythe asked.

Dickens shook his head. "Of course not. He is as honest as the day is long, God bless him. He never could have countenanced such a scheme. And quite aside from that, his loyalty to Master Peters would never have allowed him to go through with it."

"Oh, Ben, how could you?" Molly asked. "Why in the name

of Heaven would you do such a thing? What could you have been thinking?"

"He was thinking that he needed the money so that he could marry you," said Shakespeare.

Molly was struck speechless.

" 'Twas why he left, you know," Shakespeare told her, gently. "He never ran away from you; he went off to find his fortune so that he could return to England, become a gentleman, and provide a better life for you. He had even asked Corwin to watch out for you whilst he was gone."

Molly shook her head in dismay. "Oh, Ben! Whatever made you think that money mattered to me?"

"I knew that I was not your only suitor, Molly," he replied. "Corwin wrote and told me of the gentleman you met sometimes, the one who often walked you home at night. Corwin was never able to discover who he was, because he noticed that the man had servants always follow at a distance, armed with clubs and such, and he was afraid to get too close."

"Oh, good Lord!" said Smythe, as he suddenly realized to whom Dickens must have been referring. "That was no gentleman, Ben! And those were no servants who followed to provide an escort! 'Twas Moll Cutpurse and her crew of thieves!"

"Moll Cutpurse!" Burbage exclaimed. "Odd's blood! Why in the world would our Molly have aught to do with the likes of Moll Cutpurse?"

"Because she is my sister," Molly replied.

"Your *sister*!" Dickens said.

"Aye, my sister, Mary," Molly said, sighing and shaking her head in exasperation. "She did not wish anyone to know, for fear that someone might try to get at her through me. Oh, Ben, what a horrid mess you have made of things! I would have told you the truth if only you had come to me!"

Dickens gave a snort of bitter amusement. "Her sister. Fancy that."

"Well, now at least we know the truth about Master Leonardo," Shakespeare said. "We may not know for certain how the poor fellow died, though I believe that I can hazard a good guess. 'Twas a wicked scheme that Ben devised with Leonardo, and I daresay it very nearly worked just as they had planned, save for but one thing. They did not anticipate the involvement of the Steady Boys, in particular Jack Darnley and Bruce McEnery, who wanted to draw Ben back into the fold. When they were rebuffed, however, they became angry and vengeful. And because Tuck refused them also, and had the temerity to stand up to them, he needed to be taught a lesson."

"And 'twas a lesson that I shall not soon forget," Smythe interjected, touching his bandaged head. "I do not know which was worse, getting knocked upon the head or having it itch so damnably. Either way, I hope to return the courtesy very soon."

"Methinks that you shall have that opportunity before too long," said Shakespeare. "But bear with me a while longer whilst I proceed to the next act. Our friends, the Steady Boys, were angry with Ben in part for refusing to rejoin them and in part for taking Tuck's part in the brawl. He now needed to be taught a lesson, as well. To this purpose, they put a watch on Ben and his close friend, Corwin, whom they had little cause to love in any case, as he was becoming a rival to their master and thus to themselves, as well. They found out about 'Master Leonardo,' the wealthy Genoan merchant, and discovered that Corwin had become engaged to his daughter. Gossip is a scurrilous thing, my friends, and its source is often difficult, if not impossible to track, but I shall wager that the tale of Hera's sullied virtue originated with Darnley and McEnery. Corwin would doubtless never have believed it had the tale come from them directly, but they arranged for him to hear of it elsewhere. His own jealousy and

passion did the rest. And so they followed him, to see their hand-
iwork come to fruition when he confronted Master Leonardo.
And suddenly, a new and unexpected opportunity presented itself.

"I cannot say for certain what transpired between Corwin and
Leonardo," Shakespeare continued, "but I daresay that Leonardo
was alarmed at this turn of events, vehemently protested Hera's
innocence, and doubtless let it go at that. There was no danger
of them fighting any duel, as Ben knew perfectly well. Leonardo
was, in all likelihood, no duelist nor did he wish to see their plans
or his daughter's future jeopardized. He needed to confer with
Ben, so that Ben could repair the breach with Corwin. And for
that very reason, when I told Ben what had happened, he needed
an excuse not to follow Corwin on the instant, for he needed
first to go see Leonardo and find out precisely what occurred.
'Twould be best in any event to let Corwin's temper cool and
speak with him upon the morrow. Thus, he went straight from
the rehearsal to Leonardo's house, only he arrived too late and
found him dead. Was that not how it happened, Ben?"

Dickens nodded, his lips compressed into a tight grimace.
"Aye," he said. "It all went just as you said. I found Leonardo
dead and I believed that in his rage, Corwin must have taken
leave of his senses and killed him." He shook his head. "I did
not know what to do. I nearly lost my mind. I could not think.
I could not reason it out. No one was at home, so no one saw
me come there. In a panic, I fled. I needed time to think, time
to decide what I should do."

"You still felt loyalty to your best friend," said Shakespeare,
"but you also believed him to be a murderer, and at least in part,
you believed yourself to be responsible. But once you had some
time to think, you realized that with Leonardo dead, your cony-
catching scheme was finished. The only thing to do was get back
whatever money there was left. And that was what you were

doing at the house when Tuck and I came there. In truth, Ben, when Tuck and I found you there that night, I had suspected *you* of being the murderer. But I soon realized you were not. You were not searching for something to exonerate your friend; you were desperately searching for the money. Your money, that you had given Leonardo to help carry off the scheme. Only it was nowhere to be found, because someone else had been there first."

Dickens nodded, grimly. "Aye. And I know who now."

"Indeed, you do," said Shakespeare. "Oh, the comings and the goings at that house that night! The first to leave was Hera, off to visit her friend, Elizabeth Darcie. Then the servants left to have their supper and their celebration at the Devil Tavern. As they were leaving, Corwin had arrived, doubtless in a state of temper. Soon thereafter, Corwin left, after confronting Leonardo and breaking off his engagement. Leonardo was thus left at home alone, wondering what to do. Doubtless, he hoped that Ben would soon arrive. Perhaps Corwin had mentioned to him that he had left word for Ben at the theatre. Only sadly, Ben was not the next to arrive. The killers were."

"Poor Leonardo!" Dickens said. "If only I had not tarried at the Theatre!"

"The Steady Boys must have followed Corwin from the moment he was told of Hera's infidelity," Shakespeare continued, "for surely 'twas they who had arranged it all. They must have followed him to the Theatre and from there to Leonardo's house. They saw the servants leave and Corwin go inside. Most likely, Corwin did not stay very long, merely long enough to vent his outrage and announce that he was breaking off the engagement for having been deceived. Perhaps the Steady Boys listened at the window, laughing at how easily Corwin had been duped. Then, when he left, they went off to the nearby tavern to have a drink and celebrate. And there they found Leonardo's servants, having a celebration of their own. Now a devilish new idea dawned upon them.

"Darnley must have formed the plan right there in the tavern. Or perhaps they had already conceived of it and merely awaited the proper opportunity. Two of them stayed to keep watch on Leonardo's servants in the tavern. The other three went back to Leonardo's house. The plan was to rob and murder the wealthy Genoan merchant and have the blame fall upon Corwin, for he was the last one seen coming to the house, and the word had already been spread about how he had been deceived. Thus would two birds be killed neatly with one stone. Corwin, a rival to their master and themselves, would be eliminated, and Ben would suffer as his closest friend went to the gallows, the very same friend who had once persuaded him to quit the Steady Boys. And so the deed was done. They killed Leonardo, ransacked the house, stole whatever they could find, and made good their escape before the servants could return. Then Ben arrived, found Leonardo dead, and assumed that Corwin must have flown into a rage and killed him. Frantic with despair and guilt, he fled the house."

"And then the servants returned," said Smythe.

"Aye," said Shakespeare, "but they had been drinking, and so they failed to realize that their master had been slain. They never ventured upstairs, never saw the body, never realized the house had been ransacked. They knew that Hera would be coming home soon and most likely awaited her return in the kitchen. And when she came home, she doubtless went straight upstairs to say good night to her father and found him slain. Her cries brought the servants running, then in a madness of grief, she fled the house, running out into the night. Budge, fearing for her safety, gave chase as best he could, growing more sober by the moment, until he saw that Hera had reached the safety of the

Darcie house, whereupon he reported to Henry Darcie what had happened. Or, more to the point, what he believed had happened. And the very next day, poor Corwin was arrested for the murder of Master Leonardo."

"One moment, I could not believe that he had done it," Dickens said, "but the next moment, it seemed certain that he had. What other explanation could there be?"

"And so you gave up on him and went looking for your money?" Molly asked, bitterly.

"I went looking for the money, aye, but I never gave up on Corwin," Dickens said. "Without the money, I would be able to do nothing for him. With it, I could hire a lawyer to plead on his behalf, find witnesses to swear he had been elsewhere in their company that night." He sighed. "But whatever money had been left was gone. Those miserable, murdering bastards took it all."

"Which brings us to this sorry pass," said Shakespeare. "We know what must have happened, and how it must have happened, for we have used reason to deduce it. The trouble is, we cannot prove any of it. And without proof, poor Corwin swings."

"Surely, there must be *something* we can do!" said Molly.

"Methinks there is," said Smythe, thoughtfully. "Ben is not the only one who knows something of the art of cony-catching. As it happens, I have been reading up on it myself, of late. And I believe a trap set for a cony may catch a rat, as well. I have in mind a new production, Will, one eminently suited to your craft. And yours, too, Ben, and yours, my friends," he added, glancing round at all the players. "That is, if you are game for it?"

"We are!" said Burbage.

"Tell us, Tuck!" said Fleming.

"Aye, tell us!" Speed said. "What have you in mind?"

"If I, too, may help, I shall," said Liam Bailey.

"You may, indeed, Liam," Smythe replied. "But most of all, we shall have need of Molly."

"Me?" she said. "What can I do?"

"Once before we met," said Smythe. "Now you may reacquaint me with your sister."

12

✳

T HE BROOM AND GARTER WAS the sort of tavern that at-
tracted a rough and tumble crowd and notable among them
were the Steady Boys, a congregation of apprentices from various
crafts and trades who all had in common the aggressive unruli-
ness of youth and a desire to cause mischief. Here, among the
wherrymen and dockworkers and drovers, they held court like
young lords of the streets and presiding over them were Jack
Darnley and his chief factotum, Bruce McEnery.

On this occasion, the Steady Boys were spread out among
several tables in one section of the tavern, shouting and drinking
and carousing, playing cards or games of mumble-de-peg with
their daggers or bouncing young wenches on their knees and
pawing at them greedily. Most of them worked hard during the
day, from before sunup to nearly sundown, and this was their
time to play. When they played, they liked to play hard and often,
and the games they played were at other people's expense.

"Cheer up, Jacko," Bruce McEnery said, punching his comrade in the shoulder. "You have been glum for nigh on several
days now. What troubles you, mate?"

"The money," Darnley said, with a scowl. "There should have
been more bloody money."

"Are you on that again? Let it go, for God's sake. We got
what we got. 'Twasn't all that bad a haul now, was it?"

" 'Twas pathetic," Darnley said bitterly, clutching his tankard with both hands as it sat upon the well-strained wooden table into which most of the Steady Boys had, at one time or another, carved their initials—those of them who knew how to write their initials, at any rate. "There should have been much more."

"Well, we tossed the place right proper, we did. If 'twas any more there, we would have found it, eh?"

"The man was bleedin' rich, Bruce," said Darnley, with a scowl. "Everybody said so. He was going into business. He was in the bloody Merchant Adventurers Guild, trade voyages to the colonies and the Far East and all that. He was going to invest in Burbage's damned playhouse and who knows what else? He had bought a house and was going to build himself a mansion right outside o' London. You don't do none o' that on your good name, Bruce. All that takes money. Lots o' money. Gobs o' money. *So where in the bloody hell was it?*" He slammed his fist down on the table so hard that all the pitchers and the tankards jumped and everyone looked toward him.

"Steady on, mate," McEnery said, placatingly. "If there was more, well then, we never found it, eh? Like as not some merchant banker kept it for him."

"There would have been papers there if that were so," Darnley replied. He took a drink and wiped his mouth with the back of his hand. "There were no papers. We looked everywhere. We tore that bloody place apart."

"We did get some money, Jack," McEnery said. "We did not come away empty-handed."

"Bollocks! What we got was no more than a good journeyman makes in about a week," said Darnley, savagely. "Not even what a rich man would keep around the house for spending money."

"Well, so he had it stashed away, then," said McEnery.

"*Where?*" Darnley practically screamed, so that everyone

turned toward him once again. "We cut that man to ribbons," he said softly, through gritted teeth, "and he kept saying over and over that there was no more money. A pox on his lying soul! He had it hid somewhere, I tell you. We must have missed something. We *must* have!"

One of the Steady Boys came up to the table and whispered a few words into McEnery's ear. McEnery glanced up at him with surprise. His comrade nodded and pointed over toward another table that stood nearby. McEnery nodded back to him.

"Go on then," he said, "and keep an eye on him. Make certain that he does not leave." He turned to Darnley. "Jack," he said, "methinks you might want to come and have a drink or two with that chap at yonder table there." He jerked his head in that direction.

Darnley glanced at him darkly. "What the hell for?"

"Because he works for Liam Bailey, that's what for," McEnery said.

"So? Why should I care a fig about Liam bloody Bailey?"

"Because Tuck bloody Smythe works for Liam bloody Bailey now and then, remember? And because Smythe said something very interesting to this chap he works with about what happened at the Genoan's house that night, and this chap is drunk and running off his mouth about it."

Darnley sat and stared at him a moment. "Is he?" he said, after a long pause. "Well then, let us go and listen to what he has to say."

They got up and walked over to the table where the loquacious Bobby Speed sat with a couple of the Steady Boys, apparently deeply in his cups. He was holding forth with elaborate, expansive gestures that nearly caused him to overbalance on occasion and teeter on his stool. One of the Steady Boys reached out and grabbed his arm, to keep him from falling over.

"Take it easy there, friend," said Darnley, laughing good-naturedly as he clapped Speed on the back, pulled up a stool, and sat down next to him. The transformation from the dark and scowling brooder of a few moments ago to the cheerful boon companion seemed dramatic to McEnery.

It was as if Jack had become another man entirely. This was the Jack Darnley that always seemed to be the center of attention, the one the girls all liked so much, the charmer and the wit. But he knew another side of Darnley, a much more dangerous side that he both feared and respected. And also idolized. It was the Jack Darnley who had slashed away repeatedly at Master Leonardo while the others held him, demanding to know where he kept the money.

"Eh? And who might you be?" Speed asked, in a slurred voice.

"The name's Jack," said Darnley, holding out his hand to Speed. "Everyone knows me around here. What's your name, friend?"

"Bob-bobby," Speed replied. His cheeks puffed out and then he belched profoundly.

"Well, Bobby, you look as if you could use another drink," said Darnley, clapping him on the shoulder. "Something to drown that frog in your throat, eh?" He signaled the serving wench to bring more beer.

"You give him much more an' he'll pass out," one of the other Steady Boys said.

"Oh, now, never fear, Henry," Darnley replied. "Ole Bobby looks like a man who knows how to hold his drink. Is that right, Bobby?"

"*Ri . . . riiiiiiight!*" Speed belched in response.

"A ripper!" Darnley exclaimed. He took the pitcher from the serving wench and refilled Speed's tankard. "Bottoms up, eh?"

He picked up his own tankard and made as if to drink, but refrained while Speed quickly quaffed his down.

"Now that's the way to do it, eh?" Darnley said. "You know, they tell me that you work with my good friend, Tuck Smythe."

"Ah. Good ole Tuck. Here's to 'im!"

"Right, here's to him," Darnley said, refilling Speed's tankard and watching as he drank. His tone was jovial, but his dark eyes were like a predator's, sharp and intense. "You know, Tuck was saying something about that Genoan merchant who got killed the other day. Methinks his name was Leonardo, was it not? We have all been talking about that. Terrible thing."

"Aye, terrible, terrible," said Speed, nodding so loosely it seemed as if his head would roll right off his neck. "Poor bloke." He held up one finger dramatically. "But despite it all, they still didn't get 'is money!"

"They?" said Darnley, softly. "But I thought there was just one killer. And they have him locked up in the Marshalsea."

"*Hah*!" Speed barked, swaying slightly on his stool. "*Hah*! That's what *they* think!" He leaned close to Darnley, conspiratorially. "Tuck says they got the wrong man!"

"Do they, indeed?" Darnley said. "How does he know?"

"Said so. Said Corwin 'ad no money on 'im when 'e was arrested. A few crowns, is all. So if 'e robbed the Genoan, then where's all the money, eh? Where is it?"

Darnley looked mystefied. "I have no idea, Bobby. Where?"

"Need 't 'ave 'nother drink," slurred Speed.

"And so you shall," said Darnley, refilling his tankard from the pitcher. He watched intently as Speed drank with greedy swallows. "So," he said, when Speed set down the tankard, "what did Tuck say happened to the money?"

" 'Twas all stashed away, y'know," said Speed.

Darnley's eyes lit up. "Where?"

"*Ssshhh*! 'Tis a *secret*!" Speed whispered, putting his finger to his lips.

Darnley lowered his voice. "I shall not tell a soul! Cross my heart!" He performed the gesture. "However did Tuck know the Genoan's money was all stashed away?"

"The daughter told 'im," Speed replied.

"Leonardo's daughter?"

"Aye." Speed's cheeks puffed out again and a low rumble issued from his throat. He patted his stomach. "Settle down there," he said, and then broke wind prodigiously.

"S'trewth!" said McEnery, waving his hand before his face. "Smells like something bloody died in there!"

"Be quiet, Bruce," said Darnley, softly, but the tone of his voice demanded immediate obedience. McEnery fell silent instantly. "So the wench knew where the money was hidden?"

"Aye, she did," said Speed. "Gold coins, moneys o' account and letters o' credit and what all . . . a bloody fortune, Tuck said. All stashed away! An' they never even found it! Leonardo took the secret to 'is grave! The poor, old sod."

"Astonishing!" said Darnley, pouring him more beer. "And so where was it all hidden?"

"In a chest!" said Speed.

Darnley's eyes narrowed. "A chest! The devil you say! He had all that money just hidden in a chest? Why, 'tis not a very clever hiding place, if you ask me. You might think that anyone could find it in a chest."

"Ooooh, 'twas a *special* chest, this one," said Speed, leaning close to him and nearly falling off his stool. "Wif' a secret compartment inside it! *Sssh!* Mustn't let anybody know, Tuck said. 'Tis a *secret!*" He held up his forefinger and moved it around unsteadily in front of his mouth, but could not seem to make the connection between the finger and his lips.

"Mum's the word," said Darnley. "Where is this chest now? Still at the merchant's house?"

"Nah," said Speed, shaking his head, then grabbing it with both hands, as if to steady it. "*Hooo!* Head spinnin' round!"

"Have some more beer," said Darnley, pouring. "Hair o' the dog. Settle things down. So . . . what happened to this chest?"

"Tuck an' Ben brought it to the shop," said Speed, "for safe-keepin'."

"You mean Liam Bailey's shop?" asked Darnley, his gaze so intense that his eyes seemed to glitter.

"Aye," said Speed, nodding heavily. "For safe . . . keepin'." He slumped forward and his head struck the table with a thud.

"Bobby?" Darnley said. He reached out and took a handful of Speed's hair and raised his head up, then let it drop back down onto the table. "Dead to the world," he pronounced.

"The chest!" McEnery said, eagerly. "I remember that old chest!"

"Bloody old sea chest," Darnley said.

"Heavy old thing," said McEnery. "We just dumped it out onto the floor. *Damn*! We should have looked at it more closely! But who would have thought it had a secret compartment?"

" 'Twould be just like a rich man to hide all his money inside a battered old chest, where no one would think to look," said Darnley. "But now we know just where to look, don't we?"

"In Liam Bailey's shop," McEnery said, with an ugly grin.

"Get the lads together," Darnley said.

McEnery gathered all the Steady Boys and they trooped outside into the street. No sooner were they gone than Bobby Speed raised his head up off the table and glanced around. "They gone?" he asked.

At the next table over, John Fleming, Dick Burbage, Will Kemp, Gus Phillips, and John Hemings heaved deep sighs of relief and loosened their grips on the clubs and daggers concealed beneath their cloaks. "All gone," said Fleming. "Lord, I do believe it worked!"

"And the sooner *we* are gone, as well, the better I shall like it," Kemp said, swallowing nervously. "Zounds! My heart is beating like a drum!"

Tom Pope and George Bryan came over from a nearby table where they had been watching and sat down with Speed. "Bobby, you were bloody marvelous! What a wonderful performance!" Bryan said, clapping his friend on the back.

" 'Twas nothing, mate," said Speed, pouring out the remnants of the beer from the pitcher into his tankard. " 'Twould take a lot more than this weak, watery brew to get me drunk. Cheers, then!" He raised the tankard and drained it in a couple of swallows.

It was growing late by the time the Steady Boys reached Liam Bailey's blacksmith shop. The streets were deserted and only a few lights burned here and there. Darnley quickly gave commands and McEnery posted lookouts to keep an eye out for the watch. Once they satisfied themselves that there was nobody in sight, they quickly broke open the lock upon the heavy wooden door and went inside.

They made sure that the shutters were all tightly closed, and then McEnery raised the small lantern they had brought and uncovered it. It did not throw forth very much light, but it was enough for them to find their way around inside the shop.

"Right," said Darnley. "It has to be in here someplace. Look around, lads."

"Jack!" one of the others said. "There's a big chest right here!"

Darnley glanced around, saw it, and shook his head. "Wrong one," he said.

"Are you sure?"

"Of course, I'm bloody sure, you cankerous mongrel, I've seen the bloody thing, haven't I?"

"What about this one, Jack?" another one asked.

He turned. "Nay, nor that one, neither. 'Tis too new."

"Jack! I found a chest right here!" another of the boys called out.

"Be quiet, you scurvy crow! You want to bring the watch? Where is it?" Darnley went to take a look. "Nay, nay, 'tis not the one! Bloody hell! Is this a smithy or a chest-maker's shop? We are looking for a *sea chest*! An *old sea chest*!"

"Jack . . ." said McEnery.

Darnley turned. McEnery had raised an old saddle blanket under which was an old sea chest. "*That* is the very one!"

"Should we break it open?"

"Nay, 'twould make too much noise," said Darnley. "We shall take it with us and find that compartment at our leisure. Lift it up, boys."

They picked up the chest and started to carry it toward the door.

"Cover up that lantern, Bruce, 'afore we go outside," said Darnley. He waited a moment, then snapped back over his shoulder, "I *said*, cover up that bloody lantern!"

"I *did* cover it up!"

"Well, then, where the hell's that light coming from, you pustule?"

They turned around.

" 'Allo, Jack," Ben Dickens said, standing behind them with a lantern. " 'Allo, Bruce. Nice night for a break-in, eh boys?"

Smythe stepped out beside him, holding another lantern. "Good to see you again, Jack," he said. "You know, I have been meaning to speak with you about these lumps you and your boys gave me. I was hoping to pay you back, with interest."

Darnley gave a small, derisive snort. "Well, well," he said. "Are we not the clever ones? 'Tis you who shall be paying, Smythe, my friend. And as for you, Ben, you could have joined us again when you had the chance. You could have shared in all this money. But 'tis a bit too late now."

"You truly are a clownish half-wit, Darnley," Shakespeare said, from over by the door. Liam Bailey stepped out from hiding along with him and threw open the door. "There is no money. There is nothing in that sea chest but old clothes."

Darnley's eyes were like anthracite as he gazed at them with loathing. "So what?" he said. "So you have played a clever trick. What do you think that has accomplished? Nothing! The trick is going to be on you." He raised his voice. "*Gather round, lads!*"

The Steady Boys who had been waiting outside came running. They formed a semicircle in the street around the door, surrounding the entrance to the shop.

"Now so cocky now, Smythe, are we?" said McEnery, with an ugly sneer.

"I am sorry, Ben," said Darnley. "But you made your choice."

"Aye," said Dickens, "so did you, Jack."

"Now?" said Smythe, raising one eyebrow.

"Aye, Tuck," said Dickens. "Now."

Smythe raised two fingers to his mouth and gave a piercing whistle. Darnley's eyes narrowed and he quickly turned around. Beyond the semicircle of Steady Boys out in the street, figures seemed to melt out of the shadows, dozens of them, men carrying clubs and knives and staves and swords. The Steady Boys glanced all around in alarm as they found themselves suddenly surrounded and hopelessly outnumbered. Moll Cutpurse stepped out from the crowd, her hand upon the pommel of her sword.

"If there is any thieving to be done in London," she said, "you come and ask permission from the Guild. We do not look very kindly on those who come poaching on our ground."

Darnley spun around to face Smythe. "*Damn you!*" he said, with a snarl. " 'Tis all your doing! We should have killed you that night! Well, you may get in your licks in return for the drubbing that you got, but 'tis all you'll bloody get! You can still prove *nothing*! And Corwin *still* bloody well hangs!"

"Are you quite certain of that, Jack?" asked Smythe. And he raised his fingers to his lips and whistled once again.

Darnley's eyes grew wide as the clatter of hoofbeats on the cobblestones rang out through the night and Sir William Worley, leading a squad of the sheriff's men, came riding into the street. Moll Cutpurse's men parted ranks to let them through.

"What *is* this?" Darnley demanded, suddenly looking afraid.

"You said we could prove nothing, Jack," said Smythe, "but you were wrong. You are carrying the proof right there. We had placed several chests inside the shop. But only one was in Leonardo's house. You went straight to it."

"That drunken bugger in the tavern told us all about it!" Darnley protested. "He said 'twas an old sea chest that had the money hidden in it!"

"He merely said the money was hidden within a secret compartment in a chest," said Smythe. "He never said anything about an old chest, or a sea chest. He merely said 'a chest.' *You* were the one who said 'twas an old sea chest, Jack. And there was only one way that you could have known that."

"You are all under arrest in the queen's name," Sir William said. "For robbery, and for the murder of Master Leonardo."

"Nay! I never murdered no one!" Bruce McEnery cried out, in a panic. " 'Twas Jack! Jack did it! Jack Darnley killed 'im!"

"You bastard whoreson!" Darnley said, and plunged a knife deep into McEnery's chest. McEnery screamed and fell to the street, clutching at the blade protruding from his chest.

With a swift sweep of his arm, Sir William hurled his dagger. It struck Darnley in the back and buried itself deep between his shoulder blades. Darnley grunted and his eyes popped, then glazed over as he fell. He was dead before he struck the street.

The members of the Thieves Guild melted away into the

shadows as the sheriff's men rounded up the remaining Steady Boys, some of whom had started whimpering and crying.

"Thank you, Sir William," Smythe said, with a slight bow.

Worley touched the brim of his plumed hat in a salute of acknowledgement. "Your friend shall be freed within the hour," he said, then wheeled his mount, and rode off into the night.

EPILOGUE

THE DOUBLE WEDDING WAS ATTENDED by all the Queen's Men. It took place in St. Dunstan's Church, not far from where Hera and her late father, Captain Leonardo, had briefly made their home in London. The congregation was an interesting agglomeration of thespians and thieves, together with craftsmen and apprentices, for not all apprentices were hellions like the Steady Boys, many of whom would serve some time in prison, either in the Marshalsea, the Newgate, or the Clink. The chief malefactors, Darnley and McEnery, were both dead and without them, one of the most notorious of the 'prentice gangs was now no more, an object lesson to other working-class young men with too little sense and too many high spirits.

Of course, Hera could never reside with her new husband in the house where her father had been murdered. The constant memory would be much too disturbing for her. So with the proceeds from the sale of the house, Corwin had purchased a modest new home for them not far from the shop of Master Peters, where he continued to work as a journeyman, doubtless soon to be a master craftsman in his own right.

Ben and Molly were, of course, the second couple that were married at the ceremony, though much to the company's regret, Ben had decided to leave the Queen's Men once again. A player's life, he felt, was really too uncertain, and so with some of his remaining money that had been recovered from the Steady Boys, together with some money from Molly and her sister, Ben went into partnership with several journeymen and opened up a small shop selling arms and armor. It quickly became a thriving business, perhaps the one place in London where members of the upper classes could rub shoulders with members of the Thieves Guild and not be concerned about the safety of their purses.

The Queen's Men, sadly, did not fare so well. By the time the playhouses finally reopened, after numerous postponements and delays, the companies had all suffered from the length of the enforced closure. The Burbage Theatre was as much in need of refurbishing as ever, and there was simply no money to effect the necessary repairs. The chief rivals of the Queen's Men, the Lord Admiral's Men, also found themselves in difficulties. After a number of their productions had done poorly, their biggest draw, the celebrated and mercurial Ned Alleyn, had bolted their ranks and joined another company, Lord Strange's Men. Will Kemp soon followed suit, leaving the Queen's Men to join Alleyn's new company. The difficult times brought about a reorganization in which companies of players that had formerly competed with one another now combined in order to survive. The Lord Admiral's Men joined with Lord Strange's company to act together at the Rose. And this alliance made the future of the Queen's Men very grim.

"How do you feel about leaving the Queen's Men?" Shakespeare asked Smythe one night.

For a moment, Smythe did not respond. Finally, he took a deep breath and asked his roommate, "Are they going to let me go?"

Shakespeare chuckled. "Nay, Tuck, *we* are going to let *them* go. I have been invited to join Lord Strange's company. I told them that I would consider it if they took you as well."

"You did? And they agreed?" said Smythe.

"Oh, readily. Your reputation precedes you, you know. They thought that since they already had the country's finest actor, they would not be complete unless they also had the worst."

"Thank you," Smythe said, wryly. " 'Tis good to know that I have at least some sort of standing in my craft. But what about the others?"

"Well, Kemp, as you know, has already departed. Pope and Bryan are the next to go. They have already accepted offers to join Lord Strange's company, who have lost some of their members after the long closure and must now fill out their ranks."

"And the Burbages? What of them?" asked Smythe.

"For a time, we shall have to part company, it seems," Shakespeare replied. "The Queen's Men, I am sorry to say, shall not survive. And the Burbage Theatre may not, either. James Burbage does not own the land whereon the playhouse stands, you know. I have spoken with Dick and he has told me that the landlord has been complaining and may not renew the lease."

"And if the lease is not renewed?"

"Well, then the landlord shall acquire a playhouse," Shakespeare said. And then he smiled. "Or so he thinks."

Smythe frowned. "What do you mean?"

"I mean, my friend, that Dick and his father may yet have a few surprises up their sleeves. For the present, Dick has told me that we must take what offers we are given so that we may have work. The winds of change are blowing through the companies of players here in London and, like fleets of ships at sea, we shall all be blown asunder for a time. Then, when the storm has passed, we shall reunite. The formation of the fleet may not be quite the same, and some ships, sadly, may be lost, but those that will remain shall continue with their voyage. And, for some, there may be new ports of call that did not even exist before."

"New ports of call? What does that mean?"

"Well, do not go bruiting it about," said Shakespeare, leaning forward conspirationally, "but Dick has told me that his father has a plan. If the landlord refuses to renew the lease, then rather than lose the Theatre, James shall tear it down and carry off the timbers, using them to build another Theatre, even better than the first, one that shall eclipse even the Rose."

"Where?" asked Smythe.

"He has not yet decided. Southwark, perhaps. The better to throw down the gauntlet to Philip Henslowe and the Rose. 'Twould all take time, however, and meanwhile, you and I must eat. Therefore, I propose that we follow Ned Alleyn and Will Kemp and join Lord Strange's Men. Afterward, we shall see what the future may bring."

"Another Theatre, better than the first," said Smythe, trying to imagine such a thing. "And even better than the Rose? 'Twould be something marvelous, indeed. Would it still be called the Theatre?"

Shakespeare shook his head. "Nay, Dick said the name would need to encompass greater grandeur. Something better . . . something bigger. He rather likes the Globe."

"The Globe," repeated Smythe. He nodded. " 'Tis a grand name, indeed."

"Aye, but for the present, we shall be playing at the Rose," said Shakespeare. "When times are lean, a man must find what work he can. And, to that end, I am once more embarking upon my sonneteering. I have been working upon this one, tell me what you think . . ."

"Oh, Will, you are not going to read me another poem?"

" 'Tis just a short one."

Smythe rolled his eyes and lay back on the bed. "Oh, very well," he said. "You found us work, after all. I suppose the very least that I can do is listen to your doggerel."

" 'Tis a *sonnet*, not doggerel, you carbuncle!"

"If you say so," Smythe replied, wryly. He sighed. "Very well. Lay on, MacDuff . . ."

AFTERWORD

IN MY AFTERWORD TO *A Mystery of Errors*, the first novel in the Shakespeare & Smythe series, I stated that my purpose was primarily to write a work of historical fiction meant to entertain. I also wanted to disclaim having any serious credentials as a Shakespearian scholar. Teaching a college course in Shakespeare, seeing a few plays, and doing a little reading does not a serious scholar make, by any means. However, at the same time, I wanted the story to have at least a nodding acquaintance with history, insofar as it is known, before taking a certain amount (well, all right, a *considerable* amount) of dramatic license with it.

The so-called seven "Dark Years" (sometimes also called the "Lost" or "Hidden Years") from 1585 to 1592 constitute a period when absolutely nothing is known of Shakespeare's life. I chose that period as a starting point, largely because I thought it would be fun to speculate fictionally and because it offered a great deal of flexibility. (When nothing is known for certain, one has more freedom to make stuff up.) When I wrote the second novel in the series, *The Slaying of the Shrew*, it was set during that same period and I did not see any particular need for an afterword. I had, at that point, nothing more to add that I had not already written in the first afterword. But since the conclusion of this novel marks a period when Shakespeare is entering a new stage of his life, with a new theatrical company (even though we are still in the so-called "Dark Years"), I thought that a few background notes might be interesting and perhaps helpful.

To begin with, there is really no solid evidence that Shakespeare was ever a member of the Queen's Men. He *might* have been, and inferring from circumstantial evidence, a number of scholars seem to believe there is a strong probability that he was, but the fact is we really do not know for certain. We *do* know that he was a member of Lord Strange's Men, the acting company that later became known as the Lord Chamberlain's Men, and that there was something of an overlap in the membership of those respective companies. Will Kemp and Edward Alleyn, for example, were both members of the Queen's Men first and later joined Lord Strange's Men.

In an effort to control the sort of situation described in the first chapter of this novel, where numerous "bands of cozeners" (or con artists) travelled the countryside posing as companies of players, the law stated that a legitimate acting company had to have a titled aristocrat or nobleman as a patron. This was not to say that said noblemen lent any sort of financial support to the company they sponsored, so to speak (they didn't). The idea was to have such nominal patronage legitimize the companies. This program met with general success, apparently, although it did not entirely eliminate the problem of thieves and con artists travelling the countryside, pretending to be players.

Lord Strange was Ferdinando Stanley, who became the Earl of Derby in September of 1593. He did not have a very long tenure. He died in April of 1594, and rather colorfully—it was rumored that he had been slain by witchcraft. Whether this was possible or not is a matter for the reader's own beliefs; suffice it to say that this left his acting company in need of a new patron. They found one in Lord Hunsdon, the Lord Chamberlain, and it was under the patronage and name of the Lord Chamberlain that this company became, as Anthony Burgess called them, "the greatest body of actors of all time," with a resident poet (or playwright, as we would say today) who was destined to become the most famous writer in history.

Simon Hawke
Greensboro, N.C.